# night
# radio

A LOVE STORY

Also by David W. Berner

FICTION
*A Well-Respected Man*
*Knowing What to Steal*

MEMOIR
*The Consequence of Stars*
*October Song*
*Accidental Lessons*
*Any Road Will Take You There*
*There's a Hamster in the Dashboard: A life in pets*

# night radio

## A LOVE STORY

David W. Berner

*Night Radio: A love story*
Copyright © 2019 David W. Berner
All rights reserved.
ISBN 13: 9781096125617
Published: 8/1/2019



www.davidwberner.com
www.thewritershed.com

WRITER SHED PRESS
Clarendon Hills, Illinois
www.writershedpress.com

*For Casey and Graham*

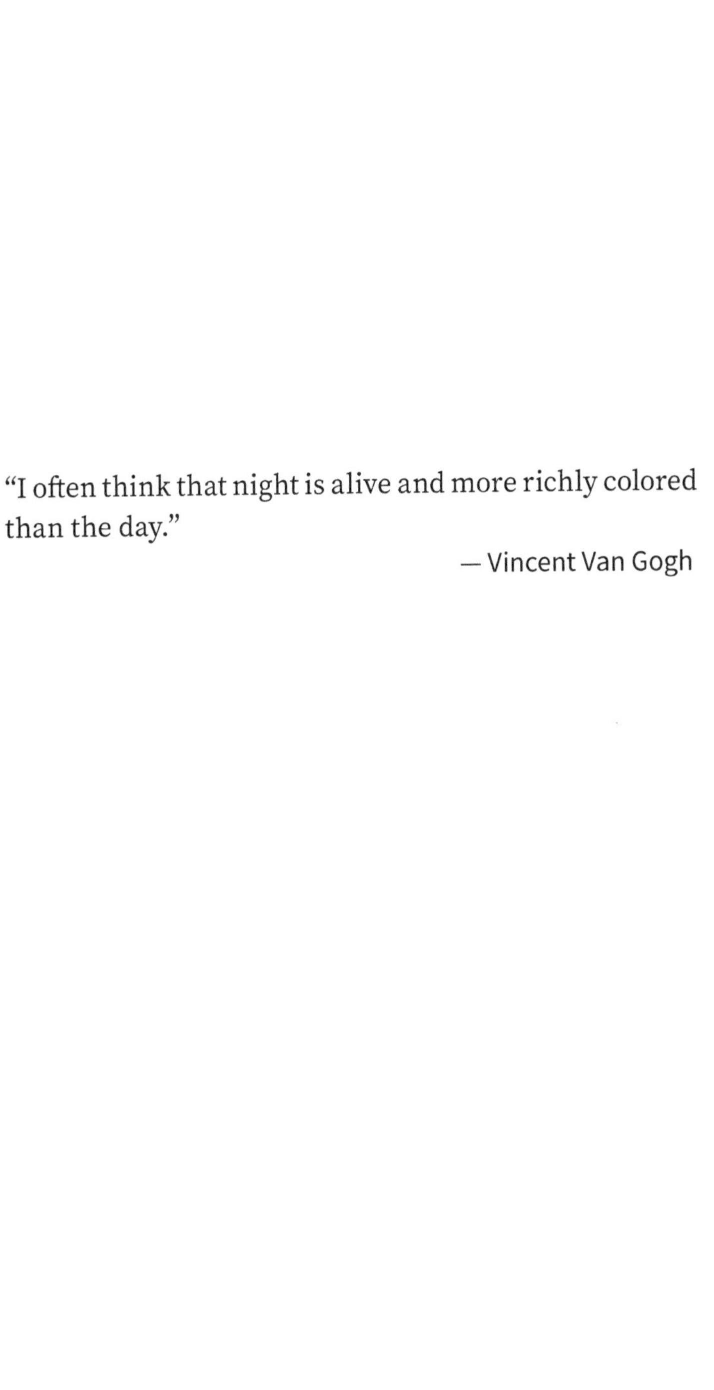

"I often think that night is alive and more richly colored than the day."

— Vincent Van Gogh

# PART 1

# 1

THERE WERE TIMES WHEN JAKE wished he and his father sounded nothing alike. When they spoke, it was nearly impossible to tell them apart. Both of their voices sounded strong and deep but not overwhelming or daunting. Like the bone-vibrating resonance of the guy who sang bass for The Temptations, their voices easily filled even the largest of rooms. Somewhere between melodic and commanding, their tones were a virtual match. Even the patterns of speech were the same. They were truly vocal twins.

Sometimes the likeness was simply a practical matter. Jake was frequently mistaken for his father, especially on the phone. When he was home from college and his dad's golf buddies would call the house, they'd go on and on about tee times and where they were going to meet before Jake could interrupt and tell them they were talking to the wrong guy. One time when his father worked for the insurance company, his boss telephoned and rattled off a list of account numbers and premium figures before Jake could interject and inform him his father wasn't home. There was also the matter of identity. Jake didn't want to be his father. No young man really does. It wasn't that he didn't get along with his dad—most times he did—but there had been battles, like the time his dad found empty beer cans in the car after Jake had borrowed it on a Friday night. His father didn't like some of Jake's friends, the way his son mouthed off sometimes, and there were those lousy grades in the sophomore year of high school. But there was little the two didn't eventually get past.

The real issue for Jake now was a matter of separation. Like so many sons before him, Jake wanted to be his own person, apart from his dad, and having a voice that sounded so much like his father's was simply not helping. So what would make him different? Both Jake and his dad had Pittsburgh accents—sort of a compressed slur with funny sounding Os. His father's was far more distinguishable than Jake's. That was the one thing Jake could work to change, train away. Getting rid of the accent would separate him from his father, and if Jake wanted to be on the radio—work professionally behind a microphone—he had to lose that vocal signature. Even Jake's college diction professor had strongly suggested he needed to sound less like a guy from Western Pennsylvania and more like one from Kansas.

Ted Lawson wasn't from Kansas, but Jake would have given anything to sound like him.

Ted had the voice of a jazz trombone, smooth and robust. Like a well-played instrument, it demanded attention. It was the kind of voice that couldn't be contained, its energy radiated through the radio station's studio glass to the outside hallways and adjacent rooms. Ted was Jake's boss, and Jake had heard that resounding voice in the office and over the airwaves at noon each day since starting his internship at the station. Ted delivered his daily newscast from the main studio. Standing inches from the microphone, he read the words he had written with effortless confidence and innate skill. He would announce the time, his name, give the radio station's identification, and launch into the first story. On this day it was an update about a tropical storm developing into a hurricane off the coast of Mexico. Everyone knew Ted was an insatiable news junkie. He meticulously prepared this daily newscast, combing the

Associated Press wire and all the papers from *The New York Times* to *The McKeesport Sun,* the town's thin weekly publication. The ritual defined Ted as a well-informed man, extraordinarily aware of nearly all that was going on in the world, except for the one thing secretly brewing on a mid-summer afternoon only a few feet behind him—the one and only thing that could throw Ted off his game.

It was the July before Jake's senior year in college, the summer before he was hired as an intern at WIXZ, a country music station in a small, fast-declining steel town some fifty miles outside of Pittsburgh. Ted, the station's program director—the guy with the booming voice—had asked Jake to return to work an air shift on Saturday mornings and manage the automation system during the week. It wasn't exactly Jake's dream gig. He wanted the job at the big Rock-n-Roll station in Pittsburgh, WDVE, but the resume and demo tape he sent there went unanswered. Still, a job at WIXZ was a chance to work on the air at a real station, not just the tiny, low-watt FM on campus. So there he was, changing the 12-inch reel-to-reel music tapes on the automation system that ran after the live weekday morning show, timing the music to end precisely at 12 p.m. for Ted's newscast, and on this afternoon, witnessing two young ladies strip the clothes off his boss.

Jennie was the station's receptionist. She sneakily entered through the heavy door that linked the studio with the offices, and Toni, the woman who scheduled the commercials, slithered in behind her, both bringing with them an infamous reputation for eliciting the most out of red lipstick and tight skirts. As Ted continued on the air, Jennie wiggled her considerable curves next to Ted's left side, put one hand on his back and with the other, began unzipping his pants. She smiled, straining to keep from laughing. Toni, now on her knees, unbuckled Ted's belt. Jake was in the room just on the other side of the studio glass—a cramped space with just enough square footage for a small desk and the Associated Press printer with its incessant clanking. From there, Jake could see Ted's pants hit the floor. The front tail of his dress shirt covered the open slit in the crotch of his blue-checkered boxers, but the rear tail was caught-up in the elastic band, the shorts puckering around his butt. Jennie spotted Jake through the studio window and placed an index finger to her lips, devilishly gesturing for silence. She winked. Jake winked back—not out of playfulness or confidence but out of nervousness. Somehow through it all, as Ted's clothes were peeled away, he continued flawlessly reading the news.

Everyone knew Ted as a solid newsman but also as a conventional sort of guy—a mix of Ivy League prep, intellectual nerd, and altar boy. Jake didn't remember a time when he saw Ted unorganized or ill prepared. *Damn* was the worst he'd heard come out of his mouth. Ted even looked exactly the way Jake thought someone with his job—the boss of what was broadcast on the air and the station's newsman—should look. He wore only white or oxford blue buttoned-down shirts, the sleeves rolled unevenly up to the elbows. And although Ted's tie—usually a preppy style with broad stripes—was rarely taut against his neck—the knot hanging just below the shirt's undone first button—it was nevertheless a tie, something no one else but the general manager and the station's two salesmen ever wore. At 8 a.m. when Jake arrived for his weekday shift, Ted was already at the station before anyone else in the office had considered the possibilities of the day. He was rarely seen without a newspaper tucked under his arm or folded and slipped in a rear pocket of his pleated khaki slacks. Ted was what Jake considered a real radio professional, unlike the station's middle-aged morning man who drank too much Canadian Club, showed up late for his air shift two days out of five, and was going through divorce number three. To Jake—a rookie part-time summer announcer—Ted was the guy to emulate. He was the only one at the station who truly had it together it seemed; he was the sole announcer who would be expected to keep his poise even on a day when his admirable composure would unravel.

Ted forged ahead, each word delivered with sharp, clear, unwavering authority.

"Jesus, how's he doing that?" Jake whispered to himself.

Jennie had already unknotted Ted's tie and let it fall to the floor, and Toni undid the buttons of his shirt from the bottom up. Jennie then moved behind Ted. She smiled at Jake through the glass, and just as Ted read the first two words of the next story, Jennie, without turning her eyes from Jake, pinched Ted's butt.

"Owww!" Ted blurted over the air, the steady cadence of his delivery hitting an audible bump, the lower half of his body squirming, twisting, in an attempt to break loose of Jennie's grasp. After a moment's pause, Ted regained his cool and started reading again. "Police say a fire in McKeesport's downtown last night has left two people injured." Now Toni was sliding Ted's left arm out of his shirtsleeve, and Jennie was teasingly tugging on the hem of his boxers as if at any second she would yank them to the ground.

"More news, sports, and weather coming up," Ted announced. "The time is 12:02." He pressed the green button to play a commercial and quickly turned off his mic. "What the hell are you doing?" Ted snapped.

His face was scarlet, a mixture of embarrassment and anger.

"Happy Birthday," Jennie giggled, giving Ted's shorts a hard jerk, the boxers collapsing on the laces of his black dress shoes.

Jennie darted out of the studio, but Toni lingered a moment to stand eye-to-eye with Ted. "Oh, come on," she throatily said, letting her black Italian hair fall from behind her ears. "Lighten up. You don't want to be an old fart at thirty-three." Toni slipped Ted's headphones off his head. Then she slid out her tongue, wiggled it just inches from his mouth and playfully licked his lips. "Don't you look so damn cute," she said, her husky voice dropping one range lower. With eyes still locked on Ted's, Toni reached down and grabbed his crotch. "And here's a present," she said, squeezing tightly. "Just a little something for the very special birthday boy." Toni then gave Ted a playful peck on the nose and scurried out of the studio.

Ted stood half-naked with his pants around his ankles and his shirt clinging to his right arm. Just as he heard the studio door shut behind him, he hit a button on the control board to play another commercial and quickly reached down to yank up his shorts and pants. He clumsily pulled on his shirt, buttoning it just enough to cover his bare chest. Then, as the commercial came to an end, he slipped the headphones over his head and ears.

"It's 12:04 at WIXZ, and I'm Ted Lawson." He completed the remainder of the newscast without a flub. At 12:10, when the automation system began playing music again—Crystal Gayle's "Don't It Make My Brown Eyes Blue"—he slowly turned and glared out the window of the studio door. There was Jennie, Toni, and Tommy—the morning host, the production director, and one of the salesmen—standing together around a small table where the flames on the candles of a homemade birthday cake sputtered in the light breeze from the office air conditioner.

Jennie motioned through the glass for Jake to join them. It was a simple, forgettable gesture. But for Jake it was a level of acceptance he was only now beginning to fully welcome.

"Happy birthday old man!" the group shouted as Ted walked out of the studio to the main offices.

"Don't...ever...EVER...do...that...again," Ted said, a wry smile slowly emerging as he released each word.

When Jake was in 8th grade, he rested his head on the pillow of his bed each night and held a transistor radio up to his ear, listening to stations in Pittsburgh and the big 50,000-watters broadcasting from Cleveland, Chicago, even Canada. Jake wanted to be one of the voices on the air, the intelligent Rock-n-Roll aficionado with the encyclopedic knowledge, a sense of humor, and a deep, resonating tone. He loved the music—songs with poignant lyrics shining a light on the discord in America, mixed with silly ditties meant for escapism. Two of the biggest songs in 1969 were "Sugar, Sugar" by the Archies and The Rolling Stones' "Gimme Shelter." If listened to closely enough, one could hear the end of innocence rising out of the speakers of car radios, the hope of Kennedy—both Jack and Bobby—fading into the tragedy of Vietnam.

Even Jake, a 14-year old boy from the leafy suburbs, knew things were changing, and in many ways had already changed. In a couple of years, he had grown his hair long, started playing guitar, smoked cigarettes and tried dope, told his parents he hated them, and watched TV news reports of college students marching against the war. Kent State—where the Ohio National Guard fired sixty-four rounds over thirteen seconds and killed four students—was a two-hour drive from Pittsburgh. But while Jake was attempting to find his place among the tormented counterculture, he was also spending a good deal of time trying to find a way to get on the radio. It was his freshman year in college when the chance arrived. The college radio station was looking for announcers, kids who could be trained to host radio shows. Jake made the cut, but he was terrible on the air. It would be a couple of years before he would improve even the slightest, eventually becoming good enough to land the internship and the summer job at WIXZ.

"See what happens when you get into this business? People take off your pants while you're on the air," Ted joked, an attempt to either scare Jake away or encourage him.

"It's exactly why I want to be in radio," Jake answered, smiling. "Who wouldn't?"

"You're next, Mister Jake Mulholland," Jennie said, pointing an index finger with its shapely nail and red polish directly at him. "When you're least expecting it."

"Some Saturday morning, we'll sneak in," Toni added, "slink up behind you in the studio . . ."

"And get you naked," Jennie interrupted, rubbing her shoulder against Jake's. "Completely and entirely naked."

All Jake could think about was how incredible that would be, how he would not resist, but he doubted that he could keep his composure like Ted. Jake still had a lot to learn as an announcer, and he had a college girlfriend; he thought maybe he was in love—although neither of them had said so out loud. Their friends insisted they were the perfect couple. *Jake and Sarah*, they'd say, *they are special.* Jake liked hearing that.

Sarah was the kind of girl who secretly slipped Hallmark cards into the pages of Jake's textbooks, the kind of girl who tried to tickle Jake when he was moody or down and followed the playful attack with a raw, infectious laugh that came from somewhere deep and hidden. Jake wasn't sure if he knew how to take care of Sarah, but she knew how to nurture him, nurture *them*, making Jake realize how he must be doing something right to end up with a girl like Sarah.

That summer there were miles between them. Sarah had a job as a low-level clerk in Cleveland at an advertising agency. They tried to connect nearly each day with a call, sometimes talking for hours and other times just a few minutes, a brief moment to touch along the phone line. The same kind of drugstore cards with the poorly written poems she had snuck into Jake's books, now came in the mail. She would draw hearts on the envelope, always in red ink. One time, when Jake had a few bucks, he sent her flowers—daisies and lilies, her favorites. Jake was her guy; she was his girl. *So, if she meant that much to me*, he thought, *shouldn't I have at least considered her a little bit when Jennie toyed with the idea of stripping me down?* Wouldn't Jake have had Sarah on his mind somehow, even just a little, as he watched two women in their mid-20s take the clothes off his boss? He didn't. Jake missed Sarah but maybe not as much as he believed. It was complicated. *If you're in love with someone, do you forget about her when it's convenient?* The question seemed to always be right there in front of him but it never lingered long enough to demand an answer.

There would be a lot of unanswered questions, misunderstandings, and missteps over time, clouding what once appeared so clear. But in the summer of 1977, there were at least a few unwavering truths: America was nursing a Vietnam hangover, the jazz-tinged sounds of Steely Dan and the California country of the Eagles owned the FM airwaves, and Jake Mulholland, a young man from Pittsburgh, was only a few months from college graduation and in love with radio.

2

IT WAS LATE ON A Thursday night when Sarah telephoned.

"Hey, I'm coming in," she said. "I have a few days off."

"Great. When?"

"I'm driving down in the morning. I assume I can stay at your parents'?"

"They'd love to see you."

Jake didn't want to spend money on summer rent, so he returned to the house where he grew up. Sarah had been there before, visiting over a few weekends and a couple of days during Spring Break. Jake's mom and dad loved her. Jake and Sarah didn't get much time alone in his parents' small Cape Cod house, but he wanted Sarah near him, and it was the best way to do it. She slept in his old bedroom; Jake spent the nights on the living room couch.

"We can hang out together," Sarah said. "And maybe I can come to the radio station with you on Saturday morning?"

"You do realize what time I get up?"

"It won't kill me," she said, smiling through the phone.

Jake looked forward to showing off to Sarah—giving the tour of the station, letting her see him perform on the air at a real radio station. She had seen Jake in the studio at the campus station, and it always made him feel great when Sarah was there.

"Let's plan on it," Jake said. "I can buy some donuts and coffee on the way, sort of soften the early morning blow, and if you get bored or tired while I'm on the air, there's a big lounge chair in the corner of the production studio. It's a little ratty, but it's a place to take a nap."

"Really?" she asked. "People won't mind?"

"Nobody's there until about 9:30 when the weekend producer comes in to set up the automation," Jake said confidently, hoping to prove to Sarah that he'd gained some clout at the place. "Really, it's no big deal."

After a few weeks, Jake had fallen into a comfortable routine. During the week, he'd come in and work the station's automation system, record a couple voice tracks for local commercials, and help Ted categorize music and write public service announcements. Jake would arrive to start his air shift at 5 a.m. on Saturdays. First, he'd look at the music log to see what songs he was expected to play, pulling each record from a rack of neatly cataloged 45s. Then, he'd tear off the weather forecast from the Associated Press printer and arrange note cards of station IDs and on-air phrases Jake was expected to read word-for-word. On the weekends, the station's format was intricately structured, and although Jake wanted to talk more, share a joke, or an obscure story about a song or artist, Ted's programming rules didn't permit it. The more Jake worked at the station, the more he realized why Ted was chosen for his job. The format fit his personality—predictable and structured. The more Jake worked his air shift, the better he got—at least he thought so. Jake also realized he didn't want to be that kind of radio announcer. He craved more freedom, wanted to express himself, wanted to play the music he loved for the kinds of people he thought would appreciate it. Jake wanted to be the most literate guy on the air, with the heart of a poet. He dreamed of being Rock-n-Roll's Ed Beach, the jazz DJ in New York.

Beach was the hippest guy on the radio, a musical professor who understood how jazz fit into the world, how its inherent irreverence was both artistic and spiritual. He knew the nuances of his genre and of those who created it. Beach had a booming voice that made radio speakers shudder, and he'd use it to carry the message of what he believed ultimately mattered most—the music. It was all about what he believed was the deep significance of jazz in America. A sophomore who grew up in Brooklyn and worked at the college radio station for a couple of semesters—a kid who was way into Miles Davis and Coltrane— had a cassette tape of one of Beach's shows on WNYC. For Jake, listening to that tape was like discovering secrets, shining little diamonds.

————

It was a couple of hours before the sun would rise Saturday morning, but the temperature was already a steamy 78 degrees. Jake drove into the tiny parking lot, the windows of his blue Chevy Chevelle rolled down. The air conditioning had gone out weeks before, and Jake didn't have the money to fix it. There were no other cars in the lot. The station ran on the automation system from 1 a.m. to 6 a.m. on the weekends, and the engineer who worked the overnight shift at the tower a mile away only came into the studio if there was a problem.

"Sar," Jake whispered, "we're here." Sarah had fallen asleep during the half-hour drive, her head resting against the door.

"Already?" she asked groggily.

"Can you grab the donut box from the backseat?" Jake had a set of keys to the station's front and back entrance. Funny how a small piece of metal on a chain can make one feel important. Jake had a set to the campus radio station, too, only one of two people the faculty advisor allowed to have them. When Jake played high school baseball, he was the team captain, a position that also came with a set of keys to the boy's locker room. It was good to be the keeper of keys. It offered privileges, real or imagined.

Jake had an hour to prep before going on the air. During that time, he double and triple checked everything, laying out all the records he'd be playing and being certain the commercials on the program log matched the audio carts in the metal rack in the corner of the studio. Advertisers didn't like when you missed playing one of their scheduled commercials. But this morning, feeling confident and proud, Jake spent most of that time showing Sarah around.

"This is where they store all the music," he said, gesturing through a door to a wall of vinyl records on wooden shelves. "And over here is the newsroom." It really wasn't a newsroom, of course. It was just that small space where the Associated Press printer was stored, from where he watched Ted lose his pants, but it sounded better when he called it a newsroom. "And this is Ted's desk," Jake said, moving down the hallway, "and over here is where Jennie sits."

"Jennie?" Sarah asked. She had heard Jake talk about Ted but no one else.

"Receptionist," Jake said, continuing to walk through the office. "And that's the automation system," he said, pointing to the wall of lights and reel-to-reel tape machines tucked behind the main studio.

"That's what you do, right?"

"Yep. My job during the week."

"Looks complicated."

"Oh, it is. Very."

Jake's pride was showing, and Sarah was beaming. She loved it when his confidence came through. Some Friday nights he would play acoustic guitar at the café in the college's Student

Center, and she always said Jake performed his best, sounded great, when he interpreted the songs with palpable self-assuredness. "Confidence," she once said, "is sexy."

Jake stacked up the records scheduled for the next two hours on the control board console and placed the weather report torn from the AP printer on the stand above it. Note cards with holes punched into the corners were kept together with a stainless steel ring. On the cards, some twenty of them, were the announcer liners Jake would read on the air: *WIXZ—Country With All the Hits, Your Country Music Connection—WIXZ, The Country Hits of Today and Yesterday—WIXZ.* The note cards were placed on the stand near the weather to remind him to read them after every commercial break and at the beginning of music clusters. That was the way Ted wanted it done.

"Can I sit here in the studio with you?" Sarah asked.

"Sure. I'd like that."

At 6:05, after the network newscast from Associated Press, Jake began his air shift with a recorded jingle, a liner from the note cards, and Eddie Rabbit's "Drinking My Baby Off My Mind."

"You sound great," Sarah said as he turned off the microphone.

"It's a living," Jake said, joking.

"Can you handle this country music all the time, though?"

"You know, some of it's not all that bad."

"That scares me," Sarah said, pretending to be horrified.

Sarah and Jake liked a lot of the same music. They listened to CSN&Y, Dan Fogelberg, Joni Mitchell, Bob Dylan, James Taylor. She was a big fan of the pop-jazz guitarist, George Benson. Jake didn't care much for him but never admitted it to her. Still, there was a lot of music that they listened to together in her dorm room or his apartment, over and over.

"Well, we do play some Marshall Tucker," Jake said, naming a progressive country rock band popular at the time.

"Tolerable," she said, laughing.

"Even the Eagles," he added.

Between live weather forecasts, liners, and song introductions, Sarah and Jake talked more about music, his job, and her internship, and how she didn't think much of Cleveland. They talked about Jake's upcoming senior year and how they were going to see each other once Jake graduated and was working, and she was finishing school. But Sarah kept bringing the conversation back to what was happening that morning, asking questions about the format at WIXZ, the equipment, what other jobs he was doing at the station, and about the people he worked with.

"Made any friends?" Sarah asked.

"Well, I wouldn't call them friends exactly, but we get along."

"What kind of people are they?"

Jake told her about the morning host who drank too much, about the general manager who didn't seem to be around a lot, and the two salesmen who both wore checkered sport coats and awful paisley ties and looked like they just walked off a used car lot.

"And then there's Ted," Jake said. "Good guy, always professional, even when things get a little nutty."

Jake told Sarah about Ted's undressing, purposely leaving out the spicy details and how it was difficult to keep from staring at Jennie and Toni when they paraded around the office in revealing skirts and tight tops.

"Jennie? That's the receptionist, right?" Sarah asked.

"Yeah."

"And Toni?"

"Traffic coordinator," Jake said. "She schedules commercials. It was a birthday prank." Jake didn't want to even hint at how Jennie and Toni had teased about how they'd do the same to him.

Around 7:15, after a couple of donuts apiece and a few swigs of coffee in Styrofoam cups, Sarah had had enough.

"Mind if I take you up on that nap in production?" she asked.

During a commercial break, Jake walked Sarah down the hall to the production studio and showed her how to work the chair's reclining mechanism. "It's a little beat up," he said, "but it works. I think you'll be comfortable."

"Wake me in an hour, okay?" she asked.

"Sure," he said, giving her a little kiss. "Now it's back to the grind."

"Knock 'em dead, superstar," she said, kicking off her shoes and curling her legs into the chair's big cushion. "I'll be right here."

The main entrance and station's small foyer could be seen from one end of the studio glass, and as Jake read the weather forecast at 7:46 a.m., out of the corner of his eye he spotted the front door swing open. It didn't alarm him that someone was coming in, but it was unusual at this time on a Saturday.

"Good morning, I'm Jake Mulholland. We should see sunshine all day today," he announced on the air. "The high is expected to be near ninety degrees."

As Jake continued, he heard muted laughter behind him. He always thought the studio glass was soundproof. Truth was, it was just doubled-paned. Real soundproof glass was too expensive, and the station owner wasn't about to pay for it.

"On Sunday, we could see a couple of late-day showers."

Jake could hear giggling behind him, morphing quickly into silly, high-pitched laughs.

"The high on Sunday again should be near ninety."

Just as Jake began to give the current temperatures around town and at the airport, he felt his entire body flush. It was in that moment that he remembered what Jennie and Toni had pledged, and Jake knew immediately who had stumbled through the front door.

"And it's already 80 degrees in downtown McKeesport at AM-1360, WIXZ."

Jake hit the button on the console to start the next record, turned off the microphone and spun around to look into the foyer. The laughter had gone silent, the entranceway empty.

Jake moved closer to the studio glass and tilted his head to peek toward another corner of the foyer. No one.

The studio door burst open.

"Hey there, cutie," Jennie slurred, sashaying her way into the studio, holding Toni's hand. "You remember us!"

"We've come to do what we promised," Toni said, winking.

A stale smell filled the room, a mixture of perfume, alcohol, and cigarettes. The two of them had clearly been out all night. There were a handful of bars, dance halls, and after-hours clubs in the Pittsburgh area. They might have been to them all.

"We're not ready to end the fun," said Jennie, playfully. She then pointed a finger at Jake and said, "And you're going to join us."

"But I have a friend and she's . . ."

The song on the air was beginning its final fade out.

"A friend?" Jennie interrupted. "A *she*?"

"Ooh-la-la," added Toni, pulling the shirttail out from the back of Jake's jeans.

"You guys doing it in here?" Jennie asked, grinning.

Jake played a recorded jingle and hit the button to immediately air the next song.

Jennie grabbed the collar of his shirt and pulled him close. "Want her to watch?" she asked, her eyes looking directly into Jake's. Jennie then reached down and began unbuttoning his jeans.

Jake could have been angry, strongly insisted they leave. He could have walked out of the studio. He could have called Ted. And then there was Sarah just down the hall. Still, with all this swirling around in his head, Jake did nothing. His instinct was to surrender.

"Jesus," Jake whispered.

Jennie wiggled Jake's jeans from his hips, and Toni fingered the elastic waistband of his underwear. With his pants around his ankles, Jake turned on the microphone.

"That was 'Lyin' Eyes' by the Eagles on WIXZ, your country music station, playing all the hits of today and yesterday." Jake played a commercial and turned off the mic, astounded he hadn't stumbled his way through the broadcast break.

"You . . ." said Jennie, slowly running the red-painted nail of her index finger down the bridge of his nose, "...are so damn kah-UTE." She left Jake with a wet kiss, and then she and Toni strutted toward the studio door.

"Bye-bye," Jennie said, waving her hand over her head.

Jake stood stunned, the sounds of their mischievous laughter fading as they weaved down the hall and out the front door.

The next three commercials—one for a car dealership selling Ford pickup trucks, a restaurant with special Italian recipes on Friday nights, and another for a Country-Western bar that just installed a mechanical bull—allowed enough time for Jake to tuck in his shirt, zip up his fly, and shake his body like a wet dog after a swim in an attempt to shed the lingering effects of what had just happened.

Undetected, Sarah quietly walked into the studio. "Was someone here?" she asked, rubbing her eyes. "I was only half awake, I think."

"Ah, yeah, one of the salesmen, checking on a spot. He wanted to make sure it was running. Some touchy client or something." It was a pretty good lie from the boy most of Sarah's friends were quick to call a "good guy." Truth is, deep down in every "good guy" was a rascal, a devilish sexual being, a cocktail of angel and devil. Every guy will lie to save himself, and every woman eventually discovers it.

"Oh," she said, sliding into the chair in the corner of the studio. "Couple donuts still left. Want one?" Sarah handed Jake the box. He chose a glazed one, snatching it with his fingers like the talons of a hawk and stuffing it in his mouth.

"Hey, you want to go get some real breakfast after my shift?" Jake asked between chews, trying to rush away from any more conversation about who had been at the station and what they may have been doing. "I want to spend some quality time together, not just here at work, you know what I mean? Wouldn't that be nice?" Jake washed down the donut with the last of his now cold coffee. "I know it's hot and all, but it's summer, and I know this place where we could sit outside in the shade."

"Sure," Sarah said, smiling. Then she paused, sighed, and stood up from the chair. "You know something Jake Mulholland? You are so damn kah-UTE," she said and kissed him on the forehead.

# 3

WHEN JAKE AGREED TO LIVE off campus, he didn't antici-pate that would mean living in a ragged old trailer three miles from school. He and his roommate, Danny, tried to get an apartment in town—an upstairs loft in one of Clarion's old stately houses—and they actually moved in, but two hours later the landlord threw them out. Somewhere on the lease Danny hadn't exactly been forthcoming about being college students. It probably was illegal, but the landlord wanted no part of that, and they had no means to fight it. So they ended up in a trailer that teetered on concrete blocks. If you dropped a ball in the back bedroom, it would roll all the way into the kitchen without assistance.

It was a cool morning in September when Jake marched off for the first time from the trailer park to the college radio station's studios. He had agreed to host the morning show from 6 a.m. to 9 a.m. each weekday and be the station's program direc-tor. He certainly didn't do it for the money, but a salary from Clarion College of eleven dollars per week was just enough for a couple packs of cigarettes and a little beer. Danny got food stamps each month, which they used to buy groceries. A couple of days a week, Sarah would steal breakfast from the school cafeteria—she had the school meal plan, Jake didn't—and would deliver it to him at the station before her morning class. It was too early for that, so on the first day back for the new semester Jake opened the door to the Student Union and the station at 5:30 a.m. on an empty stomach.

Jake worked various shifts at WCCB during his junior year, playing records on weekdays and on weekends, if they needed him. Add this to the internship and summer job at WIXZ, and he was feeling pretty confident about his abilities. Jake was hoping to log in as much time as possible during the final school year so he could pull together a solid demo tape. He was willing to go anywhere in the country. Sarah and Jake never talked directly about what that might mean for them, but she knew that he wanted to be on the radio.

The college station was on the third floor of Davis Hall, a red brick building with white windows and ivy clinging on the south wall. A photo of Davis Hall could have been used for the brochure of any Ivy League school in the Northeast. Clarion College, part of the state school system in Pennsylvania, was far from Ivy League, but with a little tunnel vision one could imagine being in Cambridge. You could say a lot about the radio station, too. It had some pretty decent equipment donated by a radio station in Philadelphia that had upgraded its own system. If one didn't know any better, any novice to the business might look at WCCB's studio and think it could be CBS in New York. And yes, of course, the students at the station didn't know any better.

All along one wall of the main offices was floor to ceiling shelving, nearly every inch taken up with albums categorized from A to Z by band name. There was a format for what to play, but it was pretty loose. The former program director told the staff to keep it current, and of course, stay away from bubble-gum crap. Jake was hoping to offer a bit more direction as the new program director, but there had only been one meeting since getting back to campus, so he stuck with the old plan and for the show that morning, pulled a couple dozen albums from the shelves—The Rolling Stones, Fleetwood Mac, Steely Dan,

Neil Young's *Harvest*—and stacked them on the big table near a wall-to-wall bay window that looked out onto campus. This was a great place to watch girls, especially in the early part of the fall semester when the weather remained warm and the girls wore shorts and halter-tops. You could stare at the co-eds studying under the trees and they'd never know. At least they pretended not to know. Sean, the station's music director, kept a set of binoculars in his desk, and a few times a week when a bunch of the guys were hanging out in the office, they'd pass around the eyeglasses and rate the freshmen.

Behind a set of doors in the rear of the radio station was the news wire machine, snapping out the latest from the Associated Press. It was tucked away in that room because of the relentless hammering of blue ink on rolls of pale yellow paper. The paper always piled up overnight, and Jake worked his way through the reams of copy to find the weather forecast. He tacked the remainder to the wall of the small room for the newsperson to go through. The station's news director had made up the schedule, and Jake wasn't sure who would be with him that semester, but he hoped it was the transfer student from Penn State who had done a little professional newscasting at a small station at State College—or better yet, Lisa, the sophomore who joined the station just last year. When she walked in the station for tryouts, Sean nearly lost his balance. Lisa had been the focus of his binoculars for months, and there she was, standing just a few feet in front of him. Before she left that day, Lisa cornered Sean in the hallway and whispered, "I know you've been watching me." Sean was speechless. Lisa just smiled. Two days later, Sean spotted her on campus from the station window and clandestinely aimed his binoculars her way. As he zoomed in and adjusted the focus, there in his sights was Lisa, sitting on the grass, smiling in Sean's direction, giving him the finger.

It was ten minutes before 6:00, the beginning of the broadcast day, and the Student Union was quiet—so unlike the middle of the day. That's why it was easy to hear footsteps echoing in the stairwell to the third floor, even if someone was wearing sneakers.

"Hey," Lisa said as she walked through the station door, flipping her long auburn hair from her face. "You doing the morning shift?"

"Yep, it's me," Jake said.

"I'm the newscaster on Mondays and Wednesdays. Early classes other mornings, so I can't do it," she said, walking quickly past Jake toward the back room where the wire machine tapped away. "Is that typewriter there okay to use?" she asked, still in motion, pointing to the old electric on a metal office desk.

"Don't see why not," Jake said. "You seem in a hurry. You know the first newscast isn't until 7:00, right?"

"Seven?" she said, suddenly standing still. "Shit, really?"

"Yeah," he said, laughing. "You got plenty of time. The casts are only three minutes long. You do have to get me headlines to read at the bottom of the hour, though. Just rip off the national heads from AP."

"Jesus, I could have slept another ten minutes, gotten a cup of coffee."

"There's that vending machine in the Union basement, you know? Shitty coffee, but it *is* coffee."

"Lisa," she said, reaching out her hand to shake mine.

"Yeah, I know who you are," Jake said.

"Yeah," she said devilishly, "you're one of the perverts with the binoculars."

"Well, that's Sean, not me." He lied. "And I don't know if you'd exactly call Sean and the other guys perverts." Jake was trying his best to defend anyone who had peered through those lenses, including himself.

"You're perverts," she said, smiling.

*Why is it,* Jake thought, *that a moment of awkward silence between two people—the two or three seconds of space—can seem like an eternity? In just those little seconds, the stomach drops below the knees, the heart misses beats, the mouth abruptly goes dry.*

"I've got to get in the studio," Jake said, turning away from Lisa.

"Headlines at 6:30?" she asked, knowing the answer.

"Yeah, bottom of the hour," he said, making his way down the short hall to the air studio.

The station's copy of Crosby, Stills, Nash & Young's *Déjà Vu* album had been played hard for several years by a lot of student disc jockeys. They needed a new copy. But the title song, David Crosby's ode to hippie paranoia, was one of the few without scratches. It seemed like an appropriate song to begin the senior year, the semester—the radio station's first song of the fall. The lyrics tumbled out of the studio speakers.

The station ID jingle played at exactly 6 a.m., and Crosby's voice took over the airwaves, the harmonies dissonant and angelic at the same time. Jake decided to keep to a loose-knit theme of hippie anthems, playing Donovan's "Hurdy Gurdy Man" next.

"WCCB. Good Morning. This is Jake and that, my friends, is Donovan with an incredible trio of backup musicians," he said into the microphone. "Bet you didn't know John Bonham is playing drums on that track, John Paul Jones on bass, and Jimmy Page on guitar. Yep. Before they were Led Zeppelin, they played hippie psychedelic music with Donovan."

For the next half hour Jake filled the airwaves with Dylan, the Beatles, Cream, and The Guess Who's "American Woman."

"An anti-war song, you know?" he announced. "'American Woman' is believed to be the Statue of Liberty." Jake didn't know that for a fact, but it was a good story.

At 6:29, Jake opened the microphone to read the weather. He should have had the headlines from Lisa a few minutes before, but she hadn't brought them to the studio yet, so he padded with the long-range forecast and some comments about how the weather should be great for the weekend's opening home football game. Jake heard the slight squeak of the studio door behind him and reached a hand behind him as he continued to talk, anticipating the headline copy from Lisa. She slid the sheet in his hand.

"So, again, a good deal of sunshine today and a high of about eighty-five," Jake said. "And now a look at the top news stories of the hour." He placed the copy on the broadcast console and began to read.

"It's been a week since the news of Elvis Presley's death, and mourners continue to flock to the area near the Graceland mansion in Memphis to take part in impromptu memorials and remembrances. The investigation into the circumstances surrounding the death of the King of Rock-n-Roll continues, and the details on the autopsy report are expected to take several more days."

*Good choice for a top story in the headlines,* he thought.

"Another wave of Vietnamese refugees is expected to arrive in the U.S. later this week," he read.

So far, no stumbles, even though Jake had had no time to pre-read the headlines. Feeling confident, he moved through the refugee story without a hitch and began the final headline.

"And in Lebanon today, where the country's civil war continues to rage, some 2,000 lesbian troops blocked off streets in the country's capital in hopes of fending off rebels."

His stomach turned hot and nauseous.

*Did I say LESBIAN?*

"Those are your headlines at this hour. The full newscast with Lisa is coming up at seven."

*It's LEBANESE, you fucking idiot! It's written right there on the page!*

Jake turned off the microphone and played a recorded public service announcement about some fraternity's charity event.

*Maybe I did say Lebanese,* he thought, desperately hoping he had.

The studio door opened.

"You do realize you said *lesbian* troops, right?"

Jake spun around in his seat. There stood Lisa, her hand on her hip and a smirk on her face.

"Shit. Did I really say *lesbian*?" Jake scrunched his face.

Lisa winked and turned to walk out. "Two thousand lesbians marching in Beirut," she said as the door slowly shut behind her. "Now *that* I'd like to see!"

This was Jake's most recent screw-up. There had been others.

One time, after playing Manfred Mann's "Blinded by the Light," he referenced the lyrics and said, "Wrapped up in a douche." It sure sounded like that's what they were singing, Jake believed. Of course the actual lyrics used *deuce* not *douche*. Jake expected a couple of phone calls on that one. Truth was, the listenership was nearly non-existent. A few students listened to the campus station, but it certainly wasn't the most popular frequency in town. Everyone who worked at WCCB thought they were hot stuff, but in reality there were fewer than a hundred people tuned in at any given time. So, although Lisa playfully needled Jake about his gaff, it was unlikely anyone else noticed. Just like when he said *douche* on the radio, the phones never rang, and this time no one had any idea that Jake had placed an army of homosexuals in the streets of Lebanon's capital city.

# 4

IT WAS SOMEWHERE AT THE tail end of the lecture in Jake's British Literature class about James Joyce's short story *The Dead* that he first imagined having sex with Lisa. It wasn't the first time he had lusted over her. But this time it was much more detailed—like scenes in a movie. It was the second week of the semester, and Jake had already fantasized about the literature professor, Mrs. Wilde. He pictured her bent over the classroom desk with him charging up behind. Wilde was probably in her 40s but looked like she was 30. Jake bet most of the guys in the class were thinking the same thing, but on that day, Lisa was winning the fantasy battle.

It had been a couple of weeks of broadcasts for the morning shift at the station. And when Lisa was there, Jake found himself intensely inspecting her walk, the sway of her hips as she stepped out of the studio after each newscast. She didn't wear perfume, but there was a sweet smell of shampoo. It was easy to imagine her naked. This was the focus of his daydreams during Mrs. Wilde's highly academic explanation of what *The Dead* was supposed to really mean, who was really "dead" in the story, and why that was supposed to matter. Mrs. Wilde was consumed with the examination of Joyce's story, first clarifying the title's significance in the previous week's session and then repeating it with more passion in the following one. The Joyce story, she explained, was about a holiday party on the Feast of Epiphany, and Wilde appeared most fixated on revealing how the "dead" in the story referred to nearly everyone in the narrative, deceased or not. The story, she continued, was really about dismissing those who have no spirit, who have no zest for a new beginning, revelations, or redemptions. Gabriel, the story's main character, planned a westward journey through Ireland, representing a rejuvenated life—new beginnings—even though some scholars believed the journey meant the afterlife—a journey to death. Wilde, however, favored the more optimistic analysis. And, since Jake had heard Wilde make this point—it seemed to him, a ridiculous number of times—his mind wandered off to think about Lisa, lying on his lower half of the bunk bed in the trailer's small bedroom.

Sarah was waiting for Jake after class on the bench near the west entrance to the library.

"Hey," she said, smiling.

"Hey. Have any smokes?" Jake asked.

"You have any money?"

"No. I'd buy cigarettes if I did."

"Let's walk up to the station. We can bum a couple from somebody." Sarah threw her backpack over her shoulder, wrapped her arm in his, and kissed Jake on the cheek. "Or maybe someone in the Quad has one. How was class, by the way?"

"I'm beginning to hate James Joyce," he said.

"But you don't mind looking at Wilde, do you?" Sarah smirked.

"Well, she ain't ugly."

"She's a knockout."

"Well, she ain't ugly."

Sarah knocked her shoulder into Jake's. "Shut up," she said. "Wilde could be your mother!"

"Best mother ever," he said, knocking his shoulder back into Sarah's.

Sarah knew Jake looked at other girls, women, and knew he had sex on the mind, but she shook it off as a normal condition, what every college boy did. "You guys are hardwired," she would say. She did get mad about it sometimes, though. Sarah was not happy when she'd catch Jake staring at her roommate, the one who walked around their apartment in nothing but a tight tee-shirt and panties. "What do you expect me to do?" he'd ask. "Why don't you try not looking," Sarah would answer. After a few too many arguments, they stopped spending a lot of time at Sarah's apartment.

Sarah and Jake sat on the stoop outside the side entrance to the Student Union and shared a Marlboro Light, a single cigarette bummed from a student who appeared half asleep, lying on the grass under a tree near the sidewalk.

Sarah puffed, blew smoke, and laid her head on Jake's shoulder. "I'm not sure it's sunk in yet," she said, passing the cigarette, a shared vice.

"I feel like I just got here," he said. Jake finished the thought with the cigarette clenched between his teeth. "It's going to be an interesting year."

"What's that mean?" she asked.

"Oh, you know, finding the energy to finish off these final classes, trying to get as much time on the radio as possible so I can get together a good demo tape."

"Think WIXZ will hire you?"

"Well, I might get some part-time work over the breaks. Full-time? I'm not sure I want to be some shit-kicking country disc jockey."

"Aren't we a prima donna?" Sarah stood up and tapped Jake on the head with her knuckles.

"Some of that twang stuff I've learned to like. But working there all the time? I don't know."

"A job's a job. It'd be a good start," she said, taking her final hit on the smoke and handing it to him.

"We'll see. I'm going to apply a lot of places." Jake stamped out the Marlboro.

"Where?"

"All over."

"Like where?"

"Wherever there are good stations."

"Alaska?"

"Maybe."

"I'm not so sure about Alaska," Sarah said.

"You're not so sure for you or for me?" Jake asked, grabbing his backpack and standing.

"Jake, do you want to be with me?"

"Of course I do."

"When school's over?"

"Yes. I do," he said, reaching for Sarah's hand. "But we don't want to give up chances to do what we love, right?

Sarah delicately tossed her head, flipping away the strands of hair that had fallen over her left eye. Whenever Sarah was particularly reflective, her long brown bangs would tumble onto her forehead, partly concealing her expression, as if masking an emotion. Then she'd gracefully shake her head, returning the hair to her temple to reveal three freckles just above her eyebrow, tiny deep chocolate dots that, if connected, would form the shape of a frown.

"Right," she answered softly.

Jake kissed her forehead.

Just before 10 o'clock that night, Jake sat alone on the ratty blue couch in the living area of the trailer, trying to get through a Dylan Thomas poem. Reading it and writing an analysis was the next assignment for British Literature.

"You know anything about poems?" he asked Danny who was standing before a tower of dirty dishes in the kitchen sink.

"Do you *ever* do the fucking dishes?" he asked. Danny and Jake got along fine, but right now Danny was pissed.

"It's not all my stuff," Jake answered.

"Some of these pots have been here for a week or some fucking thing," Danny snarled.

"I'll do them next time, honestly," Jake said, dismissing him. "You know the poem *Do Not Go Gentle into that Good Night?*"

"Nope. Never heard of it," he said, turning on the faucet and running hot water over the mound of dishes.

"Jesus Christ. You're a fucking English major!"

"Yeah, yeah, I know the poem. Just giving you shit for not cleaning up all this crap. You're a fucking pig."

"It's about his dying father, right?" Jake asked.

"Yeah, but it's really about helplessness in growing old. But it's also about how to live," said Danny. "Where's the god damn dish soap?"

"Not sure we have any," Jake answered. "So, how to live, huh?"

"There's some line in there about old age burning?" Danny asked himself. "Yeah," he added, remembering the line. "'Old age should burn and rave at the close of day.'"

"And that means?"

"Supposed to mean something about living an eventful life, sort of going out in a blaze of glory," Danny said, ducking his head under the sink. "There we go. Some Palmolive. We're going to have to buy more of this stuff," he added, holding the nearly empty bottle up to the light.

"It's not that I'm stupid about this, but like every other poem or story in this class, this is not exactly what it seems. There's something else going on."

"No good story or poem is only what it seems on the surface. The good stuff goes deeper. Think song lyrics. Think Bob Dylan," Danny said, tossing Jake a dishtowel. "I'll wash. You dry."

Jake flung the towel over his shoulder, closed the book, and leaned his head back on the couch's cushion. "We have any beer?"

Danny opened the refrigerator door. "One left," he said. "I'll split it with you. Now get the fuck over here and start drying."

At midnight, Jake placed his head on the pillow of his bed and, for a moment, wondered if when he was sucking in the air of his last breath, he'd be able to say that he had lived a full, eventful life—a life worthy of ending in a blaze of glory. For now though, Jake needed rest.

<h1 style="text-align:center">5</h1>

THE BREAKFAST SARAH WOULD USUALLY sneak out from the cafeteria was something easily slipped into her backpack—a bagel, a muffin, maybe some buttered toast wrapped in a napkin. She'd drop it off at the radio station studio before she headed to her 8:00 class. One morning Sara outdid herself.

"Here we go. Pancakes and eggs," Sarah said proudly, pulling from her backpack a small plastic plate of food covered over by a second upside-down plate. "Wahla!" she said, ceremoniously lifting the top plate, uncovering a still warm and steaming stack of buckwheats and scrambled eggs with cheddar cheese.

"Wow, you went all out today," Jake said, turning down the studio monitor that had been blaring "One Way Out" by the Allman Brothers.

"And," she added, reaching again into her backpack, "we have butter and maple syrup." Sarah flashed a grin.

"You're getting good at shoplifting, babe," Jake said, laughing.

The butter was on little patties stuck to small pieces of thin white cardboard-like tabs. Sarah had dropped four of them into one of the cafeteria's paper cups usually used for orange juice. The syrup had been poured into another cup, with a second cup turned upside down on top to keep it from spilling.

"I'm not done," Sarah said, hunting through a small compartment in her bag. "In here...we have...yes, here we go. I brought your very favorite thing in the world." In the palm of her out-stretched hand, like a jewelry store clerk might offer a diamond ring for a customer's inspection, was a large blueberry muffin.

"I thought they stopped making these!"

"I haven't seen them since we've been back. But this morning, there they were," Sarah said, pleased by her discovery.

Jake plucked the muffin from Sarah's hand and brought it to his nose. "They always smell so great. With all the shit they cook in that place, they *do* get these right."

"Better than the mystery meat," said Sarah, handing Jake a pilfered plastic knife and fork. She sat on the floor and crossed her legs. "Come on now, eat up."

"Thanks sweetie," he said, placing the food on the small table left of the studio console. "Don't you need to get to class?"

"I've got a couple of minutes."

Jake spun his chair around to face the control board and turned on the microphone. "Allman Brothers on WCCB, your campus radio station. 'One Way Out' is a classic blues song first recorded by Sonny Boy Williamson and Elmore James in 1960. That version had a full horn section blaring away in it. Pretty great, if you ever get a chance to hear it. Another one of those blues songs about the boyfriend coming home to find his girl cheating with another man. A pretty popular theme, don't you think? It's 7:55 in the morning, I'm Jake, and this is a little more of the blues to get you going on this Wednesday." He pushed the button that started turntable number-two. "It's Cream and 'Crossroads.'"

Jake turned off the mic and faced Sarah. She was standing with her backpack over her shoulder, her face catching the yellow light of the early sun through the window above the sound console. "You sound great," she said sweetly. Sarah placed a hand on Jake's cheek and kissed him. "I gotta go."

"Want to meet me here in the afternoon?" he asked. "I got class after my shift, and then I need to come back to talk to the station's advisor about the budget."

"Sounds like a great time," Sarah said sarcastically. "I'll stick my head in; see if you can break away."

Just as Sarah waved to leave, Lisa rushed in, nearly running her down.

"Oh, sorry," Lisa said, shifting her weight to avoid a collision.

"My fault. Wasn't looking," Sarah said, turning to Jake. "Bye babe. Later," she said over her shoulder as she disappeared through the door.

"Girlfriend?" asked Lisa, settling in the chair before the second microphone.

"Yep," Jake answered, taking a bite of the cheesy eggs.

"And she steals food for you, too. Nice."

"She's a keeper."

"Pretty."

"She is; thank you."

*Strange response,* Jake thought. *Why is it, when someone compliments your girlfriend or boyfriend, or even calls your dog handsome or cute, one instinctively says thank you, as if you had anything to do with it? It's as if you are praising yourself for making stunningly good choices, picking beautiful people, adorable animals with which to share your life. The choices we make on who we wish to keep close,* Jake wondered, *aren't completely and totally ours, are they? They are not our singular decision.*

Sarah and Jake were together because of many choices, some having very little to do with Jake. Jake knew that. Sarah came to the university because she wasn't accepted at her first choice, Notre Dame. She started in the education department, thinking she wanted to be a teacher then changed to communications, concentrating in public relations and advertising. Because of that choice, Sarah and Jake ended up in the same class, Journalism Writing 101, and that's where they first knew of one another, although they never talked. They would later meet more intimately, and in time, they would find something special, they believed. There would then be choices to make if they desired to stay together, decisions to make in an attempt to balance personal dreams with those they believed—hoped—they shared. There was a song Jake had always loved by Stephen Stills called "Helplessly Hoping." It was on the first Crosby, Stills and Nash album, the one with the photo of the three of them sitting on an old couch. To Jake, the song's chorus was about sharing a life with someone you love but never giving up, diminishing your own identity. He believed in those lyrics.

Jake turned on the microphone.

"It's a couple minutes before 8:00 and Lisa with a news update. But first, here are the Beatles from *Abbey Road* and 'Carry That Weight.'"

He cranked up the monitor, leaned back in the chair and sang along. The lyrics to Stephen Stills' haunting love song whispered what was in his heart, but the words of Lennon and McCartney—the lyrics of a heavy burden—overpowered all that and screamed what was in Jake's troubled head.

———

Dr. Elmore smoked More cigarettes—the long, thin cigar-like smokes—using each one like a prop, holding it elegantly between his fingers like a French artist from another era, flicking ashes into the tray on the big table in the middle of the radio station's office. Although he was a professor of communications and taught broadcast classes, he talked, walked, and gestured like he would have been far more comfortable in the theater department.

"It's your radio station, not mine," he said, "but I have to check in from time to time. Make sure you're watching the books."

"Thanks for looking over the figures," said Greg, the student general manager, a senior English major with blonde, Robert Plant-like hair. "Do you see anything that looks out of whack?"

"It seems okay," he said. "How you getting your music these days?"

"Some we have to buy," Jake said, "but much of it is coming in from the record reps. We get things later than other stations, but we eventually get the records."

"Don't spend too much on records," Dr. Elmore said. "I can't justify a lot of that to The Board of Trustees. I have to have these meetings with you to assure the administration you're not running some kind of frat house here and saying fuck on the air."

"Only once or twice a week," Jake said, smiling.

A rapid succession of footsteps could be heard climbing the stairs from the Student Union's first floor to the station on the third. It was a warm September afternoon and the door was propped open to allow the breeze to flow into the station's front office. The echo in the stairwell was familiar but different. Instead of the steady tempo of tennis or leather shoes squeaking their way up the steps, what could be heard was a slapping noise and a much quicker rhythm.

A barefoot and shirtless student burst into the office.

"I'm pissing blood," he moaned.

It was Kenny Marslender. Everyone called him Mars.

"I'm supposed to be on the air in three minutes, and I will be," he said. Mars quickly grabbed several albums from the tall music shelves near the door. "But seriously, I'm pissing blood, man."

Mars had been late before for his air shifts. Jake told him if he was late one more time, he'd have to give his airtime to someone else, suspend him. He liked his beer and his hash, but

Mars really loved being on the air, and he was quite talented. Still, he could be a screw-up, a lovable screw-up, but still a screw-up. From the time he was in middle school, his million-dollar smile, broad shoulders, and quick wit kept him out of trouble with teachers, parents, and friends. It was hard not to like Mars. Still, Jake had to play the role of the boss. And now, there was Mars, half-naked, busting in with only minutes to go before he had to be on the air, announcing to the world he had some sort of urinary tract issue while Jake and Greg sat with the one man who could throw them all out of the station and turn off the transmitter.

"I'll do my shift. I promise. But I have to go to the infirmary afterward," Mars exclaimed, rattling out his words and hurriedly stacking albums in his arms. Neither Jake, nor Greg, nor Dr. Elmore said a word. They just watched and listened. "But if it gets worse while I'm on the air, someone is going to have to take over," Mars demanded. "Honestly, I'm pissing fucking blood, man!" He rushed down the hall and slipped through the studio door, juggling the albums, dropping one on the tiled floor.

Dr. Elmore took a long drag from his cigarette and said, "Okay then, try to keep the books up to date, don't buy too many new records, don't say fuck on the air, and . . ." He stood up from the table, stuffed out his cigarette in the black, nearly full ashtray and added, " . . .try your best to have everyone here wear a shirt as much as possible. The administration isn't real big on a shirtless student body running around campus. And shoes would be good, too." Dr. Elmore walked toward the door then turned at the top of the staircase. "We'll do this again before the end of the semester." The soles of Dr. Elmore's dirty bucks tapped out a steady, slowly fading beat down the stairs.

"Jesus!" Greg cried, smacking the palm of his hand against the side of his head and sharply snapping his chair from the table, the feet of the legs screeching against the floor. "What the fuck?"

"Yeah, I wish that wouldn't have happened," Jake whispered, somehow believing if he remained reasonably quiet, it might keep Greg from throwing a stapler across the room.

"He's going to be checking on us all the time now, see if we're fucking up." Greg marched around the table, throwing his hands in the air. "He'll never leave us the fuck alone. He'll be up here all the time, watching us, asking fucking questions."

"It'll be okay," Jake said, hoping to put what happened into perspective. "It won't be that different, really. Elmore's cool."

"What the fuck world do you live in?"

"He didn't seem pissed," Jake said, knowing Elmore was not known for outbursts. He rarely raised his voice in his class, and when students were late or forgot assignments, he calmly told them not to do it again. Dr. Elmore was a steady sort of guy.

"I've got class," Greg said, gathering a thin stack of papers, a notebook and a couple of textbooks from his desk in the corner of the office. "Tell Mars to see a fucking doctor!"

"Probably a good idea."

"Jesus Christ," Greg mumbled as he exited.

The office was empty. Silent. The air monitor had been turned down for the meeting with Elmore. Jake stood before the open bay window that looked out over campus and watched the rush of students heading for classes, groups of girls on the grassy hill laughing, two frat brothers smoking near a maple tree across the walkway. He wanted a cigarette but had none. "Pissing blood," Jake said to himself. He lifted the small monitor speaker and sat it on the sill of the bay window, facing it toward campus, and cranked the volume.

Mick Jagger's vocals cut through the air and out to campus. Jake turned the volume knob as far it would go and leaned out the open window. A girl he'd never seen before walked alone along the sidewalk just below the window. She looked up and smiled.

# 6

M OST FRIDAY NIGHTS, SARAH AND Jake would end up at his trailer with a few friends. The regulars were Sean and Greg from the radio station, Danny, and Sarah's friend Lauren. They played records; Jake strummed the guitar. They smoked cigarettes and weed when they had it, and drank beer when they could afford it. Danny had a part-time job at the snack bar in the Student Union and would sometimes steal a half-dozen pizza slices to share with everyone. No one paid attention to inventory. On this night, they had pepperoni and cheese to go with cans of Iron City beer.

"Don't you think sometimes we all grew up too late?" Jake asked, swigging the last of the beer.

"You on that hippie thing again?" said Sean, sitting cross-legged on the floor, a stack of albums on his lap. "Listening to too much Dead again?" Sean held up the Grateful Dead's *American Beauty* album for everyone to see.

"The war's over, people are listening to Disco shit. I feel a little out place in my era or something," Jake said.

"You wanted to be in San Francisco in '67, right?" Danny said. "The Summer of Love."

"Don't you feel that? Like we missed out?"

"Nothing to be angry about anymore, huh?" Sarah said, putting her arm around Jake's neck. "He talks about this all the time, about not having something to protest, to care about."

"Yeah, can't really be part of a revolution when you're twelve," said Greg.

"All of us were born in '56, or something, right?" Jake asked. "If we were born a few years earlier, we would have all been in the middle of the most interesting time ever."

"Oh, come on," said Danny, "all times are interesting."

"Here we go," said Lauren, "he's getting into his Existentialism, Zen thing or some bullshit again."

"May you live in interesting times," said Greg.

"Isn't that supposed to be some sort of curse?" Danny asked. He had read that that phrase, many times said as a blessing or a wish, was really the first of three curses, the English translation of a Chinese proverb. The other parts of the proverb were about becoming the attention of powerful people and being granted your wishes, finding what you are looking for. "If you get what you want, exactly what you want, you lose your edge, your sense of longing, your adventurous spirit," Danny explained.

"So you're better off being one step behind your dreams?" asked Lauren.

"Something like that," said Danny.

"Like not being in the middle of the 1960s?" asked Greg.

"Maybe," Jake said. "I just think I was born to be part of that time somehow. I don't know. Maybe I'm nuts."

"Bingo," said Greg.

"Got to make your own interesting times, sweetie," said Sarah, kissing Jake on the temple.

"Let's put on some Hendrix," said Sean. He found *Are You Experienced* near the bottom of the stack and slipped it on the turntable.

In high school, when Jake first started growing his hair long, his friends were amazed his parents let him do it. His mom and dad barely said a word to Jake even when his wavy mop nearly reached his shoulders. Many of Jake's friends wore their hair just over their ears, but their parents were steadfast about that being the longest it would ever get. One buddy's parents threatened to throw him out of the house if he didn't go to the barber. The only thing Jake's mother ever insisted on was that he shampooed regularly. She didn't mind long hair, but she hated scruffy. His dad would joke about "getting a haircut," but he didn't really mean it, at least Jake didn't think so. His father grew up with thick auburn hair. Some called it movie star hair. But after the Army shaved his head in 1951, it never grew back. Jake's dad was essentially bald from the age of nineteen. Maybe letting Jake fly his freak flag was his father's way of thumbing his nose at the bad hair genes that had been passed on to him.

Despite being okay with the counterculture look, his dad didn't much like Jake's emerging political beliefs. Jake remembers commenting once that no man with a hippie mane would ever be elected to office, certainly not the Presidency, simply because of the length of his hair. His father didn't like that, demanding that Jake should just accept the way things were, accept that everyone had to conform in one way or another to get along in the world.

Jake and his friends drank beer and smoked their cigarettes and weed without saying much of anything all the way through side one of the Hendrix album.

"Flip it," said Greg.

Danny, Sean, and Jake, like Greg, were fans of Jimi. Lauren and Sarah, not so much.

"Maybe some Fogelberg after this?" said Lauren.

"*Souvenirs,*" Jake said. "Solid album." Dan Fogelberg was beginning to gain some popularity at the time with his country-folk and melodious voice.

"Chicks dig it," said Sean, laughing.

"Nothing wrong with that," added Danny.

They got through Hendrix, some Fogelberg, and a side of Springsteen's *Born to Run* when the beer ran out.

"You got any more dope stashed somewhere?" Danny asked Sean, the one who usually had some weed, dealing a little around campus to feed his habit.

"A little. We can all get a couple of tokes," Sean said. "Had to sell a bunch to Mars to help pay the rent."

"Mars?" Jake asked. "Okay, that explains it."

"Didn't he show up naked at the station or something?" asked Sarah, laughing.

"Not exactly naked, but close. I think he's living large right now."

"Putting his dick in anything he can, and smoking whatever he can put a match to," said Greg, shaking his head.

"Don't worry about it. I'm taking care of it," Jake said, exaggerating his influence over Mars.

Jake and Greg filled in the details of Mars' grand entrance at the station. Sean hadn't heard the complete version, neither had Danny. Jake had given Sarah the CliffsNotes story, but Lauren was hearing it for the first time.

"That's fucking hilarious," she said, holding her hand over her mouth as she giggled. "He must be a real fuckup."

"Mars is Mars," Jake said.

"Kind of a lovable fuckup," said Danny, who had heard about Mars but had never met him.

"Oh, fucking lovable, all right," said Greg, expressing his continued anxiety over how Mars' antics might affect the station. For an English major who loved Jack Kerouac and looked more like a hippie than any of Jake's friends, Greg worried like a Harvard business major.

Sean rolled a joint, lit it with an old stainless steel Zippo lighter that once belonged to his father, took a hit, and passed it to Danny. They all had a little and spent the rest of the night listening to music, talking about what plans they had, or didn't, after graduation. It was 2 a.m. when Greg, Sean, and Lauren left. Danny fell asleep on the couch. Sarah stayed over.

"You told everyone tonight you might end up back at McKeesport to work at WIXZ after graduation," Sarah said, snuggling up and resting her head on Jake's bare chest. The bed sheets were cool to the touch, and she was chilled. "You told me that probably wasn't going to happen. Couldn't stand the music."

"Yeah, but you know I'm going to take a look at whatever opportunities I might get."

"What about wanting to be part of a Rock-n-Roll station? Your dream?"

"It's still what I want," Jake said, stroking her hair. "But maybe I shouldn't say no to something right in front of me."

"Did they offer you something?"

"No, but who knows."

Sarah nestled her head a little tighter into his chest. "I could work in Pittsburgh," she whispered.

Jake kissed her forehead and caressed the small of her naked back. This was unchartered water, things unresolved, unsaid, questions unanswered.

It wasn't long before Sarah was asleep in Jake's arms, but he remained awake, his mind crowded with thoughts and emotions so silly and clichéd, the kind of unoriginal considerations every senior in every university thinks about as they approach the end of their senior year. Jake had loathed all those students at his high school who cried at the graduation ceremony and ran around getting everyone to sign their yearbooks. It was all so horribly corny. He remembered high-fiving some friends then sneaking off behind the stands in the football field with his buddy, Rick, who had slipped a pint of cheap vodka under his gown. They promised that night never to become their parents, pledged they'd see the world, do what they wanted, reject the life of the two-car garage, the picket fence, the kids and the dog. Rick had dreams of moving to New York. He'd find a studio apartment, roam the city at night, and write his novel by day.

Jake was going to write music, play the guitar at corner bars, and host a great radio show, airing the songs that mattered. He would impart wisdom over the airwaves and change the world little by little with stories about music and life. Jake didn't know what happened to Rick after high school. They didn't stay in touch. He didn't think he ever made it to New York. There was one rumor that Rick worked at a steel mill in Pittsburgh for a time, but that's all he knew. As for Jake? All that was certain was that he was awake in the middle of the night in a rundown trailer outside a small college town in Pennsylvania, nursing a head full of dreams and holding Sarah in his arms.

# 7

JAKE KEPT A BLACK-AND-WHITE PHOTOGRAPH of his mother in an old wooden frame on top of the black footlocker that doubled as his nightstand. She was probably nineteen or twenty years old at the time of the photo, just a few months after marrying his father. She's sitting at a radio control board, her hand lowering the arm of a turntable onto a vinyl record. His mother looks happy. She's smiling, almost laughing. Jake was given the photograph as a gift, after hosting his first radio show on the college station. "I was on the radio, too, you know," his mother said proudly, handing Jake the photograph.

Gloria Mulholland was a bit reserved, kind of proper. She played bridge with her neighborhood friends at the monthly card club, drinking coffee for hours and snacking on pound cake. She was also the president of the PTA at Jake's elementary school and the Catholic girl who never sang the hymns out loud in mass but instead, read them to herself. She had never appeared to Jake to be the kind of person who would host a radio program, be part of the entertainment world, or even know enough about music to pull it off. Years after Jake's brother Michael died, Jake's mother gave him that photo, seemingly compelled to share parts of her past she hadn't before. Maybe it was his mother's way of showing she had forgiven Jake. "I

just want you to have this," she said. "Think of it as something
we share."

During one summer break from school, Jake found his
mother leaning over the kitchen sink, spitting up blood. She
tried to wave him off, but Jake paid no attention and reached
out to put his arms around her shoulders, not knowing what
else to do, how to soothe her. There wasn't a lot of blood, but it
was enough to alarm him. His mother insisted Jake shouldn't
worry, it had happened before over the years, she said. For a
long time she hid the bloody episodes from Jake and his sister,
Mary, the youngest of the three children. His father knew about
them, even witnessing a few. After Michael died, the episodes
became more frequent and not as easily concealed. Jake's father
may have pretended the incidents had something to do with his
mother's extraordinary grief, but he knew they were more likely
connected to her history with tuberculosis.

When his mother was eighteen years old and newly married,
she was diagnosed with TB and quarantined in the Pittsburgh
City Tuberculosis Sanatorium. It was known as the Leech Farm
Hospital or by its nickname, the Haven of Rest. Doctors told
Jake's father, who at the time was an Army private stationed at
Fort Bragg in North Carolina, that his new bride would never be
released, never come home, and would die at Leech Farm like
the hundreds of others who were diagnosed with the disease
and brought to the sanatorium.

Jake's mother disregarded the odds, dumbfounded the doctors, and after a year-and-a-half of rest and good nutrition—the
prescription of the day for treating TB—she was deemed cured
and allowed to go home. Physicians said she'd have breathing
difficulties for the rest of her life, and at times the scarring on
her lungs might produce some bleeding, but if she tried to eat
right and take care of herself, she could live a reasonably good
life. Before she was discharged—during the eighteen months
she was confined to Leech Farm—his mother became a radio

announcer. It was a closed-circuit system heard only at the hospital, a station exclusively for the patients. His mother called herself Glorious Gloria and three times a week from 10 a.m. until noon she played Frank Sinatra and Patty Paige records and took requests from not only patients but nurses, too. She read short poems she thought would give her gravely ill and infirmed listeners some comfort. His mother also announced baseball scores and offered reading suggestions from the material in the hospital library. Something from Charles Dickens was always on the list, and on Fridays, although she was reluctant to do so, she would read the obituaries—the names of the patients who had died that week. It was what the administration insisted she do. They thought she handled it with a beautiful touch, a sense of great reverence and respect. Her voice, one nurse told her, sounded like an angel. Jake's mom played recordings of hymns and Gregorian chants before and after the reading of the names and asked for a moment of silent prayer for those who had passed. Despite that difficult chore, his mother insisted the radio show—everything about it, including the weekly list of the dead—contributed to saving her own life. "There's a reason for everything," his mother always told him. "And there was a reason I got TB, a reason why I was on the radio."

Jake's mother never said as much, but Jake believed she also trusted there was a larger, more spiritual reason why Michael had died—some purpose in it—and a reason why Jake was the last to see him before he disappeared in the shadows of the woods.

After Jake's mother revealed the full story of her radio days, the picture of her at the console became far more than a cherished, grainy, old photograph. It was now the symbol of what the music and words, radiating each day from the speakers of desktop clock radios, hand-held transistors, and car stereos, can do to a soul. Three days a week in the early 1950s inside a tuberculosis sanatorium set in the hills of Pittsburgh, Gloria

Mulholland was proof of that. She was a survivor, enduring the physical damages of TB and the awful death of a son, a mother's unending nightmare. It was the guilt she wrestled with, the guilt of putting Jake in charge of little Michael.

Jake was 12, old enough to be responsible for his 6-year old brother, his mother believed. His father believed it to. The family was in the Laurel Mountains on a fall weekend, taking in the autumn colors. His sister Mary was three years old, a toddler. The family hiked the woods, a walk not unlike the ones Jake's father took with his dog and his older son when Jake was much younger. When one grew up in Pennsylvania, the maple, pine, and black cherry forests were the playgrounds. Jake's mother and father asked him to keep an eye on Michael while they doubled-back to the campground with Mary to start a fire and dinner. "Mary's too little to keep going. Just take the trail straight back," his mom said. Jake had spent a lot of time in the woods. There was a forest and a creek across the street from his boyhood home where Michael had played, turning over rocks to look for worms and water bugs, and tossing the stones in the water. There was a dead oak tree on a hillside where they would swing from a low-hanging branch. It was familiar fun, a day in the woods. There was nothing unnerving, unsettling or unusual about being asked to hold his brother's hand and walk back along a trail to a cabin less than a quarter-mile away.

After crunching their way through the leaves and trying to climb a few small trees, Jake grabbed Michael's hand and started back on the trail. Minutes into the walk, there was rustling in the brush. Jake pushed away small low-hanging branches and trampled through groundcover, hoping to spot a whitetail, maybe a big buck. There, in a small clearing of pine, was a young doe startled still. Jake squatted below some saplings. "Michael," he whispered, turning to look behind him to alert his brother. Jake did not see Michael. The deer shuddered and sniffed the air. It then turned and bolted around a grouping of mountain laurels and small pines, the white of its tail bobbing in and around the muted reds, oranges, and browns of the season. "Michael, did you see that?" Jake said, excitedly. He stood from his lowered position. "Michael?"

A month passed before an experienced hiker found Michael's body at the bottom of a ravine near a small creek. He was partially covered by snow when they discovered him. A half-foot had fallen that early December in the mountains. A state ranger believed Michael had fallen, because of the large gash on his forehead and his fractured arm. The tumble had likely knocked him unconscious, and hypothermia weakened him. When Jake broke away from Michael that day to chase the deer, it seemed he was without his brother for only a moment. But as Jake screamed Michael's name into the thick wilderness, the silence was an eternity. Dozens of men and women—rangers, police, and volunteers from the nearby town of Latrobe—looked for many days. The numbers dwindled with the hope, both eventually disappearing. The boys' father returned to those woods alone a number of times, walking and calling for Michael, believing his son was in the shadows somewhere. Jake's mother stayed home to cry. As much as Jake wanted to join his father or wrap his arms around his mother, he could do neither. Jake was unable to find Michael and incapable of helping those who loved him, including himself. All Jake could do was sit in silence, wait for his father to return home from the woods, listen to his mother's tears, and wish he had never let go of Michael's hand.

———

It was late in the show, a couple of weeks into the new semester, when Lisa rushed in from the newsroom to the studio.

"Did you just say 'Rock Around the *Cock*?'" she asked, laughing through the question.

"What?" Jake asked, cueing up the Beatles' "A Day in the Life" from *Sgt. Pepper's* on turntable 2.

"You just said 'cock,'" she said, repeating the word cock with more deliberate diction.

"I didn't say cock."

"It was at the end of that set of 50s songs you played. You called it 'Rock Around the *Cock.*' C-o-c-k. Cock."

"No. Don't think so," Jake said sheepishly.

Greg had been working at his desk in the station office, arriving earlier than usual that morning, hoping to get the books a bit more in order per their advisor's suggestion. He was now standing behind Lisa in the studio. "I just got a phone call in the office. A listener, some student, says you said cock on the air?" he asked, disbelieving.

"Jesus, people. I didn't say cock."

"Someone called?" Lisa asked. "A listener actually called?"

"The listener said it was pretty clear. *Cock.*" Greg said the word with vibrant vulgarity.

"And if I did, what the fuck are we going to do about it now?" Jake asked, irritated and uncomfortable with the unwanted attention.

Lisa giggled. "I have to get my newscast together so I don't slip up and say *pussy*," she shouted over her shoulder as she walked out. Greg stood silently near the studio door. "Try not to say cock. Thank you very much," he said, swiftly turning and walking out.

"I'm on it," Jake said. "No more COCK!"

He switched on the microphone.

"8:47 on your campus radio station, here's what might be the most interesting song from *Pepper's*. It's the Beatles on WCCB." Jake turned off the mic. The heavy piano chords at the beginning of "A Day in the Life" surged through the studio monitor.

"Hey, babe," Sarah said, slipping into the studio. In her hand was a cinnamon-raisin bagel from Mr. Donut. "Didn't make it to the cafeteria today, but I had a coupon."

"I said cock on the air."

"What?

"Yep, cock."

"Really? At least it wasn't fuck," Sarah said, kissing Jake on the top of the head.

A friend of Jake's dad, who had been a big name on Pittsburgh radio back in the early 60s and played golf with his father every Saturday, offered to listen to one of Jake's demo tapes from the college radio station. He urged him to be more natural in his delivery, talk like he talked to friends. And he said, "Make all your mistakes now. Get it out of your system." I'm sure he would have called "Rock Around the *Cock*" one of Jake's best mistakes. He could certainly add the lesbian troops slip-up to that list, too. There would be more, he was certain. Still, Jake was weary of the blunders. He knew Sarah meant well by trying to make light of the most recent screw-up, but at that moment it wasn't exactly what Jake wanted to hear.

"Don't you have to get to class?" he asked.

"Well, aren't we touchy this morning," Sarah said, surprised at his mood.

"I'll see you later, okay?"

"Guess so," she said. "Whatever." Sarah tossed the bag with the bagel inside on the console. "Don't choke on your breakfast." She marched out the door, sidestepping Lisa who was on her way into the studio for the final newscast of the morning.

"Trouble in paradise?" Lisa asked, after waiting until Sarah was out the studio door.

"She'll get over it," Jake said. "You ready to go?"

"Yep. And when I'm done, I'm buying you a drink," she said.

"It's 9:00 in the morning."

"Coffee, you idiot. Not a cocktail," she said, smiling. "Get it? COCKtail?"

Jake opened the microphone.

"It's 8:59 on WCCB. That's it for me this morning. We'll talk again tomorrow, and always remember what Dylan Thomas once said." Jake had been paying a little more attention lately in his British Literature class, trying to spend less time visualizing what was under Miss Wilde's silk blouse, and instead, actually taking notes on what he liked and even incorporating some of it into the radio show. "'He who seeks rest finds boredom.' Now, here's Lisa with the news."

———

There were a few students sitting at the Formica booths inside Mr. Donut when Lisa and Jake arrived. Some sat alone with textbooks and notebooks opened on the light blue tables, others sat in groups, talking and drinking coffee. On a round, backless seat at the five-stool counter was an older man, probably in his forties, dressed in a grease-stained dark green jumpsuit with the name *Willy* embroidered on the right front chest. He slumped into his coffee. Jake guessed he was an auto mechanic. Behind the counter, hovering near the cash register was a woman he'd seen a couple times before. She looked to be in her mid-thirties, her mousey hair pulled back in a ponytail. She wore a dark blue apron splattered with white powdered sugar, and took orders.

"Couple of coffees," Lisa said.

"What do you take?"

"No sugar, easy cream," Jake told the counter woman.

"Black, please," Lisa added.

They took the booth near the back, facing each other at the table.

"How long you been dating that girl?" she asked.

"Couple years."

"Love her?"

"Think so."

"That's not good."

"What do you mean?"

"*Think so?* Really?"

"Yeah, I love her," he said.

"I don't believe you."

"I've known you for two months or so, and you think you got me and my girlfriend figured out?"

"I've been there."

"How so?"

"Long relationship, unsure of what we were going to do when I transferred here. We struggled with how to keep things going long distance. Truth was, there wasn't enough there to keep it going. We didn't know that until we lived away from each other."

"You got it all figured out," Jake smirked.

"Just trying to be a friend," she said, reaching out her hand to playfully touch his. "You're a good guy."

Lisa's blouse had slipped a bit from her right shoulder, giving Jake a glimpse of the strap of a pink bra that held up what appeared to be faultlessly shaped breasts, rounded and full. They were what the boys in his high school used to call a perfect handful. Jake was staring at her tits, and she knew it. Girls know when you're staring at their tits.

"I don't know about the good guy thing," Jake said, diverting his eyes to look into his half-empty coffee mug.

"Oh fuck you," she said, kicking Jake's shin under the table. "Don't play that game. Don't give me that *I'm-so-humble-that-I-don't-know-how-cool-I-am* shit," she said with a mocking, whiney voice.

Lisa made Jake laugh.

They ordered more coffee and talked for an hour about school, their tentative plans after the semester was over, and the radio station. Lisa and Jake discovered they had some mutual friends and agreed to join a bunch of them on Saturday afternoon for one of the loosely planned co-ed flag football games pulled together each weekend by a couple of clubs on campus. The games were designed to help blow off a little collegiate steam and for students to get to know each other. Plus, Jake would get to see if Lisa, a gymnast and a swimmer in high school, was as athletic as she looked—if those toned shoulders, and the kick she gave him, translated to skills on the gridiron.

# 8

JAKE'S DAD HAD PLAYED FOOTBALL in high school. He was a running back until his father walked out, and he had to quit to get a job as a member of a construction crew, building houses. Jake's grandfather left his family to live with the woman down the street, the mother of his dad's best friend. They both drank, so it probably was a better match than Jake's grandmother. Grandma didn't drink, just smoked. A lot. Chesterfields. She never divorced Jake's grandfather. She refused. She was Irish-Catholic.

Jake's father built houses for a couple of years until the Army drafted him. He was assigned to the 101$^{st}$ Airborne Division, paratroopers, but he never jumped. He became a cook instead. In fact, as the story goes, he asked to be a cook. "I wasn't interested in jumping out of airplanes," his father told Jake. Truth was, his dad was petrified. Spent his two years stationed in North Carolina, never went overseas, and was quick to say the happiest day of his Army life was the day he was discharged.

Along with the photo of his mother, Jake also had a photo of his dad from the same years. He's in his cook's uniform, a white apron around his fatigues. He's wearing a private's cap; a cigarette dangles from his mouth. He's wielding a large spatula, jokingly preparing to smack the head of another soldier. It was his bunkmate, a guy his unit called Smokey because he could blow intricate smoke rings while puffing his Winstons. Both his father and Smokey looked happy in the photo—two laughing nineteen year olds.

Happy was an emotion Jake wasn't sure what to do with at the age of nineteen, and now, at twenty-one, he was *certain* he didn't know what to do with it. Sure, there were times Jake was happy, he guessed, but he wasn't sure what happy was supposed to mean, what it was to look like or exactly how he was to feel. There were too many uncertainties to be truly happy, too much to think about. It was safe to say that most everybody Jake knew in college was in the same state of mind, believing they should be happy but not believing they were. The emotions surfaced mostly when Jake was alone. With friends, he fed off the collective hubris, the counterfeit confidences, and did his best to suffocate all the anxiety of trying to figure out what was going to happen after the diploma was handed to him. Most everyone Jake knew had some luxury of choice, the implied privilege of deciding for themselves how they were going to ascend into adulthood. That was not the opportunity Jake's father had. He was forced into his adult life. He accepted it but also resented it.

———

It had rained Friday night, producing a few puddles on the field.

"This is perfect. Football and mud, an essential combination," said Sean, tossing a football into the air and catching it.

Sean, Danny, and Jake arrived at the field just after noon. A few others, some Jake knew and some he didn't, wandered there shortly after. Greg arrived with a handful of students from the radio station. Even Mars showed up, although ill prepared in a sleeveless tee-shirt and sandals. Sarah brought her friend Lauren and her roommate, the one who strutted around their apartment in her panties. She had clothes on this time. And Lisa, accompanied by three girls from her dorm Jake hadn't met before, arrived in a pair of worn Levis, a faded and oversized Steelers football jersey, her hair pulled back in a loose ponytail, and of all things, her own football helmet.

"You know this is *flag* football, right? No tackling?" asked Greg.

"I just wanted to look the part," Lisa said, giggling through the helmet's faceguard.

"Perfect," said Mars. "You look stunning."

The several-sizes-too-big helmet slid down over her eyes.

"It was my brother's in high school. Ended up in my car somehow," Lisa said. "This is his jersey too," she added, strutting back and forth, exaggerating the sway of her hips with all the zest of a runway fashion model, flipping the strands of hair that had loosened from the ponytail.

"You, my friend, are one sexy thing," Mars said, smiling and leaning his shoulder against hers. "You sure this isn't tackle?" he asked, devilishly.

"I think it should be now," Sean answered with a wink.

"Perverts. But I knew that," Lisa said with conviction. "Probably brought those Peeping Tom binoculars with you."

Sarah came up behind Jake and wrapped her arms around his waist. "Hey babe. You on my team?"

"Always your team," Jake said. "Okay. Everyone know everybody here?"

After some brief introductions, Greg went over the rules. It was flag football, but tee-shirts were used instead, tucking them in waistbands. To tackle someone, the opposing team's player pulled out the shirt and threw it on the ground.

"Each team should have the same number of girls on it," insisted Greg. "Captains?"

"Sean and me," said Mars.

Jake ended up on Sean's team with Sarah, her roommate, and a few others from the radio station. Lisa was on the opposite team.

Lisa jabbed her two index fingers in Jake's direction. "I'm coming after you," she said, the helmet wobbling on her head. "You are going down!"

"That's my girl!" screamed Mars, playing the role of a defensive line coach prowling the sidelines.

Lisa pointed at Greg. "And I'm coming after you, too," she said. Lisa yanked the helmet off her head and tossed it toward the sidelines. She locked her eyes on Sarah. "And YOU!"

"Me?" Sarah asked, mocking Lisa's challenge. "Bring it, girlie!"

Sarah had played some volleyball in high school and had once been a regular runner but not much since starting college. She had taken some ballet classes as a kid, continued them a bit in her early teens, and now and then would go to the dance studio in the theater department to see if her muscles could remember anything. Sarah was slight—not skinny—just willowy. And she had some strength. One night in her junior year, at 2 o'clock in the morning at Mr. Donut, she was joking with some friends and started to arm wrestle. Sarah beat all the girls and a couple of the boys. It might have been more about determination, a fierce competitive nature, than real power. She didn't like to show it much, but she had determination, toughness. Lisa, however, just *looked* tougher. She had broad shoulders shaped from the butterfly stroke, toned legs, and a tight butt. Sure, she had a soft side—her silky red hair and her regularly painted fingernails, usually red. If someone had asked Jake to make a bet that afternoon, he would have put his money on Lisa kicking someone's ass.

The teams were evenly divided, seven members each with three assigned to both the offensive and defensive lines. There was one running back, two receivers, and a quarterback.

Defensive players could play just about anywhere they wanted on their side of the ball, usually picking a single opponent on which to concentrate. Man-to-man coverage. You could block and knock each other around, but no tackling. On offense you could pass or run, and because there were no markers to signify yardage, the only way to achieve a first down was to complete two passes in a row, short or long.

Mars' team kicked off. On the first set of downs, Sarah lined up as a wide receiver.

"I got her," Lisa yelled, pointing to Sarah and lining up in a crouched stance directly across from her just a few yards from the line of scrimmage.

Jake was quarterback but not because he had any particular skill. He had been a catcher on the high school baseball team but never played organized football. Still, Jake could throw a reasonable spiral, marginally better than most. Quarterback by default, one might say.

First play was a run. Jake handed the ball off to Sean, zipping to the left for an end-around, and despite Sean's reasonable speed, he only gained four yards or so before Mars, stumbling around in his flip-flops, yanked the tee out from Sean's waistband.

"We have to pass," Jake whispered in the huddle. "We'll need a first down, so we've got to throw. Sarah, you ready?"

"I'm your man," Sarah said, making fists and raising her arms into a muscleman pose.

Sarah's panty-loving roommate was the other receiver.

"I want you to go out about five yards and just turn around," Jake said to her. "Be ready, I might have to throw it to you."

"And I have to catch it, right?"

"Probably a good idea," said Sean, mocking her.

"Fuck you," she said, playfully smacking Sean on the head.

"Sarah, can you get past Lisa?" Jake asked.

There was only one other time Jake could remember Sarah giving the kind of expression she gave at that moment. When they were first dating and getting to know each other, Jake was playing his guitar for her and asked if she knew who Woody Guthrie was.

"Seriously?" Sarah asked, looking around at everyone in the huddle. "Is he really asking me that question?"

"Okay, Lynn Swan," Jake said, evoking the name of Pittsburgh's speedy wide receiver. "Go out about five yards, juke to the right, and take off."

As the ball was snapped, Sarah bolted from the line, knocking Lisa in the shoulder, hoping to slow her down. Sarah then stutter-stepped, halted, and turned on the gas with Lisa only a step behind her. Jake hurled the ball some fifteen yards down the right side of the field, trying to lead Sarah by several feet. The ball floated in an arc and descended, seemingly in slow motion, from its pinnacle to Sarah's outstretched hands. She bobbled the ball momentarily, fingertips grasping for leather, then she seized it, pulling it to her chest. At that instant, Lisa become airborne, barreling against Sarah from behind, a violent collision between Lisa's shoulder and Sarah's waist. Lisa wrapped her arms around Sarah's upper thighs, Sarah yelped, and the ball squirted out of her hands. The two tumbled to the ground, Sarah on her belly and Lisa on top of her.

"Fuck!" Sarah screamed, rolling over on the grass and popping up into a sitting position. "What the hell?"

Lisa leapt to her feet to stand above Sarah, and with little emotion, said, "Sorry. Forgot."

Jake considered running to Sarah's rescue but instead, stood frozen in the backfield, watching Sarah slowly rise from the ground. Grass and mud stained the knees of her jeans, and the wet earth had turned the palms of her hands brown from trying to break her fall. Sarah took a moment to brush the hair from her eyes and adjust her tee-shirt. Then, from somewhere in her gut came a deep growl—the yell of a warrior—and she bolted toward Lisa, who by now was returning to the scrimmage line, her back to Sarah. Somehow Lisa detected Sarah's imminent and violent arrival. Peeking over her left shoulder, she tried to scurry from Sarah's clutches. With the entire force of her upper body, Sarah thumped Lisa from behind, just below the shoulders. Lisa let out a sharp and sudden shout—an audible exclamation mark—staggering but not falling.

"I should kick your ass," Sarah roared, uncharacteristically, giving Lisa the finger. "You got some problem with me?"

Jake had never seen that side of Sarah, not that level of ferocity. Lisa had ignited Sarah's defensive instinct. She was like the cuddly cat that suddenly and angrily hisses at the dog that moves too close to her food.

Lisa shrugged her shoulders, dismissing Sarah, smiled, and said, "Let's play some football."

In Jake's kindergarten class, Debbie McKenzie and Susie Morton kicked the shit out of each other after one accused the other of kissing Joey Simpson. It rained that day, and Mrs. Eckhart kept the class inside to color and play with Silly Putty. On the playground, Debbie had done her best to kiss Joey but was never fast enough to catch him when he'd run away to the other side of the monkey bars. Susie was more understated in her approach. She'd stare at Joey, watch him eat his mid-morning peanut butter and grape jelly sandwich snack, and drink from his milk carton. Finally, Susie, after weeks of starry-eyed gazing, found an intense rush of courage. She walked straight up to Joey, waited for him to swallow, and laid a big one straight on his lips. Stunned, Joey almost dropped his milk. And Debbie, witnessing this from the adjacent table, cold-cocked Susie. It was at least a full minute before Mrs. Eckhart, another teacher in the classroom across the hall, and the school janitor, were able to tug the two apart and break up what Jake was certain was this kindergarten class's first and only raging cat fight, the same kind of battle that appeared just about to happen between Sarah and Lisa.

After more nasty words from Sarah and dirty looks from Lisa, everyone got back to the game. There were no more scuffles, but Sarah did accuse Lisa of spitting on her during one of the plays. All of this made Jake tense. For others though, the confrontation was highly entertaining. It was Sean who said, "There's nothing like watching two girls get pissed off at each other."

Later that night at Jake's trailer, while he massaged Sarah's back, still aching from Lisa's tackle, Sarah asked a sudden unexpected question.

"Do you want to fuck Lisa?"

Jake pretended to be lost in the softness of Sarah's skin, but his tiny gasp could not be disguised. And to allow a few seconds of silence between an enquiry such as that and a response—any response—would be an immense mistake. Even though Jake eventually answered her question, "Of course not," and did so emphatically, his reply was far too delayed, permitting a sliver of doubt.

# 9

JAKE'S HEART WAS FIRST BROKEN when he was a high school freshman. A tall, slim, dark-haired Jewish girl who took jazz dance lessons twice a week, the daughter of a dermatologist, told Jake her parents didn't want them seeing each other anymore. Jake carried that heartache for years, took it with him to college. He called her a couple of times, hanging up the phone as soon as he heard her voice.

Jake met Nadine in eighth grade. She was in three of his classes. Jake passed her a couple of handwritten notes on lined paper from his spiral notebook and told her friends to tell her that he liked her and to ask if she liked him. They soon started calling each other boyfriend and girlfriend. Jake gave her a cheap metal ring he bought at G.C. Murphy, a five-and-dime shop in Pittsburgh, and hung out at her house on the weekends. There was no doubt in Jake's mind that he would marry her.

Nadine and Jake had kissed a lot, necked as much as they could, slipping his hand under her bra a couple of times. Her parents certainly knew nothing about this. Not until the letter. Jake had mailed it to Nadine, detailing what he longed to do next: take off her pants, touch her between the legs, be naked with her in bed. It was explicit but romantic, Jake thought. Each day after he had sent it, Jake became more nervous. He was certain Nadine had received it, but she spoke nothing of it for more than a week. And when Jake finally gathered enough courage to ask her about it in the school hallway near her locker between biology and study hall, her answer was far from what he wanted to hear. Nadine looked down to her feet, diverting her eyes from Jake's, and said, "Yes. I did get your letter. And so did my mother." Her mother had found the note slipped under Nadine's pillow, told Nadine's father, and demanded Nadine end the relationship. When the bell rang for the start of classes, Nadine said, "I can't see you anymore." That moment was still fresh for Jake. Sarah reminded him a bit of Nadine. It wasn't that they looked a lot alike, although their body types were similar—long legs, rounded shoulders, perky breasts, blue eyes—it was more about how they viewed the world. There was an unflinching optimism, an unwavering honesty, and sometimes an unsettling frankness. Jake thought he had loved Nadine, and now he thought he loved Sarah. Truth was, Jake wasn't sure of any of it.

———

In Miss Wilde's literature class, they were discussing works that churned up the beautiful and painful; the very human stories of love. A couple of months into the semester, they read Keats. Wilde didn't adhere to the syllabus much and certainly didn't teach British Literature in some neat or chronological fashion; she just introduced what she liked and apparently what she believed she thought the class would like, or at least appreciate.

"John Keats was a romantic poet. In today's terms, you might call him a bit of a pansy," Wilde told the class. "Not necessarily a man's man. But he knew what lie deep within a man's heart, the stuff most men don't like to admit is there, and Keats knew how to write about it. Keats was a genius on love and heartbreak."

She assigned *La Belle Dame sans Merci.*

Jake read it over and over and although difficult to fully understand, he determined it had something to do with a broken relationship, a romance that never really emerged. And when Wilde lectured about the poem, Jake became smothered, buried in the heartbreak that rose up from Keats' twelve short stanzas.

The verse was about a knight, dying in the woods, who comes across a mysterious, beautiful, and wild-looking woman. She does not speak his language, but he finds her irresistible and adorns her with flowers, offers her his horse to ride, and walks beside them. He believes he loves her and she him. They stop to rest, and he kisses her to sleep. The knight also falls asleep but has a terrible nightmare, a warning that this woman will enslave him. "When the knight awakens," said Wilde, "the woman is gone." Wilde paused, surveyed the faces then read the poem's final lines:

"And this is why I sojourn here,
Alone and palely loitering,
Though the sedge is wither'd from the lake,
And no birds sing."

Most of the class didn't get it. But Jake somehow knew, intrinsically, Keats was writing about the anguish of heartbreak. Jake didn't have to understand it completely, all the poetic metaphors, allusions; to him the raw emotion was clear. Keats' poem was reawakening memories, unhealed little scars. When he was forced to try to forget about Nadine that first year in high school, Jake found himself, on a Friday night, listening to records in a buddy's basement. He bad-mouthed Nadine, trying to be a tough guy about his feelings. But his buddy knew better and asked if Jake wasn't hiding what he really felt. Jake tried to shake off the question and remain stoic but couldn't fake it for long. "I guess I just want to know when it stops hurting," Jake said. How his friend responded stayed with him a long time. "If you're lucky," he said, "never."

"Like Dylan," a student shouted from the back of the class.

"Tell me what you mean," said Wilde.

"*Blood on the Tracks*," he said. "It's an album about heartbreak."

Wilde smiled. "A modern day Keats?" she asked.

"'Tangled Up in Blue,'" he said.

Jake had worn scratches into the grooves of his Dylan albums. He knew every chord, every word. Jake quoted some words from the song.

The girl sitting at the desk in front of him turned around and smiled. And in a half singing-half talking, mildly Dylan-esque whine, Jake looked her in the eyes and recited the lyrics of longing.

It had taken some time, but Jake was becoming a little less distracted by Miss Wilde's curves and instead, interested now in what she had to say.

———

Sarah went to high school in Meadville, Pennsylvania, a small town just off the interstate between Pittsburgh and Erie. Her graduating class was small, compared to Jake's. She did well in school—As and Bs—played some sports, even had a part in her senior high school musical, *The Music Man*. It seemed every high school performed *The Music Man*. Sara played Gracie Shinn, the mayor's youngest daughter. Sarah wasn't the most popular girl, but she certainly had plenty of friends, attended all the high school football games, and dated a basketball player—losing her virginity to him—but all in all stayed out of trouble. She came home drunk once from a picnic with friends, but her parents never found out. The high school version of Sarah was a good girl, likeable and for many, forgettable. There were a lot of Sarahs in Meadville.

But somewhere in the early months of college, the Sarah Jake would know, began to develop. There was no seminal moment, no epiphany. Sarah said the shift was gradual, subtle. "My mind just opened up. The world opened up," she once told Jake. It was such a cliché, this awakening in the college years, and Jake remembered telling her so. "You sound like a commercial for the university," he said. Sarah laughed it off. She didn't care. What she said was true. "My mind is finally out of Meadville."

Jake first knew Sarah from the early journalism class but didn't formally meet her, if that's what you want to call it, until an encounter at a party.

"You're in J-101, right?" Jake asked, smoking a Marlboro and sipping a can of Iron City on the porch of a friend's fraternity house. It was early February, cold as hell, but the frat house didn't allow smoking inside the place, unusual for the 1970s. There had been a minor fire there once.

"You sit in the back, right? Always come in late?" Sarah asked. She had stepped outside with a girlfriend, a smoker. Sarah wasn't smoking yet. That would come later.

"Okay, teacher's pet," Jake said, laughing.

"Well, it's pretty obvious," said Sarah, "especially when you have to walk right by me to get to your seat."

Sarah didn't do a lot of drinking, but when she did, her confidence level jumped a bit. She wasn't cocky; she was self-assured. And when she'd have a couple of beers, her straightforwardness was more than evident.

"So what's your story?" she asked. "Got a girlfriend?"

"Well, aren't we to the point," Jake said. "To answer your question, no. Not in the traditional sense."

"Let me put it more bluntly. Who are you screwing?" Sarah never would have asked that question of anyone back in Meadville.

"Now why would I tell you that?" Jake asked.

"Because you like me," she answered with her newly gained, collegiate confidence.

"Who says?"

"There are seventy-five people in that journalism class. And you, buster, remember *me*."

"I remember a lot of people."

"And one of them," Sarah said, moving a little closer and reaching for Jake's beer, "was *this* girl." He released the can and allowed her a sip. Sarah took a long swig, her eyes remaining on his. She exchanged the Iron City for Jake's Marlboro and took an awkward drag.

"You don't smoke, do you?" he asked, smiling.

"Maybe I do. Maybe I don't. And maybe I just do right now," she coughed. Sarah didn't smoke regularly back then, never did in high school. But in college, at a party, she'd take a hit or two. She got better at it.

"I think you're a little drunk."

"Maybe I am. Maybe I'm not. And maybe . . ."

"I don't think there's a *maybe* here," Jake said playfully.

"Well, it is a party," Sarah said. "But don't worry. I'm not going to puke or anything," she added and turned to go back inside the house. "Too damn cold out here. You coming?"

Sarah and Jake hung out for much of the rest of the night. They both got a bit drunker and even made out a little, kissing in the house's kitchen right in front of everyone before she and her girlfriend headed back to their dorm around 3 a.m.

The next week Jake showed up for J-101 a few minutes earlier than usual and found a seat next to Sarah. They spent a lot of time together over the next few weeks, talking, listening to records, and examining the lyrics of the songs they loved. She learned to appreciate Dylan. Jake learned to like Joni Mitchell. "The song, 'People's Parties.' Fantastic," Sarah said. "I've never been to a party like that. Someday I will." The song spoke of the vulnerability, the frailty in all of us, even those at a high society party who hide behind the aura of manufactured coolness and pseudo-style.

One clear early spring night, sometime around 1 a.m., several weeks into their relationship, Sarah and Jake took a walk through the heart of the campus. They had been hanging out in the common area of Sarah's dorm to watch *Saturday Night Live* with some friends. Paul Simon was on the show. They didn't want to say goodnight, so when the show wrapped up, Sarah and Jake made their way outside to an oasis between the main administration building and the science center, climbed the small hill, and laid their heads on the dewy grass.

"Tell me about Nadine," Sarah said, breaking the silence.

Jake had talked about Nadine a little before, but Sarah sensed he was holding something back.

"What do you want to know?" he asked, tentative about revealing more.

"You really loved her, didn't you?"

"Whatever that means."

The night sky exploded with stars, the Little Dipper directly above them. And for many minutes, the two wordlessly stared into the heavens. Then Sarah whispered, "You know what I think? I think the very first time you fall in love is when you get it right, and it forever defines you. It becomes who you are. And you carry that with you for the rest of your life."

Sarah shifted her body to her side and nestled into Jake's, reaching her arm across his chest and nuzzling her head on his shoulder. If not for the chill in the air that had slowly found its way into that March night, Sarah would have slept in his arms until sunrise.

# 10

LISA GATHERED HER BACKPACK FROM the floor of the radio station's office. "You coming tonight?" she asked.

"I'll be there," Jake said. "Everyone's bringing booze?"

"Each of us has to bring a bottle of something," she said, walking toward the door and down the steps. "Mine's tequila," she added, pronouncing the word *tequila* with an exaggerated Latin accent.

It was the radio station's tenth anniversary, and the staff had just won an award from the Intercollegiate Broadcasting System—first place for College Radio Station of the Year. It was time to party. And what better place to celebrate the station's successes than at the radio station office; be damned the rules about alcohol on school grounds. Beer had been the cheap staple of the college drinking life, but now it was time to step it up with something better, stronger. Jake had knocked back his share of beer in high school but had shifted to some cheap whiskey and Coke when he could afford it or sneak it out of the cabinet at his parents' home. When he couldn't, Jake and his roommate frequently mixed grain alcohol in Kool-Aid. It did the trick. Drinking was fun. Jake never thought of it any other way. Nobody did. Drinking was what you did. And when Jake got really hammered, face down in the toilet bowl from time to time, he convinced himself he was only blowing off collegiate steam.

It had been several weeks since the flag football game and the little skirmish between Sarah and Lisa. In that time, Sarah and Jake found time to confront each other over what had gone on that day—her football battle with Lisa and the question of whether Jake wanted to screw her. There wasn't a lot of discussion; instead, Sarah let Jake have it. Sarah was absolutely certain Lisa was after Jake and was determined, if necessary, to put an end to it. Again, Sarah rarely showed much aggression, but she reacted like a threatened animal when it came to Lisa. And in a perverse sort of way, Jake enjoyed this. He would never admit it; it was so adolescent. But there was something exceedingly sexy about two girls knocking the crap out of each other over him.

"You were a fucking jerk," Sarah said. "Didn't help me. Didn't try to break it up. You didn't do shit." She was right. Jake just watched it all unfold, even silently celebrated it. "What does this say about us?" Sarah asked. "It certainly says something about you," she added, poking Jake in the chest. "Sometimes, you are a selfish prick." The incident with Lisa had poked a hole in a balloon that had slowly been filling up with discontent. Initially Sarah disguised her anger, but it eventually was impossible to disregard. It had been seething for a time.

Sarah no longer stopped by the radio station to see Jake, bring him breakfast, knowing Lisa would be around. In fact, she never talked or asked about Lisa again after letting Jake have it, even though Sarah knew Lisa and Jake worked together. It was as if Sarah had been holding back the waters against the dam. But when the latch was opened and a surge of anger, bitterness, and displeasure was released, the river dried up quickly, and Sarah had nothing left to say.

———

When Jake arrived at the station the night of the party, Greg and Sean were already there. They had moved several chairs around the big table in the middle of the office, and at the table's center they'd placed their contributions of alcohol—Southern Comfort and Seagram's Seven.

"Jake!" Sean shouted. "What you got there, my brother?"

"Two items for your pleasure, although both have already been tapped into," Jake said, reaching in his backpack to pull out a bottle he had stashed at the trailer, a leftover from a long-ago party, a half-empty fifth of some no-name vodka.

"Where's Sarah?" asked Greg.

"I thought this was radio people only?" questioned Sean.

"Well, Sarah's cool," Greg added.

"She's got something going with her roommate tonight." Jake lied. Truth was, Sarah didn't know about the radio party. Jake had told her it was a "guy's night out." And of course, there was Lisa.

The office began filling up. About a half dozen of the disc jockeys and another four or five producers who helped categorize the albums and keep track of the music library, and several members of the station's news team—all three of them journalism majors—came in a posse with Lisa leading the way.

"Who wants to get stupid?" Lisa asked, entering the room in a pair of jean shorts and a blouse tied just above her waist, revealing her belly button. The weather was warm but not *that* warm. Lisa pulled from her purse a small grocery bag and a large bottle of tequila. She emptied the bag—three lemons and a small shaker of salt—then she slammed the tequila on the table and shouted, "Arriba!"

"There's a fucking worm in there," said Mars, who had already spent some time with a bong earlier in the evening.

"Mexican tradition," said Lisa. "Drink the bottle, then someone has to eat the worm. Makes you crazy."

"Fucking cool," Mars said, lifting the bottle above his head to view the worm from the bottom.

"It's not a worm," Greg interrupted. "It's the larvae of an agave moth."

"What are you, some fucking biologist?" Jake questioned, sarcastically.

"It's not tequila, actually. It's mezcal," Greg added.

"Who the fuck cares," said Lisa, grabbing the bottle from Mars. "It'll make your head spin, and that's all that matters."

"Ever eat the worm?" Mars asked Lisa.

"Twice. Saw God," she answered, laughing.

"Was he a Mexican?" Mars asked.

"Juan-fucking-Valdez," Lisa answered, winking.

Sean found some plastic cups in the office closet and handed them out. Greg turned off some of the station lights, hoping the look of a vacant office from outside the building would keep campus security at bay. Mars turned the speakers that usually faced out the bay window inward toward the party. They began with the vodka, mixing it with a little cola. A few knocked back shots of whiskey. Lisa insisted the tequila was to be left for last, for those still standing late in the night. The bottle sat in the middle of the table like a holiday present under the tree. Jake had never tasted tequila or mezcal and certainly had never eaten an 80-proof worm. He did have a friend in high school who did a hit of LSD once, ending up face down on a sidewalk in the middle of the night, marveling at how sparkling butterflies were rising slowly out of the concrete, floating into the air. The same friend did some speed a few times. Jake had been a beer guy in high school, a little alcohol, and of course some weed. And now, there was this worm and the promise that eating it would make you hallucinate—your own personal "Lucy in the Sky with Diamonds." And add to this, the girl he worked with at the station, the one who tackled his girlfriend, the one Sarah believed Jake fantasized about, was egging him on, urging him to keep drinking and to stick around until the early hours of the morning to be with her and eat the liquor-soaked larva.

At one o'clock in the morning, much of the alcohol was gone and most of the staff was too. Mars, Sean, Greg, and Lisa remained at the table, licking salt off the soft spot between the thumb and forefinger, downing the tequila, and biting into a slice of lemon. Mars and Greg were familiar with the ritual. Sean and Jake were learning from Lisa.

"Take a good bite of that lemon and be sure to suck it," Lisa said. "Otherwise the tequila's going to taste like fucking gasoline."

Two, maybe three shots later, Lisa leaned on Jake and made a suggestion.

"This next shot," she whispered, "entwine your arm with mine. I'll lick the salt off your hand, and you lick it off mine."

In Jake's altered state of booziness, nothing in the whole wide world sounded better.

Lisa cut two lemons and handed one to him, pulled his hand to her lips and licked it. While she poured the salt on the wet spot, she looked Jake in the eye as if casting a spell. She then licked her hand and poured more salt.

"Ready?" she asked.

Jake tipped the tequila into two glasses then reached out his arm to wrap it around hers. Lisa smiled. "Salud!" she belted, tilting her head toward Jake's hand then slowly stroking her tongue across his skin. She placed Jake's middle finger in her mouth and flicked the tip of her tongue all around it, producing electricity that channeled through Jake's body. It was now her turn. With his finger in her mouth, Lisa raised her hand to Jake's lips, and he licked off the salt. Noticing he missed a few grains, Jake returned his tongue to Lisa's hand and consumed what remained. Then, in a quick and deliberate motion, they tossed back the tequila and bit into the lemons. They watched each other as they sucked on the bitter citrus, and then Lisa started to laugh.

"You look funny as shit," she giggled.

"What are you talking about?"

"Your lemon face," she snorted, "is so damn goofy."

"Well, your face ain't exactly perfect either, you know."

"You get this stupid squint and your nose kind of wiggles."

"My nose isn't wiggling," Jake insisted.

"Your nose wiggles, man," Mars interjected, his head resting on the table, a position he had been in for some time. Jake thought he had been asleep. "Fucking goofy," Mars added, finally raising his head, and then after a short series of slips and wobbles, he managed to get to his feet. "I'm out of here, man. You guys coming?" Mars asked Greg and Sean.

"You got some weed?" Sean asked.

"Back at the apartment."

"I'm with you," added Greg.

Sean wrapped his arm around Mars' shoulder. Greg grabbed a bottle of vodka from the table and held it up close to his face. "Couple sips left here," he said and stuffed the bottle in his backpack.

"Don't do anything we wouldn't," said Mars, directing the command toward Jake. The trio staggered their way out the door.

The night disc jockey was gone, and the station had signed off for the day. So Greg, always in boss mode, asserted his authority.

"Clean up, too," Greg said, stumbling. "Lock the door when you leave. Security will get ...ah...sup...sus..."

"Suspicious!" Sean shouted from the stairwell, finishing Greg's sentence.

"Whatever," added Greg, giving Lisa and Jake the two-fingered peace sign. "Rock on."

Lisa and Jake said nothing as they left, sitting silently in anticipation of the sound of the downstairs door clanking shut.

"Should we lock it now?" Lisa sighed.

Jake didn't answer. Instead, he stood from the chair and grasped Lisa's shoulders, guiding her body to his. Jake kissed her, and with her tongue in his mouth, Lisa kicked off her slip-on canvas sneakers, and Jake unbuttoned her shorts, letting them fall. He dropped to his knees, placed his hands on her hips and stuck his tongue in her belly button. Lisa sank to the floor. Resting on her back, she lifted her legs and wrapped them around Jake's waist, interlocking her ankles and pulling him on top of her. For nearly an hour, they consumed each other, never exchanging a word, only sighs and groans. Lisa fell asleep with her head on Jake's stomach, her hair tumbling across his thigh.

There was little warning when the overnight security guard came to check the building. The main door clanged shut when he entered and hollered up the stairwell. "Hello? Anyone in here?"

"Jake," Lisa whispered. She had been in and out of sleep for the last hour, and the guard's voice now demanded her full attention. "Hey, get up. Fuck. The guard's here."

"Hello?" the security guard asked again, beginning his ascent to the main radio office.

"Shit," Jake said, jumping to his feet. "The bottles. Shit."

With her panties still on the floor and her blouse undone, Lisa began chucking the booze bottles and plastic cups into the large garbage can.

"Who's up here?" the guard asked as he neared the radio station entrance.

"Hey, yeah, just us," Lisa answered, pulling on her shorts, stuffing her panties in a pocket and hurriedly buttoning her top.

Jake started toward the door, hopping on one foot as he pulled on his jeans and zipped them shut.

"Hey, good morning," Jake said, meeting the guard on the top landing of the stairwell. Jake had no idea whether it was really morning or not.

"What's going on up here?" the guard asked, stepping into the hallway and looking past Jake toward the office.

"Just doing some work," Jake said hesitantly. "Station stuff. Ah, re-categorizing our record library, you see, and we have to do it overnight because, ah, well, we need to do it when no one's on the air."

"Uh-huh," the guard mumbled.

"What time is it anyway?" Jake asked, trying to keep his distance, certain his morning-after liquor breath would be a giveaway.

"4:00 a.m.," the guard answered sternly.

"Hi," said Lisa, waving to the guard from behind the big table in the radio office. "Yeah, I guess we lost track of time." She smiled.

"Okay. Well, no one alerted security that you would be up here," the guard said with authority. "You're supposed to let us know."

"Oh, well, we're sorry about that," Lisa said, trying to radiate as much feminine charm as possible. "Should have told you."

"Sorry," Jake said apologetically. "We're, ah, out of here shortly."

"Okay," the guard said, poised between exiting and stepping deeper into the office. "Well, don't forget to lock up." The guard paused for a moment, looked Jake up and down, and turned to the stairs. "Have a good day," he said, like a highway patrolman after pulling you over and giving you a warning.

When they heard the main door on the first floor shut, Lisa and Jake let out simultaneous sighs and started to laugh.

"Jesus Christ," Jake said, bracing his body against the hallway wall.

"That could have been fucking bad," Lisa said, brushing her hair behind her ears and quickly walking toward Jake. She fell into his arms and softly kissed his lips.

They spent the next half-hour straightening up the rest of the office and tossing the garbage into the dumpster behind the building, doing it all as quietly and discretely as possible.

"Breakfast?" Jake asked.

The two walked the four blocks to Mr. Donut in nervous silence, timidly smiling at one another.

"You missed a button," Jake said, breaking the quiet. The middle of the three buttons on Lisa's blouse remained undone.

"Oh," she said, slipping the button through the hole. "Thank you."

They fell silent again, knowing any more talk may have led to a conversation neither was ready to have.

# 11

JAKE DIDN'T OWN A CAR, so when he was asked to fill-in at WIXZ one Saturday while still at school, he had to borrow Sean's ride, a rusted Chevy Impala with a busted radio and an 8-track stereo system Sean had hooked-up himself. Wires hung from the bottom of the dashboard, and the driver had to be careful his feet didn't get tangled in the electronic spaghetti. Sean had just two 8-track tapes in the car: Black Sabbath's *Paranoid* and Sly and the Family Stone's *Greatest Hits*. He had paid a dollar a piece for them at a garage sale. By the second hour of driving, Jake absolutely hated "Iron Man" and "Dance to the Music," but he played the 8-tracks anyway, over and over, while his mind wandered.

Lisa and Jake hadn't talked about that night at the radio station. They saw each other each morning for the show, exchanged hellos, and did their work. It was awkward. Jake ached to discuss what had happened, and other times he was ready to run and hide. But after a couple of weeks, the two of them got used to the elephant in the room. One morning Lisa asked if Jake was still with Sarah. When he told her he was, Lisa said nothing. No other questions. And Jake didn't bother to say anything more. As for Sarah, Jake had told her nothing, of course. He'd been quieter, sometimes irritable, around Sarah. He blamed it on schoolwork and worrying about what he was going to do with his life after graduation. Jake knew that didn't satisfy Sarah much, although she appeared reluctant to probe, as if she knew more than she let on. There were times Jake tried to be more attentive, forcing smiles and enthusiasm. He also worried about Sean and Greg. They had left the two of them alone that night. They had to have known something was up, still neither asked about the night. Jake felt terrible about what had happened. He'd never done that before, not with Sarah, not with any steady girl in high school. Sure, he flirted, lusted. But Sarah and Jake had been solid together, and then *one girl —a very drunk one—comes on to me, and I go to jelly*. Jake was confused, too horny for his own good, or maybe, just maybe, he thought, he really did feel something for Lisa. Whatever the answers, Jake was not going to find them during a three-hour car ride home.

Jake worked the early shift at WIXZ on Saturday, playing country music, giving the weather, and reading those lame liners. It was great to be on the radio at a real station, but the time and temperature approach to announcing at WIXZ was sucking the soul out of him. Jake wanted to say more, inspire, talk about the songs and their meaning, the artists and their lives—release his inner Ed Beach. *Radio could have such relevance if done right,* he thought. Instead, he was reduced to a machine, a single insipid voice with nothing interesting to say. Jake left WIXZ at noon, feeling down—bad radio and Sarah still on the mind. When he arrived at his parents' home, Jake found his father washing the car in the driveway, a twice a week ritual whether the Plymouth Fury needed it or not.

Jake parked Sean's car on the street and walked up the front yard.

"How'd it go?" his father asked.

"It was okay," Jake lied.

"Don't sound too excited," his dad said and then added with a deep, exaggerated radio announcer voice, "Good morning from WIXZ. This is your host."

"Dad, really?"

"Hey, I listened. I liked it."

"You like the music."

"Yep, that I do. Shit-kicker stuff."

"Mom inside?"

"I'm sure she's making lunch. I'll be in in a bit."

Some of the kids Jake grew up with had real assholes for dads. Jake's father came to his Little League baseball games, even coached a few, and when Jake was in the jazz band in high school, his dad was in the audience. His father also attended the high school plays Jake was in. Jake didn't remember his father ever saying he loved him. It was hard for him somehow. Part of it, Jake believed, was because of his dad's own father, Jake's grandfather. From everything Jake had heard, his grandfather was a stoic prick. Jake's dad was trying to do better. *A good father doesn't tell his son how he feels, how to be a man, he shows him.* And a big part of that job was simply showing up. Jake's dad did that. And there's no question Jake closely watched him, taking it all in without even realizing it. His father smoked Lucky Strikes. *So that's what a man does.* His dad could extract a hook from a small mouth bass with one flick of the wrist. *So that's what a man does.* He gave the priest at their parish a piece of his mind once when he didn't like the sermon about giving more money to the church. *So that's what a man does.* He played golf every Saturday. *So that's what a man does.* He told stories about his two years stationed in Korea in the U.S. Army. *So that's what a man does.* His father told a great joke. *So that's what a man does.* And when he worked as a sales agent for a roofing company, before he got into the insurance business, his dad was fired when the boss found out he had given a customer's $1000 down payment for a big job to a woman he had had fallen in love with. *So that's what a man does.*

Jake never knew the entire story about the woman. His mother was too proud to tell her son, and Jake was too young to understand. His father certainly wasn't going to tell Jake about it.

One evening when he was in the ninth grade, just fourteen years old, his dad came home from work stumbling drunk. He and Jake's mother talked quietly in the kitchen. But it wasn't long before her voice became shrill, and he turned quiet. For days the two of them did not talk. Jake's father ate dinner alone and sat in the basement watching television all day long, sipping from Iron City beer bottles. His mother never said a word to Jake about the lost job, insisting his father was on vacation, taking a break. She even smiled when she said it. It seemed a reasonable explanation at the time. Jake was far more focused on school and girls and baseball. But unconsciously, he was sure what happened affected him somehow, knocking him unknowingly out of balance, weighing on Jake for years before all the details surfaced. In his sophomore year of high school, about a year after it happened, Jake asked his mother why his dad left the roofing business. He can still see his mother's eyes filling with tears, her lips quivering as she told Jake about his father's affair. Jake didn't think she had spoken about it to anybody else for a long time. His mother insisted the woman used Jake's father, tricked him into giving her the money. Jake's mom was sure his father was a good man and never meant to hurt anyone. "He was weak, flawed somehow," she said. "That's what it is to be human." There was forgiveness in time, enough to carry on a marriage, but it was never quite the same. "I still love your father," his mother told Jake, "and he loves me. I know that." When she opened up that day, Jake just let her talk, asking no questions. There was too much pain. And he certainly never confronted his father about it back then. But maybe now it was time. Maybe now, with Lisa and Sarah on Jake's mind, guilt eating at him, it was time to face his father. Nothing specifically compelled him to do this. It was simply unfinished business, some kind of therapy, a necessary act in order to understand, to find answers. A large part of Jake wanted to just forget. He hadn't thought about his father's cheating in years. His father was a good dad, no matter what Jake and his mother had to go through. But it was different for Jake now; a little sharp stick poked at his gut that would no longer allow him to mercifully ignore the reality. And it was going to keep jabbing at him if Jake didn't step up and look it in the eye. Like Jake, his father had cheated on the woman he loved more than anything in the world.

His mother made a ham sandwich on rye for Jake's lunch. She had one with him. His dad never came in. Jake found him outside, waxing his car.

"How about you and I get a beer later?" Jake asked, standing at the top of the short set of steps that led to the front door.

"Me and you?" his father replied, surprised by the question. "There's beer in the fridge," he added, continuing to make circular motions with a white cloth on the hood of his car.

"Let's go out. Head up to Mitch's." Mitch's was a restaurant a few blocks away. It was known for prime rib—the kind of place people went to on Sunday nights. It had a nice bar.

"Well, yeah, okay," his dad said, hesitating. "We can do that. See if your mother wants to come along."

"I'm thinking just you and me," Jake said.

His father stopped his waxing, placed a hand on his hip, and looked Jake up and down as if to weigh his mood. He made one final swipe with the cloth near the car's right fender, put the lid on the can of wax, and tossed both the can and the cloth onto the shelf in the garage. His father smiled and said, "You drive" and tossed the keys to Jake.

When Jake was a boy, maybe about six or seven years old, his father would walk in the nearby woods with him. There were Polaroid photos of those excursions somewhere in the house. His father looked so happy in those pictures—strong, young, and virile, in love with life, in love with his son. There's a picture somewhere of Jake on his shoulders, sometime in autumn, walking through a forest of red and gold maples. Jake is laughing so hard it appears he's ready to lose his balance, and his father's hat, a hunting cap, is cockeyed, nearly falling off his head, and his mouth is opened wide, as if he were shouting out to the world how good life was. Standing before his father now, Jake saw a man with the same strong, beefcake hands, the same broad chest; a man, who at forty-six, remained physically strong. But the glow, the inner happiness so deeply apparent in those photographs was missing. It had been buried, hidden, diminished. His dad looked tired. The remaining hair he had was gray, and his eyes had sunken deeper into their sockets as if they were hiding from something. He was a different man. Jake knew his father had to quit school and go to work as a carpenter to bring money home to support his brother and mother after his father, Jake's grandfather, walked out. And Jake knew his dad never talked to his own father again or about any of what happened when he was young. Jake's mother told him that story. Jake's father never brought it up. Ever. So it certainly wasn't going to be easy to get him to open up about the affair, the indiscretion, the mistakes he'd made. And even if Jake were able to convince him, he figured it would require slow and steady nudging.

Mitch's was empty. It was too early for the Saturday crowd. The bar was nearly dark; only a few sconces around the perimeter and a couple of lamps behind the bar illuminated the edges. Jake's dad instinctively took a seat at the bar.

"Let's grab a booth," Jake suggested and pointed to one in the far corner. "That okay?" he asked the bartender, a middle-aged woman who appeared a little put out that she had customers at an off-hour.

"Be my guest, honey," she said, tapping her pack of Newports against the palm of her hand.

Jake's father pushed away from the bar and followed him to the booth as if he were being scolded. It was years since he had lost his job over the money and the cheating, but somehow he may have known that afternoon at Mitch's, after all the time that had passed, he would be asked to relive it, explain it.

"I don't think we've ever done this before, have we?" Jake asked.

"Don't think so," his father said, laughing.

"What can I get you?" the bartender asked from behind the bar across the room, her cigarette's smoke rising out of a nearby ashtray.

"Two Michelobs," Jake said, loudly.

"High class? You buying?" asked his dad.

"I got this."

His father rested his head on the back of the booth's bench and placed his hands together on the table as if he were praying. "Is everything okay?"

"Sure. All good," Jake said, smiling.

"This just seems, well, unusual," his father said, subtly attempting to prompt an explanation.

"Your son can't buy you a beer?"

His dad smiled, placed his elbows on the table and rested his chin on his fists. "Come on, Jake."

The bartender placed the bottles of beer on the table. "Glasses?" she asked.

Jake shook his head. His father watched as Jake took a swig and then another. For a moment, Jake considered abandoning the plan. What was the point, anyway, to somehow satisfy his guilt? In that second it had become very clear to Jake how he had failed to think any of this through. Sweat formed on Jake's forehead and the back of his neck.

"I was wondering what you think of my idea of maybe moving away from here when I graduate," Jake said, swiftly pulling a different topic out of the deep vessels of his brain, hoping it appeared to have some sincerity.

His father sipped his beer. "Not surprising. You've actually talked about that," he said. "You said it wasn't all that unusual for what you wanted to do."

"Uh-huh," Jake grunted, searching his mind for a way to keep this avenue of conversation going.

His dad took another sip. "You'll be fine," he added, dismissing Jake.

"Yeah. I guess so."

"You're not worried about it, are you?"

"No, no," Jake replied, shaking his head and downing a mouthful.

There were a few seconds of silence, but in that brief space of time, the movie of the night his father and mother talked quietly in the kitchen, the day his dad came home drunk, played in Jake's head. He heard their soft voices and the awful silences in between. And even though Jake didn't see them talking back then, he was clearly picturing them now, his father desperately trying to explain, an impossible task considering his drunkenness and his wife silently crying, her heart breaking. The boy she fell in love with in middle school, the teenager who asked her to go for ice cream after school—and never again dated another girl—the young man she married while he was on a weekend leave from his Army duties because neither of them wanted to wait, the man who wore a white surgical mask and visited her at the TB sanatorium every time the doctors permitted it, the one who cried, believing each visit could be the last time he'd see his bride alive, was now confessing to being in the arms of someone else, stealing money to support her, and losing his job because of it all.

"Jake," his father said, "if there is something on your mind."

Jake felt heat rise in his throat. Nothing about this would be easy, but if he didn't ask now, he never would. His father twisted the bottle in front of Jake and began picking at the label, pealing off pieces of it. "What happened, Dad?" Jake whispered. "The woman and the job."

"Shit," his father said, "is that what this is about?"

"I'm sorry. I just want to know."

"I don't want to talk about all that, Jake. Old history."

"Don't you think I deserve to know about it?"

"I still love your mother. Always have."

"I believe that."

"You better. I'm still here, aren't I?"

"But how did you guys go on? How do you live with it?"

"I don't live with it. I suffer, constantly. It won't ever go away. I'm surprised I'm not a derelict in the gutter somewhere. Your mother is a saint."

"For forgiving you?"

"If that's what you want to call it."

"What's that supposed to mean?"

His father looked toward the bar and spotted the bartender. "A couple more, please," he said.

"She *didn't* forgive you?" Jake asked.

"It's a degree of forgiveness. What do they say, 'Forgive, but never forget?'"

"Are you saying she brings it up, holds it against you, reminds you of it?"

"No. She's not like that. Your mother is the best woman in the world."

"Then what?"

His dad downed the last of his first bottle. Then he leaned forward, shook himself as if to shed the emotions building inside, and said, "The hardest thing, Jake, is not that she brings it up but that your mother *never* brings it up."

Jake remembered seeing his father cry once. It was at the funeral of his mother, Jake's grandmother. It was a soft, solitary, lonely cry. His father was at the edge of that same kind of cry.

Jake and his father drank through their second rounds, even bummed a couple of cigarettes from the bartender. Jake hadn't seen his dad smoke in years. They talked a little more about his father's indiscretion but only a little, shifting instead to baseball and Pittsburgh's season and school. The drinking moved to whiskey and Coke. Before leaving to go home, even though Jake knew the answer, he asked his father if he still loved his mother as much as he ever had. Jake just needed to hear it again. His father said he did and offered some advice, not something he did very often. "Find someone to love forever," he said, touching Jake on the shoulder, "and try not to let her down."

Before heading for the car and home, Jake's father bought a six-pack of cold Rolling Rock pony bottles from the cooler behind the bar. "Your mother loves these little eight-ouncers," he said. "We'll have a couple together on the porch tonight."

Jake had considered heading back to school that night, but one more evening at home with some Rocks and his mother and father sounded like a much better idea.

# 12

SEAN'S CAR HAD A FLAT. That meant Jake's drive back to campus on Sunday afternoon ended up taking double the time. He pulled into a service station off Route 28 somewhere near Kittanning because there was no jack in the trunk, and although there was a spare, it didn't fit the car. He had to pay the mechanic to switch the tire and the wheel, and since the man was the only one working there—pumping gas and repairing cars—the job took a lot longer than it normally would have. Jake drank Cokes from the gas station vending machine and flipped through year-old, grease-stained copies of *Car and Driver* and *Sports Illustrated*.

When Jake finally got to Clarion, Sean was waiting outside of his apartment.

"Where the fuck have you been? You told me you'd be here around 2 o'clock!"

"Might want to check your fucking spare from time to time," Jake said and told Sean the story. "And also, can Danny and I take the car to get some food at the market? He got his food stamps."

Sean was okay with him using his car as long as Jake filled up the tank and bought some milk for him with Danny's stamps. Sean liked milk. Jake agreed but never did fill his tank. You couldn't buy gasoline with food stamps and Jake didn't have the money.

Jake picked up Sarah at her place, drove by and got Danny, and headed to the Giant Eagle a few blocks outside of town. It was the only place that would take government assistance.

Jake had always loved Sarah's hands, the soft palms and long fingers. They were elegant but strong. Her nails were always painted, usually staying away from attention-grabbing colors like fire engine red and instead colored them light pink or lavender. When she handed Jake a beer or put a record on the turntable or touched his chest, he loved looking at her hands, from the wrist to the tip of her middle finger. Even when she picked through bananas at the market, Jake cherished her hands.

"Buy a couple bundles of those," Jake said. "You can take some."

Sarah smiled, noticing how his eyes were following her hands as she placed bananas in the cart.

"You like the polish?" she asked. This time the color was deeper, something Jake hadn't seen before, a smoky blue.

"Ah, sure, yeah," he said.

"You okay?" Sarah questioned.

"Just tired."

Sarah touched his cheek, a request for Jake to say more. He just smiled a crooked smile and pulled her fingers to his lips to kiss them.

The two filled the cart and calculated how much the stamps would get them. They had to put back some paper towels and some laundry soap. Danny said the stamps wouldn't cover those, but they did select good ground beef, kidney beans, and tomato sauce for making chili. Danny made a pretty good chili. He would make a big pot of it and they'd have it for days, even eat it for breakfast.

After dropping off Danny, Sarah and Jake headed to Sean's place to return his car.

"How was your trip?" Sarah asked. "Radio go okay?"

"Uneventful," Jake said.

"And the 'rents?'" Sarah always shortened the word parents to 'rents.'

"They're good."

"Your mom make you potato soup?" Jake's mother was famous for that dish. It was his grandmother's recipe. When friends were in town over a break from school, his mother would invite them for "Potato Soup Sunday." Jake's dad set up card tables in the living room, and a dozen or so of Jake's friends would load up on the soup. His mother and father loved having his friends around, even if his father complained about all the peeling he had to do to fill up three big stovetop pots.

"No soup. Wasn't enough time for it, I guess. She did make cookies though. There's a tin for you."

"Well, where are they?" Sarah asked impatiently, pretending to be mad.

"Shit, left them back in my bag at the apartment."

"Tomorrow."

"Yeah, tomorrow."

Jake parked the car in front of Sean's place, a small duplex apartment in the downtown area a couple blocks from campus. Sarah opened the car door to step out but realized Jake wasn't moving.

"You coming?" she asked.

"Sarah," Jake sighed and leaned back against the headrest. "You think we are supposed to be together forever?"

Sarah shut her door, put her hands in her lap, and looking bemused, said, "What's going on?"

"Nothing," Jake lied again. "Just saw Mom and Dad together, you know, living their lives."

"Wondered if we're going to be like that?" Sarah asked.

He nodded and smiled.

Sarah placed a hand on Jake's chest over his heart.

"I'm usually the one talking about this," she said, "asking questions about how we're going to be together or not."

Jake tapped his head against the headrest a few times as if to rattle loose what was floating around in his brain.

Sarah caressed his cheek. "I know what I want. I want us. I think you want me, don't you?" she asked, attempting to show confidence.

Jake turned away to look out the driver's window.

"Jake?" she asked.

"Of course, Sarah," he said, turning toward her, embracing her hand. "What is it they say, 'I want to grow old with you?'"

"All wrinkly and shit," Sarah said, grinning.

Sean was now standing outside the driver-side window. "About fucking time," he belted, a little pissed. "What the hell you guys do, buy the fucking store?"

Jake tossed Sean the keys. He offered a couple of beers, and they drank them on his front stoop. Sarah and Jake shared a cigarette. It had been a long day. Jake stayed at Sarah's apartment that night. It was closer to campus than his place. Her roommate was away for the weekend and wouldn't be back until Monday sometime. Sarah set the alarm. Five a.m. Jake was exhausted but still had enough in him to pull Sarah's naked body on top of his. She did all the work.

———

Jake was usually the first person at the radio station in the morning, but on Monday when he walked through the door, Lisa was already there.

"Early start?" he asked, sleepily.

"We need to talk," Lisa insisted, pulling up chairs for the two of them.

Jake craved coffee, but right then a stiff drink seemed the better idea.

"Maybe after the show?" he asked, nervously.

"Now," she said, pointing to a chair. "Sit."

Jake leaned against the chair. "I'll stand," he said.

"Are you going to just fuck me and forget it?" Lisa asked angrily.

"That's not how I see it," Jake said.

"That's what it was," she quickly answered.

"We were drunk."

"You've been avoiding me for weeks."

"I work with you almost every morning. How can I avoid you?"

"Seriously, Jake?"

"You've been avoiding it, too," he said.

Lisa stared directly into his eyes. She did not blink.

"Did we make a mistake?" he asked.

"You tell me," she answered.

"Well, there's Sarah." Jake wasn't sure what he meant by saying that. It was instinct.

Lisa shook her head.

"I think you need to rethink all this," she said. "Think about it hard." Lisa turned and walked toward the room where the wire machine noisily tapped out the news.

"What's that supposed to mean?" Jake asked, taking a step toward her.

"I have to get ready to be on the air," Lisa said dismissively, disappearing through the doorway to the wire room.

For a split second, fear raced through Jake's body. *Lisa wasn't thinking about telling Sarah; surely not,* he thought. *What good would it do? But, if Lisa wanted to be vindictive—find another way to tackle Sarah—telling her everything would certainly do it.* For a moment, Jake considered confessing to Sarah, exposing it all. His father made a mistake. Jake made a mistake.

"Lisa? Why are you so pissed?" he asked, raising his voice, hoping she could hear him over the clanking news machine. She didn't answer.

For the next three hours, Lisa did her job and Jake did his and nothing more. He played a lot of Dylan that morning, cranking up the monitors in the studio so "Early Morning Rain" —a song of travel and regret—could be heard through the doors and all the way down the hallway.

Jake stepped lightly that morning, and Lisa remained matter-of-fact and reticent. And there were subsequent mornings when it was almost as if she had forgotten what had happened. Before the night of tequila in the radio station, Jake had learned some things about Lisa, tidbits of information that had trickled out in workday conversations. She had been on the staff of the high school newspaper. She said something once about being on a girls' softball or swim team. She had been in a couple of plays in high school but had only a few lines. She was a cheerleader in junior high, although Jake wasn't sure cheerleading in junior high counted. She beat up a boy once who teased a friend with a speech impediment—a neighbor girl with a lisp. The boy said the girl sounded "like she was spitting" and got that way from sucking cock. Lisa was suspended from school for a couple days for punching the kid. There were a few times she mentioned her parents' divorce. Lisa never said anything good about her dad, calling him "an anal asshole," "abusive," and a "cheater." But she was a different person when she talked about her mother, laughing her way through a story about how her mom would rise on Christmas morning when Lisa was a little girl and dress up like one of Santa's elves—wearing a homemade red felt hat and a green tee-shirt—and give out the toys that had been stuffed the night before under the six-foot white pine in the family's living room. One morning when the Pope was in the news, she commented about attending Catholic grade school and how her parents were pretty religious. "But they still got a fucking divorce," she said angrily. "Catholic Church is going to send them to hell, you know?" she added sarcastically. Lisa had a brother but didn't talk much about him. She didn't talk much about her college classes, either. Lisa could tell a good dirty joke. They were the kind young boys tell when they're hanging out late at night in a buddy's garage. "A dog, a cat, and a penis are in a bar," she began one morning. "The dog says, 'My life sucks, my master makes me do my business on a fire hydrant.' The cat says, 'Mine's worse. My master makes me do my business in a box of cat shit.'" Then, with the skill of a nightclub comic, Lisa finished it off. "The penis is ticked off and says, 'At least your master doesn't put a bag over your head and make you do push-ups until you throw up.'"

And then there were Lisa's hands. Like Sarah's, Jake noticed them.

Every morning for weeks she had brought news headline copy into the studio, handing it to Jake once an hour. He watched her fingers and noticed her skin close-up over and over again. Her hands were different than Sarah's, larger fingers and stronger, the nails trimmed and shaped like a woman's but never any polish. And there were times Jake imagined those hands on his skin again, like the night at the radio station.

After the radio show on the morning Lisa confronted Jake, Sarah was waiting outside the Student Union, still not willing to come inside and risk running into Lisa. Sarah and Jake shared a cigarette on the grass near the walkway. It was mid-November but unusually mild. Sarah stood close, her shoulder, arms, and legs taking turns touching him. She brushed her hand through his hair. Jake said little, and he was sure she wondered why. He told Sarah he was tired, needed a nap, and decided to blow off class and head for the trailer.

"Forgot to tell you. My parents want to know if you'll come for Thanksgiving," Sarah said as Jake began walking away.

"Yeah, I guess," he said, stepping backward and facing her.

"Think about it, okay?" Sarah asked.

"Yep." Jake turned and continued down the walkway toward the library and the road that led to the trailer.

The last thing he wanted to think about was Thanksgiving, all the expected appreciation and gratitude. At that moment, Jake wasn't at all certain what he was thankful for anymore.

# 13

J AKE DIDN'T HEAR THE ALARM. He was certain he'd set it, but restless sleep and then a fitful afternoon nap had thrown off his biorhythms. And Danny was no help. He never got up early. Jake arrived at the radio station with only ten minutes to spare.

"Jesus, man. I didn't think you were going to make it," Sean said anxiously, stepping out of the wire machine room with a handful of copy just as Jake bolted into the office.

"What're you doing here?" Jake asked.

"Lisa's not coming in."

"Good," he murmured.

"What was that?" Sean looked puzzled, but Jake knew he heard him.

"Nothing," Jake said.

Sean was the music director, but someone had to be there to do the news. Again, the station had few listeners, but most of the staff took the work seriously, trying to be on time, do the work well. There were some students who just wanted to play around, get their kicks out of being around radio, all those hundreds of record albums and the energy. But for Sean, Greg, and Jake, and even Lisa, it was different. So, Sean stepping up and filling in wasn't unusual, even if he didn't know how to write copy and never read news on the radio before.

"You're not going to fuck up, are you?" Jake asked, feverishly pulling albums from the library and stacking them on a chair.

"We're going to find out," Sean said. "Thanks for the vote of confidence, fucker."

"Always," Jake said. "When did you get word about Lisa?"

There had been a knock on the door at Sean's apartment at about 4:30 in the morning. Scared the hell out of him, he said. It was a guy he hadn't seen before. He looked like a student.

"Said he was Lisa's boyfriend," Sean continued. "Said he just left Lisa's place. She gave him the address and asked if he'd let me know she wasn't going to make it."

"Really?"

"Yeah. Thought it was a little weird."

"Her boyfriend, huh?"

"Yeah. Jim, I think he said his name was. No, Tim? I don't fucking know. Remember Suzi last year?"

A student named Suzi, who was doing the morning news the previous semester, showed up drunk at the station. The girl literally stumbled her way into the studio. She was fired, as firing goes at a campus radio station, and eventually left school. Sean was program director then and had to scramble to find a last minute replacement.

"So this boyfriend said she was sick or what?" Jake asked, lifting the bundle of albums and walking quickly toward the hallway that led to the studio.

"Shit, I don't know. Just told me she wouldn't be in."

"I'll need headlines at 6:30," Jake said over his shoulder, leaning his thigh on the studio door to push it open. "Is she coming back tomorrow?"

"Come on, man. Don't you want me around instead?" Sean asked, frowning, sniffling, and pretending to wipe away a tear. "I thought you loved me, man."

Lisa did not return to the radio station the next morning. She wasn't there the morning after that, either. The weekend came. So did Monday. No Lisa. Sean filled in one more day then got a new student at the station, a sophomore, to take over. Jake asked Sean several more times what he had heard about Lisa. "Very little," he said. "Might have gone home," Sean added.

———

On Tuesday, Sarah had a night class, so Jake headed for Lisa's apartment, the third floor of a house in the oldest part of the town. He climbed steep wooden stairs to the side entrance and knocked on the door.

"Hi. I'm Jake. Lisa here?"

Standing at the door was a girl he had seen on campus before but had never met.

"She's not. Sorry."

"When will she be back?"

The girl looked puzzled, as if Jake should have known the answer.

"And you are?" she asked.

"Jake. I know her from the campus radio." She leaned her head against the half-open door and ran a hand through her short, Twiggy-like hair. "Something wrong?" he asked.

The girl began slowly closing the door "Look," she said, "Lisa's just not here. I can't help you."

Jake stood still, his feet steady on the small wooden porch, arms hanging limp at his side. The door shut, and he heard the double click of a deadbolt. For a moment he was paralyzed. Then, he rapped again on the wooden door.

"Is there a way to get a hold her of her?" Jake asked, adding volume to his words, hoping someone on the other side would hear him.

No answer. Another woman peeked out from the curtains in the second floor window near the steps. Their eyes met and she disappeared. Neither the girl at the door nor the one at the window could know how much disappearances troubled Jake.

Jake smoked a cigarette. He finished it and lit another. The late fall sun had vanished hours ago. It was cold and a light fog was forming. Not a star in the sky.

———

Danny kept a BB rifle at the trailer. He grew up in central Pennsylvania, hunted with his father every fall. His dad gave the roommates some fresh venison one time. They made chili. Jake didn't like it much. He liked the chili they made from food stamp food, ground beef. He also didn't like the BB gun around much, either. His father hunted years ago, and there were rifles in his house when he was growing up, but he never fired one. His dad gave up hunting before Jake was old enough to hold a shotgun or a .22 rifle in his arms. But he wasn't going to tell Danny he wasn't a fan of the rifle in the trailer, as relatively harmless as it was. And Jake certainly wasn't going to tell him he had never fired a gun. Boys from Pennsylvania were supposed to shoot guns.

Jake found Danny outside, smoking weed and shooting BBs at milk cartons he'd balanced on rocks in the field on the other side of the gravel road in front of the trailer. The glow from the street lamp offered little light.

"Who goes there?" Danny asked in his best western rancher imitation, lifting the barrel of the BB rifle to his hip.

"You've seen too much *Gun Smoke*, man," Jake said.

"Where you been?" Danny asked, offering a hit.

"Had some stuff to take care of." Jake inhaled, held it, and blew the smoke out his nose.

Danny presented the rifle. "Shoot?"

"It's fucking night time. How you seeing anything?"

"I know where the cartons are," he said confidently. "Go ahead."

Jake took the rifle from Danny's hands, fumbling with it a bit. It was heavier than expected, far heftier than the toy guns—plastic and wooden—he had as a kid. He loved those guns then and even had a cowboy holster that held a fake metal revolver. It was the era of the TV Western. His father thought for sure he would become a cop or a soldier, or at least take up deer hunting. Pretending was enough for Jake, it seemed. All those years of playing with fake guns made it look like Jake knew a little of what he was doing when he had the real thing in his hand, although Danny would never have considered a BB gun a *real* weapon.

Jake lifted the rifle toward his face, placed the butt against his shoulder, and looked down the barrel toward the rocks about thirty yards away.

"I can barely see a thing," Jake said, waving the barrel back and forth in search of the cartons.

"Left," Danny directed.

Jake adjusted.

"Little more," he added.

"I think I got 'em," Jake said, the rifle's barrel still in the air.

"Hit that fucker," Danny commanded.

Jake fired. Missed. Pumped the rifle. Fired. He heard the snap of a steel BB striking the waxy cardboard carton.

"Fucking Matt Dillon," Danny belted.

"How the hell'd I hit that in the dark?" Jake asked.

"We all see things in the dark. See more than we know," Danny answered, in his best Zen master tone. He took the rifle from Jake's hand and fired off two quick shots, hitting one of the cartons in its center.

Later that night, Danny and Jake walked to a bridge about a mile from the trailer. Everyone knew it as Piss Bridge. It was on the road that led out of campus and up to the Allegheny National Forest and over the Clarion River. After 10 o'clock on some nights, when there was virtually no car traffic, kids would hang out on the outer walkway off the bridge, and guys, after pounding several beers, would piss into the river below. Some warm nights in the spring and fall, kids would jump the fifty feet or so into the river to take a swim. It was too cold for skinny-dipping that night, but it didn't stop people from showing up. Weekends were busier, but there were always a handful of students around, drinking beer, smoking weed, making out. Jake brought his guitar there a couple of times. It was usually a good time. A few years ago, though, a drunken student died at the bridge, slipping and falling, hitting his head on one of the steel buttresses. For a few months, county cops would come by at night and chase kids away. But after some time, the cops stopped coming.

Mars was at the bridge that night with a few unfamiliar guys. Two of them sat a few feet from Mars near the far side of the bridge. He sat in the middle, wearing a wool cap, his coat draped over his shoulders, a bong between his legs. He was on one of his dope-fueled spiritual soapboxes.

"When scientists finally figure out there's a Fourth Dimension out there, when they discover it and can detect it, they'll see people's souls walking off into the night when they die," Mars said.

"Hey man." Danny greeted Mars.

"They'll just fade away into the ether," Mars said, staring in Danny and Jake's direction and then out into the dark water.

"People don't just fade away, Mars. People die. They just die," Jake said, stepping onto the wooden planks near the west end of the bridge.

"There's far more than just what's in front of us, man," said Mars. "The Indians believed that."

"You can smell the weed halfway down the road," Jake said, trying to change the subject.

"It's cool," Mars said. "What's going on?"

On the walk to the bridge, Jake had filled Danny in on the Lisa story but not all of it, of course. He told him about her disappearance and about going to her apartment. How strange it all seemed. Danny agreed but asked why Jake appeared so worried about it. Jake didn't tell him—nothing about the tequila night or the argument at the radio station—but he did remind Danny that Lisa did the news with Jake at the station.

"You haven't heard anything, have you?" Jake asked Danny.

"I heard she has a sweet ass," said Mars, interrupting and hitting the bong.

"She's missed a bunch of days at the radio station. Haven't seen her or talked to her," Jake added.

"You fucked her, though." Mars coughed, dope smoke rolling from his nose and lips.

"Truth's out," said Danny.

Jake leaned against one of the bridge's metal beams and lowered himself to Mars' level. "What did you hear?"

"Come on, man. We left you guys alone at the station that night," Mars replied. "You guys were fucked up, horny as shit."

"I didn't fuck her," Jake said curtly.

"Really, man?" Danny asked. "You got to give it up," he added, encouraging Jake to tell more.

"Well, if you didn't, you should have," said Mars.

"Seriously, man. What's the deal?" Danny questioned.

"Nothing," Jake said.

"Does Sarah know?" Mars asked.

"Nothing to fucking know," Jake said bluntly.

"Fuck. That's why you're so weirded-out about what's going on with Lisa," Danny said with revelation. "Now I fucking get it."

"I'm not worried. Okay?" Jake snapped. He reached a hand toward Mars. "Give me a cigarette."

"This is a serious conundrum," Danny said, pretending to be pompous.

Mars fumbled in his coat and pulled out a smoke and a lighter.

"Maybe Lisa just faded away, man, into the Fourth Dimension," said Mars.

"Maybe she...just...vanished. Gone. Poof."

Jake inhaled tobacco smoke deep into his lungs and held it for a long time.

# 14

THANKSGIVING HAD ALWAYS BEEN SPENT at home, at Jake's parents' house, but this year would be different. His mother wasn't thrilled about the idea, but she understood, at least that's what she said. Jake tried to make it better by agreeing that on Friday night he and Sarah would come down from Hermitage and stay for the rest of the weekend. Sarah was okay with it. Hermitage was near the border of Ohio, nearly a straight shot westward along I-80 from Clarion. Sarah and Jake were able to bum a ride from a couple of students going the same direction on the Wednesday before the holiday. On Friday they bought a couple of cheap last-minute bus tickets and took the two-hour ride, including a scheduled thirty-minute stopover in Youngstown, to the Greyhound terminal in Pittsburgh. His father picked them up.

"Hey there," Sarah said, tossing her backpack onto the car's floor and sliding into the front seat. She liked Jake's dad and joked how his father's picture should be in the dictionary next to the word dad. He fixed things around the house, worked on his car, watched football and golf on TV, and sat at the head of the table for supper. She even called him Dad now and then.

"Good to see you," he said.

Sarah reached across the seat and kissed Jake's father on the cheek.

"Hey Dad," Jake said, slapping him on the back from the rear seat.

"Hope this wasn't a big deal getting down here."

"Had to dodge some shoppers in the city, but it was okay."

"Mom good?" Jake asked.

"Cooking up a storm. Hope you guys are still hungry."

"Let me guess, she's planning a full Thanksgiving meal for Saturday, right?"

His father tilted the car's rearview mirror and smiled at Jake.

"She's cooking a full dinner?" Sarah asked.

"It's just Mom," Jake answered, smiling back at his father. "What'd you guys do yesterday?"

"She made a meal for me and your sister. Turkey, sweet potatoes, green beans, some salad thing."

"And she's doing it again?" Sarah asked.

"Sure is," Jake's dad said. "Mary won't be there. Your aunt invited her to come up to the mountains to spend some time with the cousins. You know how that goes. Your sister loves skiing." Mary rarely missed an opportunity to get on the slopes, and it wasn't unusual for her to head up there over a holiday break.

"Mary's quite good," Jake said to Sarah.

"It was a small turkey yesterday, and it'll be another small one today," his father continued. "A meal for four this time. Plus, you guys might get a few leftovers. But, yeah, I guess your mother is doing it all over again," his father said, laughing. "Strap on the feed bag."

The meal was everything his dad had described, plus, two pies—pumpkin and blueberry. Jake had a sliver of both. Sarah had pumpkin with whipped cream on top. They had coffee in the living room. His father sat in the rocking chair, Sarah and Jake on the couch, and his mother in the blue wingback where she could reach around and slip her dog—a Yorkshire-Maltese mix—some of the crust from her pie.

"I can't believe you two will be done with school in a few months," his mother said. "Graduates. My goodness."

"Hasn't hit me yet," said Sarah, tucking her legs under herself on the couch. "I think Jake has been thinking a lot, though," she added, peeking at Jake over the lip of her coffee cup.

Jake had avoided talking in any depth to his parents, especially his mother, about looking for radio work, about how he'd take a job in Alaska if it were the right one. His mother would certainly want him to find something close. She never said as much, but Jake knew his mother. And now Sarah was putting Jake on the spot, a tactic, he assumed, to try to pin him down about the two of them.

"What is it you're thinking about?" his mother asked Jake. "Surely the two of you are going to try to find work in the same place, right?"

"Mom, I don't know exactly," he answered, swirling the remaining coffee in his cup.

"Probably should think about it more than that," his dad interjected.

"Well, I am thinking about it. But I'm just not sure what it's all going to bring."

"Are you thinking about here, Pittsburgh?" his mother asked.

"You do have a job already. Would they offer full-time?" his father asked.

"I don't know."

"You going to ask?"

"Well, of course, Dad. I'm going to ask. I just don't know."

Sarah shifted anxiously in her seat, pulling her legs tighter into her body. Jake's mother lifted her cup to her lips, hiding her expression. His father quickly finished what was left of his coffee, stood from the rocker and asked, "More anyone? I'll add a little whiskey."

"I think Sarah and I are going to take a walk. Burn off some of that good food," Jake said, taking Sarah by surprise.

Sarah did not look at Jake. She simply placed her cup on the coffee table and said to his mother, "Don't start cleaning up yet. Jake and I will do it when we get back."

"Oh honey, don't worry about it," his mother said. "Take your walk. Enjoy. Looks like a nice night."

"Dinner was great," Sarah said, touching Jake's mother's shoulder. "Pie was incredible."

Jake handed Sarah her jacket and slipped on his. "We won't be long," he said, stepping through the small foyer.

"What the fuck was that?" Jake asked as soon as the door was shut behind them.

"What?" Sarah asked innocently.

"Give me a break. You hung me out there, bringing up the future with my parents sitting there. Jesus, Sarah."

"Well, we have talked."

"I don't know what I'm doing, okay?"

"And you and me? It always comes down to that. But you never answer."

"You're with me. Here. Now. Right?"

"And that's supposed to be enough?"

Jake put his hands in his pockets and walked a few steps ahead of Sarah as they climbed the hilly street, both of them silent.

"You going to talk?" Sarah asked from behind.

Jake stopped and turned. "Look. I want to be with you. But I don't know where things will take me, and maybe you don't want to go along."

"Do you *want* me to go along?" Sarah whispered.

Jake sighed and then smiled, feeling cruel that he'd snapped at Sarah. He put his arms around her and pulled her to him. She placed her head on his shoulder. The late November moon was bright, casting shadows on the black asphalt street. A dog barked in the distance. Sarah and Jake walked around the remainder of the block, saying little else, holding each other's hand.

When Sarah stayed at Jake's parents' home, she slept in Jake's old bedroom while he took the couch in the basement.

"I'm going up. Long day," Sarah said.

"It'll be okay," Jake said, kissing her and gently touching her cheek. He watched Sarah walk up the stairs to the second floor.

In the dining room, his parents kept a small cabinet of liquor. Jake poured Canadian Club into a tumbler and added cold Coke from the refrigerator. He sat at the table and drank. He made another and a third and took a fourth to the basement. His mother had tucked sheets into the cushions and placed a blanket and two pillows on the couch's arm. Jake slipped off his clothes, slid under the bedding, and downed the last of the smoky, sweet drink. Sometime past midnight, after Jake had fallen into a boozy sleep, Sarah softly crept into the basement, quietly crawled under the blanket, and edged her body between the back couch cushions and Jake's naked body, sleeping in his arms until morning.

———

Jake awakened early, slid out of Sarah's arms and pulled the blanket over her exposed bare feet, tucking it around her shoulders. She opened her eyes for just a moment and caught his eyes then rolled over to face the rear cushion and nestled her head into the pillows. Jake climbed the stairs to the kitchen to make coffee.

Inside a chest in his parents' living room, his mother kept photo albums and boxes overflowing with dozens and dozens of snapshots. During the holiday seasons, his mother would take handfuls of them out, and the family would spend hours laughing and crying over black-and-whites, old faded Polaroids, bad hairdos, awful fashions, moments lost in time. It was a tradition. In the quiet of that early morning, with a strong black coffee in his hand, Jake started in on those photos. He wasn't sure what compelled him to delve into the old pictures before anyone else, at that moment, especially alone. Maybe he was fueled by what faced him—graduation, new beginnings, and intimidating uncertainties. Maybe some connections to the past were necessary to move forward.

Jake lifted two shoeboxes out of the chest, being especially careful with one that had a torn corner, and placed them on the coffee table. He sat on the floor, slipped his legs under the table, and pulled himself close. There was nothing that categorized the photos, no system; they appeared to have simply been heaped into the boxes. At least one had a series of color photos pulled together with a rubber band—the kind of photos printed with the white trim around the edges. They were pictures of his mother and father in England, a trip they had taken during Jake's freshman year. His mother had the address of his grandfather's boyhood home on the Isle of Wight and wanted to find it. It was still standing, even after the bombing of the island during World War II. One of the photos is of his mother and father in front of the small house. His mom is smiling broadly, and his dad appears to be amazed that he's found himself on an island in the English Channel, sharing this adventure. The Englishman who now lived in Jake's grandfather's old home had taken the picture.

Underneath the trip photos were three or four photos of Jake and his sister playing in bathing suits near the backyard pool, one of those air-filled wading types his parents bought at Kmart. The smiles are genuine; one could almost hear the laughter. Michael would still have been alive at that time, but curiously he was not in any of those photos. Jake worked his way through the rest of the box and still nothing of Michael. He dumped the contents of the two boxes on the carpet and shifted through the pictures. No Michael. On the corner bookshelf, there were framed photos of his high school graduation night—Jake in his cap and gown standing near the maple in the front yard, one of his sister when she played on her pee-wee softball team, two of his mother and father at their wedding, and a single small wooden-framed photo of Michael in front of his elementary school, a Flintstones lunch box in his hand. It must have been his first day at school, his only first day. But in the shoeboxes, Jake could find no photos of Michael.

There were pictures of Jake in his pajamas at Christmas, one of him in a red sport coat at his First Holy Communion, another of his dad holding him on his shoulders on a beach somewhere, his mom on a chaise lounge in the backyard, wearing Jackie Kennedy sunglasses. There were several of Mary and her friends on a ski trip to the mountains several years ago. No Michael.

Jake sipped his coffee then placed his hands behind him and leaned his body backward. *In all the years of looking through these photos, were there ever any of Michael? I must have missed something,* he thought. *Am I not remembering? Certainly there were photos of my brother. Wasn't there one of him with birthday cake all over his face, the one of him in the little baseball suit and hat?* Jake grabbed the photo albums and scanned through them. No Michael. He looked inside the chest again. No Michael.

"What's going on?" Sarah said groggily. She stood near the entrance to the kitchen and the basement door and wiped her eyes, a blanket wrapped around her shoulders and draped to her knees. "What's with the photos?"

"Do you ever remember seeing a photo of my brother?" Jake asked.

"There's that one," Sarah said, pointing to the bookshelf.

"Other than that."

"Well, I'd have to think."

Jake rose from the floor, emptied the remaining coffee into his mouth, and turned toward the kitchen for a refill. "You've been here when my mother does her photo thing at the holidays, right?"

"Yeah, all the old pictures."

"Do you remember seeing any of Michael?"

Sarah sat in the blue wingback and wrapped the blanket more closely around her body. "Last time we looked, was it last Christmas? Yeah. Sure. I think so."

"Like what? What do you remember?"

"I can't be certain, but there must have been some."

"Then where are they? None in here," Jake said, pointing to the piles of photos scattered on the floor. "Not a single photo."

Sarah sank to the carpet and sifted through some of the pictures. She scooted to the others nearer the couch and examined those then quickly skimmed the same photo albums Jake had. Sarah looked up and shrugged her shoulders.

Over the next half-hour, Sarah and Jake carefully filtered through several more boxes of photos and still no Michael. Giving in to the futility, Jake reached for the photo on the bookshelf and carried it with him to the rocking chair. With the picture resting in his lap, he stared into Michael's eyes. Jake had thought deeply about Michael before of course, but for those few silent moments that Sunday morning, his brother had returned from wherever he had been.

# 15

JAKE AND SARAH HEADED BACK to school Sunday evening. A friend with a car had room for them, and they could help with gas money. They spent the last day in Pittsburgh playing with Jake's mother's dog in the yard, doing laundry, and watching football, Pittsburgh was playing Cleveland. His mom made dinner before they headed north. Curiously, over the entire Thanksgiving weekend, his mother never brought up the photo tradition, never insisted it was time to look at them, and Jake never mentioned it. *She might do it at Christmas time,* he thought. After his empty search for a photo of Michael, Jake was relieved the tradition had apparently been postponed.

Jake slept in the car's backseat with his head against the window nearly the entire ride to school. Sarah sat beside him, studying for a Monday morning test. They arrived at Sarah's place in the early evening and sat on the stoop outside with a couple of beers. The mild November weather continued.

"Turned out to be a nice weekend, don't you think?" Sarah asked.

"It was good, yeah."

"I don't think I'll ever be hungry again."

"Mom likes to cook," Jake said, reaching for the cigarette and taking a long deep drag. He held the butt close to his chest and then took another quick hit, slowly letting the smoke filter from his nose and surround his face as if he were trying to hide behind it.

"You want to stay tonight?" Sarah asked softly.

The cigarette's tip glowed a deep orange as Jake sucked in the last of it. He flicked the butt to the street.

"I've got the radio tomorrow, and I want to stop by a friend's house on the walk home," Jake said, standing from the stoop. "You're right. It was a nice weekend."

Sarah stood and leaned into him, taking his hand and placing it on her cheek. "Who's the friend?" she asked.

"Guy from class. We have this group project."

Sarah kissed Jake's hand. "Tomorrow after your show?"

"I'll see you outside the Union." He kissed her on the forehead and grabbed his duffle bag from the porch.

Sarah handed Jake a cigarette and a pack of matches. "One for the road," she said.

"Thanks." He tucked the cigarette behind his right ear and stuffed the matches in the front pocket of his jeans. "Good night." Jake could feel Sarah's eyes on him as he moved under the streetlight and across the road to the other side. A block away, deeper into the night and nearly out of sight, he turned to look back. Sarah was still standing in front of the apartment, a fading silhouette. She lifted her hand halfway to her chest to offer an uncertain wave. Jake pretended not to see her and rounded the corner toward Lisa's apartment.

Jake could see a dim flickering blue light through the window, shadows of TV images on the glass. He knocked on the door, waited, and knocked again. The door cracked open, and a face appeared.

"She's not here," the girl said, the same girl Jake had encountered once before at this same door. "She's not coming back."

"Not coming to school? Not at all?"

"Look," she said, opening the door wider and placing both hands on her hips. "I don't know what you know. But she's left school."

"I don't want to keep bothering you," Jake pleaded, "but can you tell me how I can reach her?"

"Who are you?" she asked suspiciously.

Jake ran his hand through his hair and took a step back from the door. "A friend."

The girl returned inside the apartment with the door still open then reappeared with a small piece of paper from a notebook. She handed it to him. "I don't know how long she'll be there."

"Is it home?" Jake asked.

"That's all I have," she said and shut the door.

On the paper was a phone number. Jake had the immediate urge to crumple it in his hand and heave it into the dark, to let it all go and forget about Lisa. Instead, he stood silent on the porch, looked to the starless sky, neatly folded the paper twice and back again, and slipped it into the pocket of his jeans, next to the matches, tossed his duffle over a shoulder and headed for campus.

———

Patty was the radio station's night disc jockey, a big-breasted hippie girl who wore fringed, nearly see-through blouses and spoke with a deep, raspy voice. She was quite aware of the power of her sexuality. It was hard to miss the bare nipples straining at the fabric of her shirt. She was made for night radio, perfect for playing deep cuts from blues and jazz-fusion albums from 9 p.m. to midnight, the station's sign-off time.

Jake used his key to the Union and the station and tried slipping into the office without Patty seeing, but she liked keeping the studio door open when she was on the air. Few people ever came into the station at that time of night, especially on a Sunday, and she liked the open-air breeziness, even in November.

"Who's here?" Patty asked from inside the studio.

"Hey," Jake said, retracing his steps from the hallway to the office and peeking around through the studio door. "Just me. I have a couple things to take care of."

"Kind of late."

"Yeah. I'll only be a couple minutes."

"Just getting back from break?" Patty asked, raising her voice over Steely Dan's *Aja,* pulsating through the monitor's speaker.

"Yeah, got in a bit ago," he hollered from the hallway, attempting to answer but dissuade more conversation.

Jake sat at Greg's desk in the corner and pulled the paper from his pocket, unfolding it before him. He lifted the telephone's black receiver and dialed the number. It rang twice and then an answer.

"Hello," said the drowsy voice of what sounded like a middle-age woman.

"Yes. Lisa there?" Jake whispered.

He could hear the woman breathing.

"Who's this?

"I'm a friend. Jake."

"Jake from school?"

"Yes."

"I'm sorry, it's late."

"Is she there?"

The woman exhaled. "She'll call you some other time," she said.

"Is this her mother?"

"No."

"I don't want to pry. But we work together at the radio station on campus."

"Jake." The woman paused. "Lisa has some things to take care of. Please respect her privacy. Can you understand?"

"Yes. Certainly. I just wanted to know if she was all right."

"I'm sure she'll appreciate that. I'll tell her."

Jake heard a click, silence, and then a dial tone.

He continued to hold the phone to his ear, as if time had been paralyzed. Then the recorded voice of the operator came on the line, "If you'd like to make a call, please hang up and dial the number again." Jake hammered the phone back on its cradle. "Shit!"

"You all right?" Patty stood in the entranceway to the office.

"Oh, Jesus," he said, startled. "Yeah, I just, well, I had to make this call, and . . ."

"I know you worked with Lisa," Patty said, walking slowly toward him.

"Yeah, yeah, I just wanted to see what was going on, you know," Jake said hesitantly. He reached for the cigarette behind his ear and the matches in his pocket. Then he rose from the chair and cracked open the big window overlooking the campus, leaned on the sill, and turned toward Patty to light the smoke.

"You look rattled," Patty said, reaching to pull a couple of albums from the library shelf but keeping an eye on him. "It happens, you know?"

Jake shifted his weight, took a long drag, and spoke through the smoke. "What happens?"

"I don't know Lisa all that well, but she was in a class with me. Her roommate's there too."

"Yeah?"

"I knew a girl in high school who got pregnant. It was tough for her," Patty said.

Jake's face flushed.

"Lisa was part of a group project with me. It was for a grade, so I guess her roommate felt she had to let me know something."

"The roommate said this?" Jake questioned, trying to clarify. He took another drag and turned to the window. The lights along the walkway below were shining off the glass window, blinding his view to the outside. He closed his eyes.

"Yeah. Her boyfriend, or something, came to get her."

"Boyfriend?" Jake continued to face the window, eyes still closed.

"Some guy from high school, I think. Hometown."

He blew smoke at the glass.

"I figured you knew, you know, working with her and all," Patty added.

"Yeah. Sure," he mumbled.

Jake could see Patty's reflection in the window glass. He could see her watching him for a long moment then tuck the albums under her arm and move toward the hallway. "Not sure what I'd do," she said. "Got to get back on the air."

Jake rested his forehead on the window and tapped the glass three times, each one a little harder. Patty's sultry voice soon came over the air monitor in the office, "It's a good night for cuddling with a friend and letting this beautiful vibe roll over your bodies, through your ears, and down to your soul. This is *Night Radio*, I'm Patty, and here's something from Tom Waits. 'Blue Valentine.'"

# 16

LISA NEVER RETURNED JAKE'S PHONE call, and he never dialed the number again. She never came back to school. Part of Jake wanted to know more; part of him was afraid to know anything. He ran into Lisa's roommate, the girl Jake encountered at the door of her apartment, outside the library late one night early in the spring semester. She was still reluctant to tell him much, but by then Jake had heard stories about the pregnancy from two others, giving it credence. The roommate did tell him one thing, though. Lisa wasn't staying at home but at her boyfriend's parents' place, at least for a time. The boyfriend's mother was likely the one Jake spoke with the night he called from the radio station.

Of course, Sarah had soon heard the news about Lisa too and asked Jake what he knew, what he'd heard. He nervously shrugged it off, telling Sarah he didn't know any details and was surprised by it. He didn't know if Sarah believed him. What was most important is that she stop asking questions, and she did. Meantime, Jake desperately wanted to hide from all the talk, brush away thoughts of Lisa, so he put all of his attention into the radio, the occasional weekend air shifts in McKeesport, and doing his best to keep his grades from tanking. His relationship with Sarah was slowly improving after the angst of the holidays. They were finding better times, laughing, and making love; they went to parties. Jake stayed over at her place more often. The panty-wearing roomie found a boyfriend and stayed many nights at his place. Sarah was bringing Jake breakfast again to the radio station, and they were talking more about being together, maybe finding jobs at least within a day's drive from each other. Jake was trying to do the right thing, whatever that was, even though he remained uncertain about everything except the music he loved and how alive he felt behind a microphone. He kept the uncertainty to himself.

At the evening dinner celebration after graduation ceremonies, Sarah and Jake sat together with their parents over a steak dinner at a restaurant a block from campus. Maury's had been there for years—a paneled place with red leather booths and chairs. The restaurant had linen napkins and served Caesar salad with real anchovies. The new graduates' diplomas sat atop the seat of the only empty chair at the corner table.

"I have a couple resumes out to ad agencies in Cleveland, Philadelphia, and Pittsburgh. No responses yet," Sarah said, answering Jake's father's question about her job hunt.

"No rejections yet, though, right?" Jake's father asked, sipping from his bottled beer.

"What about you, Jake?" Sarah's dad asked, pouring more red wine into his wife's empty glass then adding to his own.

"Pittsburgh, Cleveland, but I also have tapes out to stations in New York, Los Angeles, and a few in obscure places—a station in Asheville, North Carolina, some station in the Florida panhandle that says it pays in sunshine."

"You ready to make that kind of move?" Sarah's father asked.

Jake brought the tumbler to his lips, the ice clinking in the glass, and tossed back the last swallows of Jack Daniels and ginger ale. A piece of ice slipped into his mouth, and he played with it between his tongue and cheek. "I think so." He hadn't the courage to say more.

Sarah scooted her chair from the table and stood. "I'm going to the little girls' room." She placed her napkin near her dinner plate, took a sip of her father's red wine, and with her eyes alone, asked her mother to join her.

Jake felt the hot spotlight on him and lifted his glass again to his mouth, hoping to find one last drop of whiskey.

"I'll join you," said Jake's mother, reaching for her purse under the seat. "Can you order me another gin and tonic?" she asked Jake's dad.

"I'll have another," Jake said to the waitress standing out of his mother's view. He pointed to his glass. "Jack and ginger."

"And a gin and tonic, please," his father added. "When did you go to liquor, Jake? I thought you were a beer guy."

"I like beer. Can't afford Jack."

"Can't afford it now," said Sarah's father, joking.

"Ah, but he doesn't have the bill tonight. I do," his father said, tapping his glass against Jake's. "Time to celebrate."

When Jake's mother walked through the door of the women's room and disappeared, Jake could only imagine what the conversation in there might be like among the three of them. Sarah knew what he had said at the dinner table was less than true, and she had every right to be upset, even angry. Sarah might be crying, Sarah's mother trying to console her, and Jake's mother would ask if she wanted to talk, reveal what was so heavy on her mind. And Sarah would do exactly that, open up in between the tears to say what was hurting her heart. His mother would be surprised at the news but would remain stoic, calm for Sarah's sake. And his mother would undoubtedly be empathetic as Sarah's mother attempted to soothe her daughter's pain, maybe even place an arm around Sarah and dab her cheeks with a tissue. "Maybe he's not ready," his mother might have said. "Maybe he's waiting for the right time to tell us," she might have added, justifying her son's reluctance to divulge his plans. Then, as a way to change the subject and offer relief,

Jake's mom might have asked Sarah a question that had little to do with any of this. "Did you like your meal?" his mother might ask. "Yes," Sarah would answer. "Yes, I did."

After one more drink and Jake's father paid the bill, Sarah and Jake stood together outside the restaurant in each other's arms. They kissed. He stroked her hair. She cried quietly. Sarah was going back to Hermitage with her parents that night, their station wagon already packed with Sarah's suitcases, a box of books, and bags of linens and towels. They promised to talk on the phone late that night or early the next day and see each other in a couple weeks.

"Please tell me everything," Sarah whispered into his neck, her arms around his shoulders, her body sinking into his.

Their parents waited near the cars, giving the two some space. But Jake could see his mother glancing toward them.

"I promise," Jake said, not completely believing his own words.

"And Jake," Sarah said, lifting her head to look in his eyes, "be honest with yourself about what you're doing, where you're going. Figure it out." He stepped back from her embrace. "Jake?" Sarah asked, suddenly anxious.

"Yeah," he said, forcing a smile. "I know." Jake kissed Sarah and held her hands in front of him, lightly shaking them as if to add emphasis to internal uncertainties.

"Whatever it is that's keeping you from me, being totally and completely *here,*" she said, "whatever it is that's got you locked up," she added, pointing to Jake's head, "I just want you to understand it."

"I know. I know."

"I love you, Jake," she said, sliding her index finger down his nose, stopping at his lips. "But I worry."

He kissed her finger.

Jake planned to stay on campus a few more days before going home and packing for Cleveland. This is what he hadn't revealed at dinner, what Sarah knew and no one else. It was a job as a production assistant at a radio station. He'd work three days during the week, handle the weekend night air shifts, and get paid $4 an hour, more than Jake had ever made—more than the summer work at WIXZ, more than the grass cutting job at the golf course the summer before his freshman year of college.

His parents were headed to Pittsburgh that night but first drove by the trailer to drop Jake off and grab a cup of instant coffee for the road. He put water on the stove to boil. His father sat on the living room couch. His mother stood next to him.

"So what aren't you telling us?" his mother asked, knowing some of the answer after her talk with Sarah in the restroom.

"Telling us what?" his dad questioned.

Jake's mother took a seat next to his father. "Your son apparently has some news," she said.

Jake stretched out his arms and pushed against the kitchen counter.

"Okay. I was going to tell you," he sighed. "I got a job." Jake gave them all the details. Cleveland. Production. Rock station.

"Congratulations," his father said proudly. "Are you looking for a place?"

"I don't start for a month. But I thought I would go up there in a week to look around."

"Cleveland." His mother pondered the word for a moment, crossed her legs, and looked at her husband.

"It's two hours," Jake's father said, touching her arm. "Two hours, right?" he asked Jake.

"Not far," Jake said.

"And Sarah?" his mother asked.

"Well, she knows, and I guess she's looking."

"That's great," his father said.

Jake's mother uncrossed her legs then re-crossed them. She gently touched the corner of her mouth with her middle finger, as if to wipe away something invisible. "Honey?" she asked. "Are you two doing okay?"

"Mom, there's a lot going on, and I . . ."

"You'll figure it out," his dad interrupted. "Be good to her. Be good to you. Take care of *you*, Jake." It was rare when his father offered relationship advice, or any advice, really. It was his own fatherless teenage years that made him cautious of asserting parental counsel. He feared alienation. He feared Jake running away.

"She's a wonderful girl," his mother said with a familiar firmness, the same that had tinged her demands for Jake to finish his high school homework, clean his room. This wasn't a statement; it was a directive.

As his parents stepped out the trailer door to head back to Pittsburgh, his father handed Jake a folded white envelope. "A few bucks to get you through," he whispered. "It's a gift. You need it for Cleveland now, I guess."

His mother blew Jake a kiss from the passenger side window of the Plymouth Fury as it eased out of the space in front of the trailer; the only thing one could hear was the sound of wheels on the gravel road.

———

Jake was sitting outside, smoking and drinking a beer when Danny returned. It was midnight. Danny was still wearing his mortarboard.

"Fucking A, dude," Danny said, stepping out of an unfamiliar car. "You're still up. Perfect."

"I see you're still celebrating," Jake said.

Danny shut the door and thanked the driver. The car sped up the road, spewing dust toward them.

"I have weed," Danny said, pulling a joint from underneath his gown. "And you are just the guy to help me get rid of it." He took a seat next to Jake on the step.

"You smell like a keg," Jake said, smiling.

"I have not stopped drinking since they handed me that fucking diploma." Danny lit the joint and inhaled deeply. "Here," he croaked, handing Jake the weed.

It was hours later when the townie police drove by and asked them to take it inside. The weed was long gone, thank goodness, but they'd finished several beers apiece, the bottles littering the steps. None of it mattered to the cop. It was the guitar and the singing someone had complained about. In the cooling night air, they had belted out dozens of songs and grown progressively louder.

Danny fell asleep on the living room floor and Jake on the couch, the neck of his six-string across his chest.

———

There was a celebration at his parents' home before Jake left for Cleveland. Neighbors, a few relatives, some old high school friends came by. It was sunny and breezy, and much of it was held outside in the backyard and on the side porch. There were grilled burgers and roasted corncobs. Jake's mother made chocolate chip cookies; his father picked up a few cases of beer and bags of ice. His sister asked a few of her friends to the party; a good excuse for teenagers to get together. It was Mary's way of distancing herself from the family, a kind of buffer. Her ski trips weren't always about skiing; sometimes they were just about getting away. As far back as Mary could remember, Michael's death lingered in the shadows of her childhood at every family gathering. She detached herself to escape the sadness.

Jake had seen Sarah only once since graduation, driving to Hermitage for a day. No job yet for her, so Jake was certain it was unnerving for her to endure all the talk and the questions about his new job. As soon as people would stop asking about Jake, they'd turn to Sarah. *So what's going on with you? Any prospects? Are you going to Cleveland?* The questions were exhausting, even as she smiled through the answers. There were times during the party when Sarah would disappear, hide in the house, the garage, or the downstairs bathroom.

"I think I need to go lie down," Sarah said early in the evening. "I'm not feeling all that well."

Jake knew she wasn't sick.

Around 10 o'clock that night, most guests had left, but a few remained on the porch: Jake's older cousin Walt, a couple of old friends from high school, his dad, his mom, a reluctant Mary, and Betty, a widowed neighbor Jake's mother had known for years and had once been part of a regular neighborhood card party. Jake sat on the floor, leaned against the porch railing, and downed another Budweiser. Sarah remained upstairs, sleeping in Jake's old bedroom. Lots of beer and sun had mellowed most everyone, everyone but Betty, who had been drinking lemonade and continued talking about the recent falling out she had had with her daughter. This time it was an argument over church and religion, something about baptizing her daughter's baby. Most tried to ignore Betty but attempted to remain polite.

"It's what you do when you're a Catholic, I told her. You get the damn baby baptized," Betty demanded. "But I guess she doesn't even want to be a Catholic anymore."

"Ah huh," Jake's mother graciously acknowledged.

The story of Betty's daughter was a little close to home. Cynthia got pregnant in high school. She was just sixteen and was sent away to have the baby, a boy. She put it up for adoption. There had been some brief discussions about an abortion, Cynthia's idea. But her father had been an usher and a highly regarded member of St. Sylvester's parish for more than twenty years. Nothing was ever the same for that family after that. Cynthia got in trouble at school, nearly flunked out of tenth grade. She was arrested for selling dope on school grounds, twice for driving drunk. It took her an extra year to receive her diploma, and one month after graduation she married a local fireman, a man nearly ten years her senior. Cynthia's father had long stopped talking to her, saying nothing to or about his daughter until the day he died. After his death, Betty tried to communicate, keep the channels open with Cynthia, and was still trying several years later in the best way she knew how. Sometimes it worked; most of the time it didn't.

"It sounds like Cynthia has some things to work out in her own head," Jake said.

"You'd think she would have worked all that out by now," Betty said. "Jesus, that girl has been a burden."

Jake swigged a mouthful of beer and caught his mother's eyes just as she rolled them. She wasn't mocking Betty's anguish; she was just done hearing about it. Jake was done hearing about it, too.

"Jake, can you come with me for a moment?" his mother asked, standing up from the red Adirondack chair, a staple on the porch for as long as anyone could remember.

He followed his mother through the side door to the living room, believing she had had her fill of Betty and wanted a way out of the conversation. She shut the door to the porch behind them. "I have something for you," she said, putting the Rolling Rock pony bottle on the coffee table and kneeling before a small cabinet near the couch. "I've been working on this for months."

From behind the doors, she pulled out a leather-bound photo album, bulging with pictures. "It's a graduation present," she said, handing Jake the album.

When Jake graduated from high school, his parents designed a large poster board collage of photographs—Little League baseball games, birthday parties, sunny Saturdays in the backyard pool, the first middle school dance, Senior Prom, and the proud graduate in his gown, standing next to his mother. What she was handing him now was the continuation of that tradition, he believed—another collection of photos, a this-is-your-life assembly of memories.

"Mom," Jake said, "you are so good at this." He kissed her cheek and opened the album. On the first page were three neatly printed words: YOUR BROTHER MICHAEL. Below the words, a snapshot of Jake's brother, a smiling 3-year old, holding a plastic toy truck, a child's trophy.

"I wanted you to have all of these, Jake," she said. "I wanted you to remember Michael, and I thought now would be a good time to give them to you. He would be so proud of you, you know?" She gently touched the photo of Michael.

Jake gingerly sat down in his father's rocker and placed the album in his lap.

"Open it up," his mother said, leaning from behind the chair and over Jake's shoulder.

There were pages and pages of photos. One of Michael as an infant, sleeping in the wooden crib his father had made, another of Michael wearing a straw cowboy hat and wildly riding a spring-loaded rocking horse in their living room, and a snapshot in front of the house, near the bottom of the driveway, of Michael in a clean white shirt and neatly ironed khaki pants—the first day of pre-school.

Jake achingly turned the pages. He looked at his smiling mother above him. There were no tears, no sadness.

"I really love this one," she said, pointing to a photo of Michael in a light blue shirt and red bow tie, an Easter basket in his hand. "He hunted for over an hour for the one last egg,"

"Mom, why are you giving me this?" Jake said cautiously.

"It's your brother," she said.

"Sure, yes."

"And if he can't be here to share this day, to see his big brother and be proud of college and a job, well then, maybe through these photos Michael can somehow, through the grace of God, share this moment with you."

"And you, Mom, don't you want these?" Jake asked, tapping the album, remembering the shoeboxes void of photos of Michael.

"They're yours," she snapped, her mood quickly altering. She stepped in front of the chair, snatched the album out of Jake's hand, shut it, and handed it forcefully toward him. "It's a gift."

Jake placed his palms on top of the album, as if to ensure it could not be opened.

"There's more cake. You want some?" his mother asked, walking toward the kitchen. "I think there's a corner piece left."

Jake stood from the rocker and tucked the album in his duffle near the door. He had packed a light bag for the trip back to Sarah's in the morning. His father was allowing him to borrow his car for a one-night stay. Sarah was beginning a part-time job in a couple days at a Dairy Queen while she kept looking for advertising work and a real job.

"What you got there?" Sarah asked sleepily. She had descended the stairs from his old bedroom and saw Jake place the album in his things.

"A present," he said reluctantly.

"Let me see," she said, reaching for the album.

"No," he blurted, stepping in front of her and lifting the duffle and its contents off the floor. "Not now," he added, less abruptly.

"What's going on?" Sarah asked.

"Nothing." Jake threw the duffle over his shoulder and stepped out the front screen door to the small entranceway landing. "This is going in Dad's car so we're ready to takeoff in the morning. If you can get most of your stuff ready, that would be good." Jake headed down the steps and tossed the duffle into the trunk. But before shutting it, he hesitated and lifted the album from the duffle, opening it somewhere in the middle. There was Michael, probably the summer before he was lost—a plastic baseball bat in his hand, and a several-sizes-too-big baseball cap balancing on his head—posing for the camera in a crouched stance like a professional on a baseball card. In the background was an out-of-focus image of Jake, leaning an arm against the trunk of the cherry tree in his parents' backyard. Jake was unable to distinguish his expression or detect a mood in that split second of captured time. It was the only photograph in the collection with the two of them together.

Certainly no one can ever truly predict the end of anything… not the final drink of the night, one's last cigarette, joint, or song on the jukebox…not the last summer party or last love. Nothing really ends. There are always remnants left behind. And there was no way to know that Jake's drive back to Pittsburgh from Hermitage after returning Sarah to her parents' house would be his final trip home for a long time. And Jake would never have believed that after stopping for coffee at a truck stop near Grove City, he would take one more last look at the photo album his mother presented to him, gently place it on the diner's counter and intentionally leave it behind, an unforgivable act but the only one that made sense to him. And no one could have ever told Jake that the kiss he gave Sarah in front of her parents' home before leaving Hermitage might be their last.

PART 2

# 17

JAKE DIDN'T LIKE IT WHEN someone was sitting in his seat at Tina's Coffee Café. It unnerved him. Funny, when one gets older, how routine is so much more important. But this was about more than that. Routine was now part of Jake's recovery, helping to keep him from falling apart.

The olive green cloth chair, frayed at the tips of the arms from years of comforting caffeine lovers, had maintained its overstuffed qualities despite its age. It had been positioned near the big picture window of Tina's, turned just right to watch 2$^{nd}$ Street and the sea just a couple of blocks west. If one leaned slightly forward in the chair they would see the century old Bandon Lighthouse where the Coquille River empties into the ocean. That's why Jake liked it, he would tell people. It was the reason he always sat there, he'd say. And that is why when Brenda was in Jake's chair when he arrived a few minutes after 11 a.m., nearly a half-hour late, Jake could offer only a prickly hello.

"Do you mind moving?"

"There's a table with a couple of chairs in the corner; that okay?" Brenda asked.

"No, I mean can *you* move?" Jake asked edgily, standing before her, shifting his weight from foot to foot. "That's where I sit."

"Well, Jake, I thought we might try something different this time. Break the sameness."

"I like my chair. Thanks."

Brenda smiled and stood from the seat. She pulled a wooden chair from a small table close by and sat down. Jake settled in.

Jake had been seeing Brenda for nearly a year. It's not something he necessarily wanted to do. But Sean told him he would only hire Jake if he took a blood test for drugs and agreed to see a therapist on a regular basis. If that was the way to get back on the radio, then Jake was going to comply. What Jake didn't know is how much he would dislike his time with Brenda. He liked her as a person; she was pleasant enough, had a bright, toothy smile and was reasonably sweet on the eyes, despite the untamed, shoulder-length hair and her age—nearly a decade older than him. It was the therapeutic process he despised, the incessant talking, the achingly slow method of dredging up of all the debris he had left behind, littered in his path. Intellectually, Jake knew it was the right thing to do, what one has to endure to repair wounds, but he didn't have to enjoy it. It helped to meet at Tina's, a compromise Brenda agreed upon, although not what most therapists would have agreed to. For Jake, her office was too much of a cliché. It had newer, cleaner furniture than Tina's, but the instant coffee was lousy, and the pastoral posters on the walls and a pillow on the couch embroidered with the words *Think Happy Thoughts* nearly gave Jake enough reason to skip out to the Bandon Tavern a block down the street and get hammered.

Sean, Jake's old buddy from college, tracked him down when Jake was working outside Memphis in a meat market. It was an unusual kind of place. Jimmy's Meats sold the basic stuff—steaks, chops, lunchmeats—but it also offered live turkeys and kept them in pens inside a big garage in the back of the shop. Jake's job was to clean the place, hose out the turkey shit, and when a bird was chosen by a customer and slaughtered by one of the two older black men who worked with him, Jake had to hose out the blood. He got used to watching turkeys with their heads cut off prance around the garage with plasma spewing from the neck until the bird tipped over and died. And the machine they used to de-feather the bird was pure entertainment.

The meat market job was one of three Jake took on after being fired from his last radio gig in New York City. He packed bicycle pedals in a warehouse in Jamestown, NY for a time and spent three summer months at an amusement park near Toledo as the vomit guy. The place would hire someone each season to do nothing but mop away the throw-up of sickened riders who couldn't stomach the rollercoasters, especially the biggest one that twisted and turned upside down. Jake had at least ten clean-ups a day, fifteen or so on the weekends. There were some perks to being around the coasters, especially the twisting coaster. It flipped the riders over, flinging pocket change, wallets, small purses, and necklaces into the heavy bushes surrounding the ride. If Jake found anything while cleaning up the puke, he was supposed to take it to the lost-and-found office. He didn't always.

Sean had heard about what Jake had gotten himself into—the on-air breakdown, the firing, the mess he'd made. Sean was surprised, certainly. Family members and college friends Jake hadn't talked to in years had been shocked. They had heard the rumors, the stories. *What the hell happened to Jake?* If you were in the industry, you couldn't miss the news. *Radio and Records* published a front-page story entitled "The Epic Downfall of Rock Radio's Superstar Voice." Jake never read the story. *There's no good in that,* he thought. But nearly everyone else in the business did read it, including Sean. The two didn't run in the same radio circles back then, during the crazy 80s and early 90s. While Sean was on the air in Sand Point, Alaska and Cave Creek, Arizona, programming a station just outside Boulder, Colorado and then in Bandon, Oregon, Jake had worked to eliminate the sound of Pittsburgh from his voice, the only part of his father he had control over, and found commercial and intoxicating fame. He had become a star, was making big bucks, going to record company parties, snorting coke in the back of limos, and waking up at least once in a hotel room in SoHo at 3 o'clock on a Sunday afternoon with a half-empty bottle of Jameson whiskey on the bedside table and a pair of black panties tangled in the sheets. His life ripened then began to rot like fruit. From a distance, it appeared to happen in an instant, quick and dirty. But in reality, it was a slow decay. Jake was living an increasingly heady Rock-n-Roll radio life with each new market—first in Atlanta, then San Francisco, L.A., and finally New York. And at the same time, his old friend Sean was living the life of a radio prophet, a voice of spiritual, mystical qualities, talking about the meaning of life and playing music that melded seamlessly with philosophy. He was a rare talent in those soulless days of time-and-temperature DJs, promotional liners, and the mandatory announcements of songs and artists' names. Sean flew under the radar in small markets known for liberal thinking and progressive thought, where programmers, owners, and general managers let you play nearly anything you wanted and talk when you thought it was necessary, needed, made sense, or when it complemented the music or helped seize the day's unique vibe, a vibe Sean had an uncanny way of unearthing. He mixed Zen-like musings with meaningful music. He played old Dylan and new Talking Heads. He even found mystical meaning in Poison and Aerosmith. Sean knew his audience and knew himself. He once spent two weeks meditating at a Buddhist temple. Sean didn't like to label himself a practicing Buddhist but, instead, called his spiritual life a "work in progress," saying he had a lot to learn. But he was certain of one thing, how the human voice and the beauty of thoughtful music could be a healing mechanism. What he had been doing on the air was the kind of radio Jake and his friends dreamed about in college, the kind of art they believed radio could encourage, radio that was expressive, eloquent, consequential, relevant.

Sean had found a place to cultivate that art while Jake—after leaving college—never really bothered looking, allowing money, sex, drugs, and Rock-n-Roll to numb him, burying stuff Brenda was now working hard to bring to the surface. Jake was beginning to understand why things turned out the way they did, although Jake thought he already knew how he got there. Jake deserted the loves of his life and his family, never came to terms with death, sold out, and lost his dreams. It was that simple, a clichéd story of a failure. Jake used beer and then cheap whiskey to soothe him in his college days and then drugs and sex to forget the missteps and miscalculations, to medicate the mess he'd made. But *why* it moved to that level of debauchery was a harder question. That's why there was Brenda. But it didn't take therapy for Jake to come to understand at least one thing: we all are capable of fucking up. All of us are just a few wrong turns away from tumbling into a cavernous and ugly trench from which we will forever struggle to crawl our way out.

Still, even after Jake hit bottom, Sean somehow detected the embers of those early idealistic days still smoldering in Jake, submerged under the damaged and jaded psyche. Jake trusted Sean, certainly enough to have come to Oregon—a small coastal town, a kind of artist colony—and attempt to shake away the past, become the radio voice he always wanted to be.

"How you been, Jake?" Brenda asked.

"Gettin' it done, I guess." This was Jake's standard answer when Brenda asked that question, a catch-all phrase that meant he was staying straight, continuing to try to come to some kind of understanding despite the fear of confronting it.

"Are you still having the dream?" Brenda asked.

"Nearly every night."

The dream was always the same. Jake is in a small, cramped radio studio and nothing works. He flips switches to play records and hears nothing. The microphone won't turn on, and no matter how frenetically he works the on/off button, there is silence. Jake is desperately trying to manage the show, get his voice and music on the air, but no matter what he tries, nothing will save him.

"When you get up in the morning, are you writing down your thoughts, how you feel after the dream?" Brenda asked.

"I'm keeping a journal."

"And have you thought about the letter?"

"I have."

"Have you written it?"

Brenda wanted Jake to write to his dead father. His dad died a couple of months before the New York firing. He had talked to him on the phone off and on for several years, but after his mother died, Jake never visited again. He didn't know why, really, only that he was too self-absorbed or embarrassed with what he'd become. His father didn't like doctors, hadn't been to a doctor in the decade before he died. So when they found the prostate cancer, it was far along and unusually fast moving. He was dead in fewer than five months. Jake made it home to tell his father he loved him four hours before he took his last breath.

A few days before the funeral, Jake needed to find his father's social security number for some paperwork, details to the affairs he and his sister were trying to finalize. Jake searched his dad's wallet for his social security card. It was there, along with two bank cards, his driver's license, a frequent-buyer punch card for an auto parts store, and two small photos—one of Mary at her high school graduation and another of a faded and cracked black-and-white picture of a young woman, a photo Jake had never seen before. The woman sat on a bench in front of a group of trees, her legs crossed. Her hair appeared dark in color. She was attractive but not necessarily pretty. She wore a sleeveless blouse and jeans rolled up at the ankles. And she had a sad smile, one Jake believed might have been hard to forget.

"Who is this?" Jake asked his sister.

"Some relative?" she answered curiously.

It was impossible to tell how old the photograph was, but an intelligent estimate would have put it sometime in the late 1940s.

Several of his father's friends from the old neighborhood came to the wake. When they were just boys, Martin and Jake's father fished together in the streams over the hill from their childhood homes, shot BB guns in the woods, and got into some boyhood mischief. Once they poured gasoline into coffee cans and pitched lit matches at the cans as the boys swung high in the air from a big tree vine in Martin's backyard. Jake's dad loved to tell that story. The two also played football together in high school before Jake's father had to quit school.

"Do you know who this is?" Jake asked Martin, leading him to the funeral home's hallway and showing him the photograph.

"Where did you get this?" Martin asked, smiling and taking the picture in his hand.

"You know her?"

"That's Joanne from high school."

"It was in Dad's wallet," Jake said.

Martin contemplated the photo for several seconds then exhaled. "He had this for all those years?"

"Who was Joanne?"

"Your dad was head over heels for her. Met her the first year in high school. They hung out together," Martin said. "Your dad got his first car, a piece of shit with holes in the floor. You could see the damn road zipping by underneath. Your father offered her a ride before any of his buddies."

"Girlfriend?"

"Probably his first love. You say you found this?"

"Yeah, Dad's wallet."

"Amazing." Martin handed the photo back to Jake. "Joanne Wozniak," he said, remembering her full name. "Damn."

Jake leaned against the hallway wall, holding the picture in the palm of his hand. He tried to see deeper into Joanne's eyes. *Was she looking at my father when this photo was taken? Was he the one with the camera? Was that sweet smile for him?*

Martin placed his hand on Jake's shoulder. "Long time ago."

"Yeah, long time," Jake said.

"He loved your mother, you know. More than anything."

"I know, Martin. Thanks for saying that." Jake slid the photo into his shirt pocket and smiled. "Whatever happened to Joanne?"

"When your dad had to leave school to work, they went their separate ways, I think. Not sure."

"Did he ever talk about her?"

"Several years ago someone from the neighborhood was talking about old school buddies, where they were and all that. Your father was there. I think we were at a bar or something. This was, oh gee, twenty years ago. Somebody mentioned Joanne, said she married some guy from Ohio right after high school. But I couldn't tell you where she is or anything."

"Did Dad know that story?"

"I don't know. I don't think he said anything about it that night."

"Nothing?"

"After he left school," Martin said, thinking aloud, "I don't think I ever heard your dad say anything about Joanne."

Jake shook Martin's hand and thanked him.

"Your dad was a good guy, Jake," he said.

Since the day his father was buried, Jake carried the old photograph of Joanne in his wallet.

Brenda asked, "Do you want to read the letter to me, Jake?"

"I think I'll just give it to you," Jake said, pulling several pages of folded lineless paper from his back pocket and handing them to Brenda.

"Tell me, what did it feel like to write this letter?" she asked.

"There were a lot of questions. Did you love her? Did you love Mom? Why didn't you marry Joanne?"

"And what about you?"

"What do you mean?" Jake asked, even though he knew exactly what Brenda meant.

"Jake?" she asked.

"You know I struggle here."

She leaned forward in her chair and said nothing, waiting and watching, a technique to get Jake to fill the empty space.

"It's in the letter," he said uncomfortably.

"Words on Sarah, how you loved her. Words on Lisa and all that may or may not have happened. How did you address this with your father?"

Jake shifted uneasily in his chair. "I asked him what it was like to love someone and leave them behind, forget them, dismiss them from your life. And not know why."

"Like Sarah? Or maybe Lisa?"

"Yeah, although I don't know about Lisa. I still don't know about Lisa."

"Whether you could have loved her?"

"I know I loved Sarah. Shit, I probably still do."

"And Lisa?"

"I guess I need to know."

"Know what, Jake?"

"Jesus, Brenda. You're a pain in the ass." Brenda was used to hearing this. Jake said it often. She usually smiled when he lashed out. For Jake, that was annoying.

"You know the story. Lisa left school, probably to have a baby. That was the rumor. Never heard a fucking thing more about it."

"And?"

"I don't know. Jesus. I've said it before. I still have this feeling, you know. It's a possibility, you know."

"And?"

"An abortion, maybe. Fuck, I don't know."

"How does this relate to the letter to your father?"

"Look. Dad had his issues with women. It wasn't like he was whoring around or anything. But he cheated on Mom once, and he carried a fucking picture of his high school girlfriend in his wallet until the day he died."

Again, Brenda watched and waited.

"Maybe he could give me some insight into my own shit," Jake said.

"And you asked him what?"

"How do you know you love someone? How do you let it go when you need to let it go? Why did I run from it? Why didn't I keep searching to find out what happened to Lisa? Why did I just walk away from Sarah?"

"And your father would know the answers to these questions?"

"Well, *I* sure as hell don't have them."

Brenda reached out and touched Jake's arm. "Why your father? Why not a friend, a buddy?"

Jake shook his head and let out a hard sigh. "I think he knew something about longing—wanting but not getting. And I don't think I ever really knew how human Dad was until he died. And all those years I didn't visit, all that wasted time when we could have talked. He had answers, maybe not solutions—not sure there are any of those."

"And why didn't you reach out to him then?"

"Easier to hide in coke and sex and Rock-n-Roll radio."

"And now?"

Jake placed a hand across his mouth, a gate to block the emotions. Then he gathered himself and said, "I have a little work to do before my show, Brenda. Can we give it a rest?"

"Sure. We've done plenty."

Jake walked her to the door of the cafe and agreed on another meeting the following week and another letter, this one to Sarah.

"You did well tonight, Jake," she said. "You still want me to read the letter to your father?"

Jake silently nodded and watched her walk around the corner and out of sight.

Jake ordered a double espresso and sank back in the green chair, his chair. The summer sun was sinking low toward the Pacific, and the lenses in the lighthouse had begun to rotate, refracting light into the gray clouds of a darkening evening sky.

# 18

"WE ALL JUST GROPE ALONG, don't we?" Jake asked his audience. "This is what life is, continual groping. Sometimes I wonder if we all concentrate too hard on the vision—what we want to be, what we hope to be, what's next—that we forget that the groping, that crawling around trying to find it, the 'it' Jack Kerouac's Sal Paradise searched for, is the one beautiful and true thing."

It was a few minutes before midnight, a time on Jake's show when he performed what some listeners had come to call "Jake's Sermon." He took pains to prepare this segment, contemplated and meticulously worked through it for hours. It was a performance from the heart, taking about five minutes of airtime. Jake never used a script, only notes. And on this night, after his session with Brenda and the letter to his father, Jake was thinking about answers and whether there were any, and if we, as human beings, spend far too much time hoping we'll find them when it is the searching, the long painful looking, that is the essential path to the illusive solution.

"As Kierkegaard said, 'The self is only that which it is in the process of becoming,'" Jake said softly into the microphone. He paused and added, "Maybe we are simply defined by what we are *trying* to be, not what we are at any given moment—slaves to our own visions and whatever the gods are asking us to discover."

Ever so lightly, under his voice, came the acoustic guitar introduction to Dylan's "Every Grain of Sand."

"Listen to the master," Jake said. "In his most mystical, biblical period, comes a song of Zen-like salvation for all of us on the journey, all of us who are groping." Dylan's music took over the airwaves. Jake turned off the mic and leaned back in the studio chair.

"You killed it, Jake." Angela, his producer, always had something to say about the sermons. But she was far from a kiss-ass, like some radio producers. One time when Jake mused about how some of the basic tenants of Marxism were actually good things, based in Christian belief—even the words of Jesus—she told Jake he was missing the point. "Marxism," she said, "might have had an altruistic idea. You can argue that, yes. But the reality is human nature gets in the way." Angela was smart, and she adroitly supported her opinions. "Look at Che Guevara," she said. "He's a hero to so many for giving power to the poor, but he was also ruthless. The dual nature of man."

Angela was a pretty girl in the hippie sort of way. She had attended USC and had a job at a big publishing house for a time in Los Angeles, working in the acquisitions department. Got the job right out of college. Thought she was going to work with brilliant writers who had something unique and substantial to say but, instead, slogged along in the division that published romance novels. At twenty-four she got tired of the schmoozing, the fake smiles, and telling all the "hacks," as she called them, how great they were. "Soulless writers of soft porn," she called the romancers. She left to work in radio. First it was part-time at a station in San Francisco, writing copy for the advertising department and living in a tiny two-bedroom near Golden Gate Park with three girlfriends. She ended up in Oregon after following a boyfriend who took a job at the *Portland Tribune*. He dumped her. "Long story," she once said, never wishing to go any deeper. Angela couldn't afford Portland on her own, headed for Bandon for a producer job the year before Jake arrived. She liked working at night. She and Jake ended up together on the 10 p.m. to 2 a.m. air shift.

"If I please you, Angela, I please them all," Jake answered through the intercom to the small adjacent studio where she worked during the show, taking phone calls, preparing guests for their time with Jake on the air—mostly by telephone since Bandon is in the middle of nowhere—and helping with song selections. Even though the sermons were all Jake's, there were times he would ask Angela to conduct some research. She was good at it.

"I don't know if that's a compliment or a complaint," she joked, her honey-toned voice still clearly evident through the crackly intercom system.

"You are the higher standard, baby," Jake said with an exaggerated pompousness. "I am not worthy of your intellectual companionship."

Through the studio's soundproof glass, Jake could see her smirk. She mouthed *fuck you* and gave him the finger.

Angela could point out the holes in Jake's thinking, the deficiencies in his knowledge or the blindness in the assertions. For one, she made fun of Jake's Dylan obsession, pleading with him many times to pay attention to some of the newer songwriter/poets. He did and liked a lot of them. Kurt Cobain came up in those conversations. But he reminded her that there are scholars, professors at universities, who have made a living studying, writing about, and researching Dylan's lyrics, like the poems of Shelley, Keats, or Whitman. "When another songwriter reached that level of admiration and impact," Jake would frequently tell her, "that's when I'll take a hard look at them. Until then, they are just wannabes."

"You're old," she'd respond. "But I get it. I like Dylan, too. I'm just saying, okay?"

"So happy you see it my way," Jake would answer, grinning.

Jake wondered sometimes what it would be like to sleep with Angela. She had long, lean legs, and even though she wore earthy shoes—like Birkenstocks or something that didn't necessarily show off how smooth and toned those legs were—her legs still looked lovely coming out of a pair of shorts or a sundress. It was likely the way she walked that did it. Her hips swayed just enough to be subtlety alluring, as if she were teasing and knew it—a bit of a wiggle. Her breasts were small, like that of a teenage athlete, a soccer player or sprinter, but they fit her body, perfectly proportioned to her stature. She had a cute off-center nose and thin lips. Her eyes were deep brown and smallish, not necessarily interesting or sexy but certainly expressive. Her hair, though, is what people most noticed—long, silky, and coal black, unfolding to the middle of her back. It shimmered, light reflecting off its thick strands. It begged to be touched.

Sean let Jake do his thing each night on the radio. And frequently he would remind Jake that his air work was what they had always wanted to be a part of, what they talked about in college, the kind of radio they imagined.

"That guy Ted, the one who gave you your first job," Sean once said to Jake. "I'm not that guy."

Sean knew Jake was thankful for Ted's early encouragement, but he was quick to remind him that Ted was part of the corporatization of radio—the faceless, straight-laced guy who saw radio as a business, not an art form, a guy who meant no harm but had no spirit. Jake agreed but still defended Ted for having confidence in him, a young kid with little more than passion. Sean called his loyalty admirable. Still, Sean believed there had been far too many Teds in the radio business over the years, people who had sucked all the life out of the work. "Do you know where else in the country they would let you do what you do each night?" Sean once asked emphatically. "Nowhere. That's where. Do you think a guy like Ted would let you rant and muse and play the music you want?"

Sean was right. But Jake remained grateful for Ted's support, although he never told him so. Ted was not at the station on his final day at WIXZ that summer after graduation in 1978, two decades ago. Jake didn't remember why not. But he did speak to him on the phone after he'd landed the job in Cleveland. He asked Jake to do one more weekend shift at WIXZ, and he agreed. A year or so later, Jake heard Ted left radio for a TV news job, an assignment editor position. It was the kind of work that fit his personality. Maybe we all eventually end up in the places we're supposed to be. That's what was on Jake's mind when he returned to his apartment at 3 a.m. and began writing the letter to Sarah.

Jake's apartment was in an old house two blocks from the ocean. The small cottage had been converted to two flats for summer renters, but the landlord had agreed to allow Jake to lease year-round. Jake had to climb a small flight of stairs to a tiny landing and the front door. There were three rooms: the living area, where he had a twin bed, a small kitchen, and the bath. He bought a simple wooden desk at a yard sale and placed it near a window that looked east, over part of the town. The lower apartment had a great ocean view, but it cost too much.

Jake made a small pot of coffee, put a Tom Waits CD in the player, and sat at the desk to write.

Unlike the words for his father, these came effortlessly, although not painlessly. Apologies are simpler when you know the letter will never be delivered. Jake told Sarah he regretted abandoning her. He told her he loved her then and believed he still did but didn't know what to do with that. He didn't know what that meant twenty years later, if it meant anything. Jake told her what he was doing, where he lived and wrote that he'd heard recently through Sean that she was married, had a child, and lived somewhere in Pennsylvania. Jake thanked Sarah for the time they had together, how he cherished it still, and how the memory of watching her grow to be a woman would always be a treasured time in his life. Jake would understand if she never wanted to see him, talk, or think about him again. He would understand, Jake wrote, if she hated him. He told her he hadn't been the best person in the world and that he'd lost his way but was trying to find it again. Jake wrote about his failure to be a committed man, an honest man, a faithful man, and as he penned the words, the echoes of the past reverberated in the recesses of his head. Jake knew it was the right thing to do, to come clean, if that's what it was. But as painfully self-satisfying as it might be, he still couldn't tell all. Jake could not reveal Lisa's name, instead, referring to the object of his indiscretion as "another girl at college." The letter would never be sent. Sarah would never see the words on the lineless pages of a Moleskine journal. It's easy to be honest, vulnerable, when you're talking to yourself.

By 5 a.m., Jake had 27 pages, 631 words, several underlined or capitalized phrases for emphasis, nothing scratched out, and no re-dos. He had been more contemplative with the letter to his father, reworking and rewriting entire paragraphs. The letter to Sarah was a continuous stream directly from inside darkened rooms of the heart, like opening a once locked storage vault and watching the contents tumble out to the floor.

Jake closed the journal and caressed its cover. He placed it in a corner of the desk and hit replay on the CD player. Tom Waits' sandpapered voice sounded somehow different, haunting.

# 19

J AKE WAS LIVING IN ATLANTA when John Lennon was shot. Howard Cosell announced his death on *Monday Night Football*, and Jake was working morning drive back then and in bed when the phone rang.

"Someone shot Lennon." It was the radio station's music director. He was shaken.

Jake sat up on the mattress and wiped his eyes. "John Lennon? The Beatle?" He asked. Later, it seemed such a stupid question.

Jake was drinking then, three or four glasses of Jack Daniels most nights. He was functioning though, making it to the studio on time. He was young, able to shake it off. The coke would come later.

"Saw it on TV. We have to do something in your show," the music director insisted.

"Are we doing something now?" Jake asked.

"Carrying live coverage from the network."

"No music?"

"Not yet. No one knows the whole story. Just happened."

"Is he dead?"

"That's what they're saying," the music director whispered.

For several hours the next morning, Jake played Lennon's music, took calls from fans, and updates from the network news.

The radio station had someone at its New York sister station standing outside the Dakota Hotel with the hundreds of fans who had gathered there. Jake put him on the air, live, several times, from the street outside Lennon's apartment. If historians say the Kennedy assassination was the end of America's innocence, Lennon's death was the end of a generation's hope. Some might say anything that was left of the idealism of the 60s died with Lennon that night.

When radio is one's life work, it's easy to index your existence with the events of the day. Jake was still in Atlanta when Reagan was shot, on the air in Los Angeles when the Space Shuttle Challenger exploded, and in New York when the riots broke out in L.A. after the Rodney King verdict. In each case, his work, he thought, was strong. At music radio stations, Jake had to make the initial call on when and if to stop playing music, when to make news the priority, to allow for listeners to react, to solicit their phone calls and put them on live—to be a shared community of sorrow, shock, and rage. Jake had to make quick judgments that eventually would be managed and adjusted by program directors and general managers. But that first reaction, the first move, was his. In 1995 when the Oklahoma City bombing happened, Jake was on the air in NYC. And it would be the beginning of the end.

First reports suggested a local tragedy, an accident, maybe a natural gas explosion. Jake didn't stop the music that morning, not at first. Then over the next couple of days, the death count reached over 160 people, some of them children who had been at a daycare center.

Timothy McVeigh and Terry Nichols were arrested and charged with planning and carrying out the attack. McVeigh, a member of an American militia movement and also a Gulf War veteran, had detonated a Ryder truck stuffed with explosives in front of the Alfred P. Murrah Federal Building in downtown Oklahoma City. McVeigh and Nichols hated the federal government. During Jake's show—just a few days after the bombing, when it was still so fresh and raw—he interrupted the flow of music and openly asked listeners what they thought was happening to America. *Who are these people? Does the government overstep its boundaries? Is McVeigh nuts? What have we come to in this country? Where are we heading?* He began to put listeners on the air. There was intelligent discussion, although the program director had already been to the studio to insist Jake put an end to it and get back to the music. Despite what had happened, the boss felt a Rock-n-Roll station should be about the music. "People want to hear Bon Jovi," he demanded. Jake ignored him. And when his boss walked out the studio door, Jake locked it.

"We have become a violent nation," Jake said into the microphone. "If it's not nutcases blowing up buildings and people in the name of freedom, then it's cops storming establishments, groups that believe they have a right to assembly or to create a church of their choosing or protect themselves." He was referring to the claim by some that the FBI had been overstepping its authority.

Jake continued to rant.

"Look, I don't believe in militias. I want controls on guns. The NRA is a freakin' terrorist group. But aren't its members allowed to be wrong? Isn't that part of the freedom we have, to be wrong?"

Jake had no clear idea where he was going with any of this, but he kept going anyway. He was amped, angry, and fueled by drugs. The coke he had done before the show, and the pills and Jack Daniels he'd ingested for years had rushed together at this moment to unravel him. He snapped. Jake's train was off the rails. The senselessness of Oklahoma City, the meaninglessness ignited suppressed rage and bitterness. Until then, Jake had managed to keep his job, get good ratings, and make big bucks. In the 80s, everyone in Rock-n-Roll radio was high, jacked on coke and anything else they could get. It's what they did. It's what Jake did. But it was now distorting his life; the synapses in his brain were rapidly misfiring.

"When will we learn? When they blow up all the federal buildings in the country?" he blustered, his words slurring now. "America learned nothing from Vietnam; we learned nothing from Watergate. We are a country that has lost its way." Jake's speech was quickly losing its earlier fluidity and gaining a threatening, frenetic edge. "If you think JFK's assassination was a mob hit, certainly Robert Kennedy's death was the mafia's doing, too."

Jake saw the program director and general manager standing outside the studio door—one pounding on the window, the other violently shaking the handle.

"The Vietnamese were just trying to find a better life. They thought communism might be it. Maybe it would be, but in our righteous American way we thought we knew better."

The maintenance engineer now stood at the door, quickly working through dozens of keys on his chain. Standing beside him were two building security guards.

"There's no reason marijuana shouldn't be legal. All drugs should be legal. We all have the right to do with our bodies what we want."

Jake heard the metal key twisting into the door's double lock.

"And women should always have the right to choose to do with their bodies what they fucking wish."

The door burst open and the program director swiftly moved to the control board.

"Good listeners," Jake screamed, "management is trying to silence me, silence you!"

The program director reached for the microphone's on/off switch. Jake shoved his hand away.

"We all have the right to speak, say what we want, be heard!"

Security guards flanked Jake. They grabbed his arms and pulled him out of his chair and away from the controls.

"In the words of Howard Beale in the movie, *Network*," Jake screeched, "'I am mad as hell and not going to take it anymore!'"

The guards slammed Jake's face into the soundproof glass, squishing his mouth and nose. The program director flipped off the mic and hit *play* on CD player #1, and roaring from the air monitor speakers came the blaring guitars of "Blaze of Glory" and the raspy voice of the man the listeners apparently couldn't live without, Jon Bon Jovi.

Jake was fired the next day. A breach of contract, they called it. In two days he was formally charged with simple assault. The program director insisted Jake struck him. Jake pleaded guilty before a judge, paid a $5000 fine, and was sentenced to mandatory rehab.

# 20

JAKE DROVE TO OREGON IN the BMW-318 he bought back in 1985 before things got crazy. He purchased it with cash. It was one of the only things he owned outright. After paying the fine and attending the court-ordered in-patient rehabilitation, he sold a bunch of furniture, an old audio system, and brand new golf clubs he'd never used, and drove the BMW as fast as he could out of Manhattan. It was Jake's getaway car, packed with all he had left: two suitcases—one full of books and the other with clothes—a Yamaha acoustic guitar, a PowerBook G3 Apple laptop, a few old vinyl albums he couldn't bear to part with, including the Beatles' *White Album,* Dylan's *Blonde on Blonde,* and a box of CDs. One thing he purposely left behind—a clock. Jake gave away his Movado wristwatch to an old woman on the highway who carried her belongings in a red wagon, tossed his wall clock into the dumpster behind his high-rise New York apartment, and dropped his alarm clock over his 14th floor's balcony to the street below, watching the plastic fragments explode across the concrete pavement. Jake's life had become knotted by time. Everything was a deadline—start the show on time, air the advertising on time; when you produced work it had to be timed perfectly to the second, play the songs exactly as they were scheduled. Even off air, time was insidious. He had a specific time to meet his coke connection—every Thursday afternoon at 2:30. Jake was always on time. The dealer was nearly always late. It was only after Jake left radio and began to work those other jobs that he learned to no longer be a slave to time. He had his doubts about returning to the radio, but with the bike pedal, puke, and turkey herding gigs behind him, Jake looked to Bandon for peace.

It wasn't long after the firing and Jake's goodbye to NYC that he learned to love morning again, especially with no more clocks to startle him into the day. Being sober helped. His inner time machine had somehow taken over. Coffee became a joy again, a treat for a new day rising, not a medicine for easing the sins of the night before. And after living in the Memphis area for a while, working at the meat market and chasing turkeys, Jake began to find himself at Graceland, sitting silently alone near the entranceway in the early mornings. Despite the heavy commuter traffic on Elvis Presley Boulevard, he was able to find tranquility near the gate to the home of the King of Rock-n-Roll. It's where Jake first began to meditate, if one could call it that in the early going.

Jake's first experience with meditation was when he read about it in Jack Kerouac's *Dharma Bums*, and he knew about the Beatles and their trip to India and all that Transcendental Meditation stuff. But of course, he really didn't understand a thing about the practice, the true discipline. Jake did, however, know enough to close his eyes, sit silently, and try to sink into what he had heard a yoga teacher once call nothingness. It was difficult, hard to quiet the head. But he eventually found his own primitive, private version of Nirvana with the help of a CD of Gregorian Chants playing through the headphones of an old Walkman he bought at a Sunday morning flea market. At first, Jake struggled with focus, but in time, he was reflecting for as long as an hour, cross-legged in front of Graceland's large metal gate, the big, flowing two-foot-tall musical staffs and the image of a guitar player looming above him. Why Graceland? Why not a quiet park or a church or temple somewhere? He didn't have an answer. Jake was simply drawn to the place. It might have had something more to do with Paul Simon than Elvis. Jake was a big fan of Simon's *Graceland* album. *It's an inspired work of genius,* he thought. And then there were those words, the simple lyrics that may have unconsciously helped him find new footing in Memphis, words that hinted at salvation.

———

In Oregon, Jake took his morning meditations along the Pacific coastline on the rocks across from the Bandon Lighthouse. He'd reflect alone in clear, cool ocean air, in mist and fog or in the middle of a blustery storm, wrapped in rain gear. Jake tried not to miss a morning. And afterwards, it was Tina's and coffee, sometimes to meet Brenda but more often than not to sit silently to read, write, or just be. After rehab, simplicity drove his days. Minimalism meant more to him than ever before. He had found beauty in it. During the intoxicating, drug-soaked radio days, Jake believed he had to experience everything in a flash, all at once, in an explosion of sensations. And by the time he was in Bandon, contemplation, reflection, and the slow, steady work of introspection had become vitamins for a new life.

It was late on a Friday night, actually early Saturday morning following the show, when Angela and Jake headed over to Morgan's, the all night diner in Coos Bay. It was a regular destination at the end of each week and the only restaurant within dozens of miles still open at 2:30 in the morning, catering mostly to workers at a timber mill a few miles outside of town. Several days a week, when business was good, the mill scheduled a number of employees on evening and all-night shifts. Morgan's was a beneficiary.

"I heard you tonight, talking about that 'Paul is dead' stuff." Stacey was always at Morgan's when Jake and Angela came in, frequently working the night shift. She listened regularly to the show. "I never knew about all that. Amazing."

"Too young, huh, Stacey? What were you in the late-60s? Six years old?" Jake joked.

"Wasn't even born yet."

"Nice job, Jake, you just told Stacey she's an old hag," said Angela, pouring honey into her hot tea.

"Ah, you know I didn't mean anything by it. You know I love you, Stacey," Jake said, reaching out to touch her arm.

"Yeah, yeah you fuckhead," Stacey teased. "More coffee?"

"Please."

"So did the Beatles do that on purpose?" Stacey asked.

"McCartney and Lennon never said, although their management denied it. I think John and Paul played along with the mystery for shits and giggles."

"Jake put a new spin on it tonight," said Angela.

It was the fifth anniversary of McCartney's solo album, *Paul is Live*. The cover was a parody of the *Abbey Road* cover that contained clues of Paul's apparent death. Paul is in bare feet on *Abbey Road* as he walks out of step with his band members across the London street, a symbol that he was the corpse. Jake dedicated part of the show to the aftermath of the Paul is Dead rumors with the songs and all the talk that came after the initial mystery broke, including, "So Long Paul," recorded by Werbley Finster, who was really Jose Feliciano. Jake asked listeners to call in, wonder aloud on the radio what it would have been like if Paul had really been dead. How would a generation steeped in music have dealt with such a tragedy? It was nearly two decades after Lennon's shooting. What did it mean to lose a hero? What would it have meant if McCartney's death had been real and kept from us, altering reality, playing with our emotions? And what does death really mean? What is it? Where do we go? How do we say goodbye?

"When my mother died," Stacey said, "my father didn't call me for a week."

"Really?" asked Angela.

"I had just moved out here to Oregon, literally days before she died. Just quit school, my fiancé left me, and I was heading out on my own. Dad said he didn't want to stress me out anymore than I already was."

"Sounds like he cared," Jake said.

"I have a hard time forgiving him for it. He should have told me. We needed each other."

"Not to make light of all this, but if Paul had really been dead, you would have never forgiven the Beatles?" asked Angela, smiling.

"Probably would have wanted to kill John," Stacey said, laughing and then catching herself. "Oh shit, well, I didn't really mean that. Not like I wanted to shoot him or something."

"I lost a cousin to leukemia, and I kind of watched him go. He was so young," said Angela. "Anybody ever *not* tell you about a loved one's death, Jake?"

He lifted a coffee mug to his mouth as if to hide behind it.

"Nope. Death was always right there in front of me," Jake murmured.

Stacey glanced behind her, making sure the manager didn't see her spending too much time at one table. "Who'd you lose?" she asked.

No one in Oregon knew about Michael. Very few people anywhere knew. Of course Jake's sister did, and Danny, Jake's old college trailer mate who he hadn't talked to in years. Jake told him fragments of the story one night in the spring semester of his junior year when they were drunk on Captain Morgan's rum. And then there was Sarah. She knew everything about Michael— how he disappeared, how Jake panicked, how he believed it was his fault, how Jake suffered, believing his mother never truly forgave him, and how maybe he didn't deserve to be forgiven. Sarah knew more about Michael and Jake than anyone. Even when Brenda eventually was able to unearth the story, it was little more than an emotionless account, like reading a list of facts from a police blotter. It was different with Sarah. She had watched Jake cry.

"Someone close," Jake answered faintly. "Can I get a little more?" he asked, raising his mug off the table, hoping to redirect the conversation.

"I'll take another tea, please," Angela said.

Stacey smiled and turned to leave. Angela sipped the last from her cup and asked, "You ever talk about it?"

Jake placed his elbows on the table, brought the mug to the height of his chin, and looked out the window just left of the booth. "It's amazing how many stars you can see in his part of the country."

A light fog had already moved in over the coastline. There wasn't one visible star in the sky that night. Jake knew it, and Angela knew it, too.

# 21

IT WAS RARE WHEN SOMEONE came to Jake's apartment door, especially on a Sunday. He had returned from his morning on the rocks near the lighthouse and was tossing laundry into the tiny washing machine stuffed inside the bathroom closet when two light and reluctant taps echoed through the small apartment.

"Hi Jake."

Angela had never been to his place. Jake hesitated with hello, as if needing a moment to recognize her.

"Hey," he said tentatively.

"Hey."

"Everything all right?"

"Oh sure," she said. "I was at Tina's this morning to meet a friend and thought you might be around."

"Well, sure, yeah. Come on in."

Angela wore make-up, something Jake had never seen on her before. And her hair, usually hanging straight and long, was pulled up on the back of her head, a scarf around it to keep it in place. She smelled of musk.

"Hope I'm not interrupting," Angela said, stepping through the door.

"No, no. Just doing a little laundry." Jake reached over to turn down the CD player offering up the opening acoustic guitar riffs of Zeppelin's "Over the Hills and Far Away." He always loved it when Jimmy Page and Robert Plant mixed country-ish licks with Blues and Rock-n-Roll.

"Want some coffee?" he asked.

"Had plenty of tea, thanks. I like your place."

Jake appreciated the comment, although he thought she was just being polite. He was proud of the simple life he'd taken on: two chairs, a twin bed, a simple chest of drawers he found for a few bucks at a thrift shop, a small desk. No TV. No kitchen table. There were just enough clothes in the closet to get him through a week: jeans, tee-shirts, one pair of khakis, two long-sleeved oxford shirts. No suit. No sports jacket. Three pairs of shoes. Not much on the walls. There was a 2x2 photo of Hemingway's studio that he'd picked up on a trip to Key West and a framed replica of the original Woodstock poster, the one with the dove sitting on the neck of a guitar.

"I like it," Jake answered, motioning for her to sit in the more comfortable of the two chairs, a gray upholstered seat with big arms and overstuffed cushions, another good thrift store find.

There were a few moments of silence before Angela spoke up.

"I have only a small group of friends in Bandon. You may be the person I spend most of my time with, actually."

"I guess so."

"And I thought, maybe, you could offer some advice."

"Really? Me? About?"

"A relationship."

"I don't know if I'm the guy," Jake said, shaking his head.

"Well, I don't know really a lot about your past loves, girlfriends, whatever. But I do hear what you have to say on the air every night."

"I guess I do give away a little from time to time."

"Little slivers, yeah."

"Okay." He smiled.

"I get the sense you have had your heart broken."

"Who hasn't?"

"And from what I can figure, you kind of forced the issue."

"What do you mean?"

"You made the decision to break off a relationship with someone you cared deeply about. You broke your own heart."

Jake sat down in the other chair and crossed his arms across his chest. He heard the buzz of the dryer, signaling the end of a cycle.

"How do you figure?" he asked.

"You left someone, and you don't know why. You abandoned love."

"You think you know me, huh?"

"Jake, you wear it on your sleeve. It comes out on the air."

"And what else do you think you know?"

"There's another relationship somewhere that haunts you."

"Haunts me, huh?" Jake stood and walked to the kitchen to refill his coffee mug, avoiding Angela's eyes.

"Your life does show up on the air, you know. And I'm sorry; I don't mean to be intrusive."

"Then what are you trying to be?" he asked from the kitchen entranceway.

"You know I left Portland after my boyfriend left me."

"Yeah."

"Well, that's not exactly the story."

"What do you mean?" Jake asked, sitting back down in the chair.

"I left *him*."

"Okay," Jake said, sipping coffee. "And?"

"I left because I didn't know how to handle being in love while trying to deal with life and everything else I wanted."

Jake's body sunk deeper into his seat. The coffee suddenly tasted cold.

"He came looking for me," Angela added.

"He did?"

"That's who I met at Tina's this morning."

"He's here? In Bandon?"

"Came down for the day."

"You met with him?"

"He pleaded with me."

"And you wanted to see him?"

Angela ran her hand over her hair and tightened the scarf. "Guess I did."

"So you're asking me...what?"

"Has the girl you left ever reached out?" Angela said softly, easing carefully into the question.

Jake crossed his legs, took a large drink of coffee, and swallowed hard. "Angela, I don't know if . . ."

"I have no right to ask this, I know," she said, interrupting.

"It was a long time ago."

"I'm sorry," Angela said.

Jake leaned forward and sighed. "We were in separate cities. I stopped phoning. Never returned her calls. She wrote letters, all of them full of questions. Questions she had every right to ask. They were sad at first, and then she was angry. She told me she was coming to see me. She never did."

"Just cut her off?"

"Cold turkey, I guess."

"Do you understand why you did that?"

"I was selfish, afraid, unsure."

"Are you still?"

"Don't know."

"And what if she showed up here tomorrow?"

"She has no idea where I am."

Angela smiled. "Oh, she knows."

Jake looked puzzled.

"She knows, Jake," Angela added.

Angela's words were more about a woman's intuition than solid evidence. At least that's what Jake suspected.

For another half-hour, they continued talking about Angela's old boyfriend. How he asked her that morning at the café to move back to Portland with him. How she didn't answer. Whether Angela loved him. She said she thought she might. Jake asked her why she was in Bandon if she loved a man in Portland.

"Same reason you're in Bandon, Jake, and love a girl in... wherever."

"Got it figured out, do you?"

"Maybe."

Jake had a similar conversation with Brenda. But talking about it with Angela was less clinical, less like treatment.

Angela rose from her chair. "I've gotta go," she said.

"You okay?" Jake asked, walking her to the door. Angela smiled. He placed a hand on the small of her back. "I wish I could say you'll figure it all out."

"I know," she said. "I know."

As Angela stepped through the door, she removed her scarf and allowed her hair to cascade over her shoulders and down her back. The late morning sun danced off its silky blackness.

———

Just after 10:30 p.m. Monday night, a half hour into the show, Angela pressed the studio intercom button.

"His name is Mark," she said.

Jake gave a perplexed look through the studio glass.

"Mark," she said again. "The guy in Portland."

Jake nodded.

"You never asked," she said.

It was true. He never asked.

"Sarah," Jake said through the intercom. "Her name was Sarah."

"Always liked that name," Angela said.

Jake smiled, sliding the CD of the Beatles' *White Album* inside player #1 and cueing up the second song. As R.E.M.'s "Night Swimming" faded out, Jake pressed the CD's start button and heard Harrison's haunting, metronomic lead guitar and then Lennon's vocals, words to a lonely, troubled young woman.

"At least it wasn't Prudence," Jake said through the intercom.

"I think Prudence is a great name," Angela answered, laughing. "How cool would it be to share your name with one of the Beatles' coolest songs?"

"Let's do that at midnight tonight. Names. Songs and people's names. Ask listeners to call in if their parents named them after a great song."

"Just women?" asked Angela.

"Just women," Jake said. "Can you work on some songs?"

"Peggy Sue"

"'Layla.'"

"Is that a real name?"

"Of course it's a real name!"

"'Mandy.'"

"Oh, Jesus. Let's leave that one out. No Manilow."

"'Maggie's Farm.'"

"There you go! 'Mustang Sally.' Wilson Pickett."

"Mustang or Sally?" Angela asked, grinning.

"I must someday meet a girl named Mustang."

"Probably a stripper."

"Even better," Jake snickered. "Let's get together a bunch of good ones, and I'll work on something to wrap around it, see if we can get some good phone calls for this one. And better yet, great stories about why parents named their kids after songs."

Angela went at it, sorting through the music catalogue, searching the internet for stories of people who named their daughters after rock songs. "You cannot believe the number of girls who were named Rhiannon after the Fleetwood Mac song.

After 1976, it just took off. Before that, nothing," she said, walking in Jake's studio with a fresh cup of coffee for him.

"Thanks," he said. "In a way, the woman's name in whatever song it is becomes a lover, of sorts. Yes, a love. Someone we fall in love with, and then we give our daughter the name, and it makes us feel like we are always in love. Don't you think?"

"That is completely a guy's perspective, you know," Angela said, dismissing him. "How does the mother fit in here?"

"I'm just thinking out loud."

"Think harder," she said, playfully slapping him on the head.

"Yeah, yeah, okay," Jake said. "Geez, do you have to hit me?"

They laughed about all the kids who were saddled with the name Delilah after the Tom Jones hit. Or a real boy named Sue, who will forever hate Johnny Cash. They bantered and joked and kidded each other about names and songs and mothers and fathers. Angela then returned to her side of the glass, and they worked separately and silently, preparing for how to present the theme on the air.

During a commercial break, Angela pressed the intercom button.

"If you had a daughter? Would you name her Sarah?" she asked softly.

Jake was motionless.

"Don't have a daughter, don't plan to," he said resolutely. Then, in an attempt to take the edge off, he added, "Plus. Has anyone ever written a Sarah song?" he asked, already sure of the answer.

Without hesitation Angela replied, "'Sara' Dylan."

Jake closed his eyes and rubbed the lids with his fingers then brushed the back of his neck with both hands. "Of course, no H. Better than that Sarah song by Hall and Oates," he said, smiling warily through the window at Angela.

"I have it cued up in here. Ready to go," she said.

"Dylan?" he asked.

"Of course," Angela answered. Jake looked surprised. "You all right?" she asked.

Jake nodded. "Play it next."

"Don't you want to save it for midnight?"

"Next," he said.

Angela pushed the start button on the CD player in her studio, Dylan's lyrics cut through the night like a pinpoint beam from a lonely lighthouse on a very dark ocean.

———

It was 3 a.m. when Jake unlocked his apartment mailbox and pulled out all that had been bent and stuffed inside. He didn't make daily mail checks. There was no need. Promotional flyers and store coupon sheets addressed to "occupant" were jammed inside. There were some utility bills and what appeared to be a letter from Greenpeace, undoubtedly asking for a donation. All the way in the back of the box was a light blue envelope, soiled at the bottom right edge and slightly torn along the top. It was an old-fashioned licked-on-the-flap letter with the mailing address handwritten in dark blue ink. The writing was smudged from moisture, most likely rain. The address on the envelope, however, was not Jake's apartment in Bandon but rather the old apartment in Memphis. And it had been stamped across the front at least twice with the words "Please Forward." There was no return address in the left corner or on the back, and the artwork on the oversized postage stamp in the upper right corner was that of a flower, a white orchid.

Jake held the letter in his hand for several minutes, fingered the edges, raising it up to the light in the entranceway. He placed it in the center of the kitchen counter, being certain it was exactly in the middle, and headed for bed without opening it.

# 22

I T WAS SOMETHING A COUPLE of tourists might do, but Sean insisted they do it anyway.

"It's out on the dunes, the big ones. The dunes are part of Oregon's coast, man," he said, sitting behind the wheel of Jake's old BMW, as they made their way north on US-101. Sean had asked to drive.

Jake had found comfort in Bandon's cooler weather, the frequent fog and mist, and the dunes. One evening he walked the beach north of Bandon and sat on the enormous sand hills overlooking what's called Haystack Rock, falling asleep against the cool grains. He dreamt he was lost on an island where only children lived. There was something soothing about that.

"It's not going to be a bunch of out-of-towners, is it?" Jake asked, facing the wind as it rushed in through the passenger window. "You know what I mean?"

"Come on, man. The buggies are great, and you can get them really going. You fly up to the top of the dunes, launch to the other side. You'll love it."

Jake didn't see Sean at the station much. He was gone when Jake arrived each night. Sean wasn't the kind of program direc-tor who hovered, micro-managed, but he knew people, and he knew Jake.

"Never been on a dune buggy," Jake said.

"Go-cart? One of those metal cars you drive around at bad amusement parks?" Sean asked.

"When I was a kid."

"Not much different, just faster." Sean hit the gas and moved to the left to pass a slower vehicle. "Thing is, you can die if you don't know what you're doing out there," he added, smiling devilishly.

"Fuck you," Jake said.

"There are roll bars. Helmets. You'll be fine."

"Just fuck you, man."

Sean didn't know about the letter. He didn't know Jake had left it on his kitchen counter for two days and even considered burning it. He didn't know that when Jake finally found the courage to read it, he read it over and over and over. And Sean didn't know Jake had carefully folded and slipped it in his wallet to carry with him. Angela knew, though. Jake had let it all out at Morgan's one early morning. Angela listened without reaction, without judgment, as he told her how he'd cheated on Sarah with a girl named Lisa all those years ago. He told her about the tequila and the sex at the radio station and how Lisa disappeared, never returning to college. Angela watched Jake's eyes, his hands, as he unfolded the story. Then, during a pause, she gently touched his arm and asked, "Pregnant?" *It had been a rumor*, Jake said.

"Sundays are never crowded at this place, so it'll be good," Sean said. "My treat, by the way."

"Bill it to the station."

"Shit, no. The owner would shoot me. This is out of my pocket, my brother. It's my personal present to you."

"Maybe I'll drive into the ocean."

"You want to talk about it?" Sean watched Jake lean his neck against the headrest and recline the seat a bit so he could feel the force of the wind. "A few beers after the dunes?" Sean asked, joking.

"Non-alcoholic beer, asshole," Jake said. "Meantime, you got any weed?"

"Good plan, man," said Sean, sarcastically. "Let's get stoned then drive buggies as fast as we can over 400-foot tall dunes into the blinding sun. Perfect." Sean laughed and punched Jake on the shoulder.

"Yeah, I guess I'm not really thinking of dying," Jake said.

"Not today," Sean quickly added.

"Not today."

They spent nearly two hours on the dunes, rocketing the buggies off the steep pinnacle and into the salty air, along winding trails and the flat hard sand near the ocean's edge. Jake left with grains in his shoes and a wind-burned face. For a short time, everything was about today, not yesterday.

"First game of the World Series in a few days," Sean said after ordering a Coors for himself and an O'Doul's for Jake. They had stopped at Goonie's, a tavern in Coos Bay. It rarely bothered Jake that people drank in his presence, and he'd frequently let them know he didn't see their drinking as insensitive. People drank; friends drank. He'd learned to deal with it. And he'd told buddies like Sean that strangely, *their* drinking was in a way, empowering.

"Think San Diego has a fucking chance in hell?" Sean asked.

"Yanks in five," Jake said.

"San Diego's going to win a game? Really?"

"Everyone deserves a little respect." Jake glanced up at the television set behind the bar.

"When is Pittsburgh playing?" Sean asked.

"Not sure." Jake took a swig from the bottle.

"Can't shake the connection, even after all these years away."

"Babies are tattooed with the team's emblem in the hospital," Jake said, his eyes on the TV.

"They started hot this season; hope they can keep it up."

"I haven't been paying a lot of attention."

"What? You sick? Need a doctor? A Pittsburgh fan not paying attention?"

Jake shrugged and tipped the bottle back again.

"Okay. What's the deal?" Sean asked, turning the barstool toward Jake.

"It's just harder to pay attention out here. West Coast and all."

"Not football, asshole."

"Ah, it's just old stuff," Jake said, trying to dismiss it. "No worries."

"Fuck you, man. Come on."

There was a part of Jake that wanted to talk like he'd done with Angela. A part of him wanted to read the letter out loud over a microphone to everyone in the bar. Another part wanted to tear up the letter into the tiniest pieces and bury it in the sand dunes.

"I got something in the mail," Jake said softly. "A letter. It was forwarded from Memphis and finally found me."

"Says something shitty about the postal service," Sean laughed, sensing Jake was reluctant to say much more.

Jake took a long sip from his O'Doul's, glanced again at the television screen, and turned to Sean. "It's from Lisa."

"Lisa?"

"College. Radio station."

"Jesus, Lisa? I thought she melted into thin air. Why is she writing you?"

It had been over a year since Jake had a cigarette. Gave it up in Memphis. Still, whenever he smelled the sulfur from the strike of a match or the sweet, peppery aroma of a freshly lit smoke, he craved the taste and the light-headedness it delivered. There were times after late night coffee when he desired the burn in his throat. And right then he wanted that; he wanted to draw deep, hold it long, and let it seep out the corners of his mouth.

"She had my son." The words came out like an unstoppable sneeze.

"Jake?" Sean appeared to teeter on his stool.

"It's in the letter. All of it."

"Jesus, Jake."

"He's nineteen or twenty, I figure."

"So, it happened at school?"

"That party at the station. Remember? Tequila?"

"Long fucking time ago. We left you there with her, right?"

"Security almost caught us."

"And the boy? Where is he?"

"I don't know."

"What do you mean you don't know? She wouldn't tell you?"

"Oh, she knows."

Sean tipped the palms of his hands toward the ceiling and shook them. "What the fuck?"

Jake pulled the folded letter out of his wallet and tossed it on the bar. "She gave him away."

"What?"

"Adoption. Minutes after he was born."

"Jesus." Sean stared at the letter.

"Left school, had the baby, gave it away."

"So the rumors back then were right." Sean picked up the still folded letter. "This is it?"

"That's it. The word back then was some guy from high school knocked her up."

"She had a boyfriend?"

"Back home. He came up to get her from school. They stayed at his parents until Lisa got the guts to tell her mother and father."

"Maybe the baby is his?" Sean asked, slowly unfolding Lisa's letter.

"It's not. It's all in there. She knew it was mine."

Sean held the letter's three pages in his hands.

"Go ahead," Jake said. "Read it."

"She waited twenty years to tell you this; didn't bother to tell you back then before she gave it away?" Sean scanned the pages.

"Catholic parents," Jake answered.

"That's why the adoption," Sean added.

"That's what she says," Jake said, signaling the bartender to bring them two more.

"Like fucking turn-of-the-century shit. Girl gets pregnant, they send her away, tell everyone she's sick or something. Gone to live in a nunnery." Sean was trying to make sense of it.

"Not quite, but close."

Sean began to read, glancing up at Jake every few seconds as if to make sure he had permission to keep going.

Jake took a long swig of his second O'Doul's.

"Jesus," Sean murmured, his eyes remaining on Lisa's words.

Jake's urge for a cigarette returned.

"Jake," Sean blurted. "What the hell?" He looked up from the letter.

"You got to the Sarah part."

"Jesus."

"Yep."

"She told Sarah, not you?"

"Keep reading."

Lisa told her boyfriend it was his baby, to perpetuate the twisted illusion. She couldn't tell him it was someone else's, but of course that made him angry about the adoption. Lisa insisted her parents wouldn't permit her to keep it. She and her boyfriend struggled to stay together, splitting up several times. They did eventually marry, but her parents weren't happy about it. *A mistake*, Lisa wrote. After three years living outside Akron while he went to law school and Lisa worked part time at a camera store, they split for good. *For years*, she wrote, *the truth, lying just under the skin, plaguing me, infecting everything I did, had to come out. But I couldn't do it. The lie had become reality.* Then

Lisa's parents died—a car crash at a train crossing in Florida. *I'm a terrible person for writing this,* she wrote, *but I finally felt free.* This prompted the letters. First, she wrote to the old boyfriend, confessing, telling the truth. Then she found Sarah in Cleveland. The alumni association helped track her down. *I wanted Sarah to know,* Lisa wrote, *not because I wanted to hurt her, but because I wanted to apologize. I wanted to tell her I was sorry.* Jake wasn't sure if he understood that. Why so many years later? And why not tell him? Find Jake first? *I planned to tell Sarah only about the night at the radio station but not the baby,* Lisa wrote, *but when I started writing, there it was, all of it gushing out of me.* A month after mailing the letters and more searching, Lisa found Jake in Memphis and sat down to write what she believed were the most difficult words *of my life. I kept hearing that Robin Trower song in my head, the one from college,* Lisa wrote. *"Shame the Devil" is about telling the truth.*

Sean shook his head, tossing the letter on the bar. "Wow."

Jake drank the O'Doul's as if at the bottom of the bottle he would have an answer.

"Still not sure I get it, you know, not telling you first," Sean continued.

"It doesn't matter now, does it?"

"What are you going to do?" Sean asked.

"What the fuck am I supposed to do? Get mad? Go look for my son? What?"

"You got to do, I don't know...something."

"What's the fucking difference?" Jake asked edgily. "It's hanging over me now like some black sheet. Forever. Always. It'll smother me. Getting mad, writing a letter, screaming at Lisa, going on some wild chase for my son isn't going to change one fucking thing." Jake picked up the letter, refolded it, and slipped it back into his wallet.

"Okay, okay." Sean placed his hand on Jake's shoulder.

Jake stood up from the barstool. "I got to get a fucking cigarette."

"There's a machine at the door," Sean said, tilting his chin toward the bar's entrance.

Jake used to smoke Marlboro Lights. But that afternoon it could be nothing less than Marlboro Reds.

———

The radio station received an advance copy of the new R.E.M. CD, *Up*. It had nothing to do with the status of the radio station or the market, tiny as it was. They got the copy because Sean knew record company representatives from his days in Arizona. "It's not your usual R.E.M.," Sean wrote in a note he left with the CD in Jake's mailbox at the station. "More electronic. But they do this song with Leonard Cohen, one of your favorites, and I think you'll like it. Play as you wish."

A couple hours before the show, Angela and Jake listened to the tracks in the production room

"Ooh, I like that," said Angela, listening to "Daysleeper," a song Michael Stipe wrote about a woman in a New York City apartment who worked the nightshift. The song turned out to be the album's single.

"Not sure I'm sold on this electronic sound," Jake said, tilting back against his chair and lifting his feet to rest them on the sound console. "I liked the acoustic, folky thing they had been doing."

"You would," Angela said, mocking him. "Hippie."

Much of the new album was either sprinkled or drowned in digitally produced tones and drum machines.

"Stipe can write great words; why lose them in noise?" he said. "Play 'Hope.'"

The song had composition credits that included Stipe and the Canadian poet turned songwriter, Leonard Cohen. It's the one Sean recommended. He heard Jake play Cohen's "Suzanne," on the guitar many times back in college. And despite what Jake thought was a badly over-produced electronic arrangement, the words still rose from the monitor speakers and settled somewhere inside him.

"Angela, play that again," Jake asked urgently, pointing to the CD player and the green button that selected the track. "Pay attention to the lyrics."

They sat and listened again. Angela had a pair of headphones over her ears, and he stood just inches from the monitors, eyes closed. After Stipe sang the final words, the song lingered in a flurry of electronics, ending after a crescendo of digital racket.

Jake was still. He looked at Angela.

"It's about illness?" Angela guessed.

"Don't think so," Jake said, reading silently the lyrics from the CD's inner sleeve.

"There's a line about doctors and surgery or something."

"All allegory, symbolism. Read this." He handed her the CD's liner notes and the lyrics.

She rested the headphones on her neck, placed the CD sleeve on her lap, and whispered the words the way a child does when she's told to read quietly to herself.

"It's about trying to make sense of things," Angela said, her eyes remaining on the lyrics. Then she lifted her head to look at Jake. "It's about struggling with why things happen the way they do."

Jake smiled.

"About searching for logic in the illogical," Angela added.

"I think so," he said quietly.

"About how to justify why things happen—lost love or death," she said. Angela picked up the liner lyrics and held them close to her chest.

"Yes."

"It's about the hope for an answer, for salvation," she said.

"Forgiving."

Angela returned the lyrics to her lap and smiled. "Like God."

Jake ejected the CD, slowly placed the disc and the sleeve inside, and closed the case, handing it to Angela. The silent space began to fill with sadness, like the smoke from a fire in another room.

"You okay?" Angela asked.

"Let's do something with this tonight. Salvation. Hope. Making sense of all the shit that happens to us," Jake said.

Angela stood, placed her hands on his cheeks, and maneuvered his head so she could look directly in his eyes. "You're a good guy, Jake. And it's going to be all right."

He took her hands in his, their eyes remaining on each other. He thought about Michael, Sarah, Lisa, his mother, and his dad. He thought about Sean and his friendship. He thought about Ted at WIXZ, about the boss in New York who fired him, and about the woman now before him—how in some other place and time, falling in love with her would be the one true thing to do. And Jake thought about a young man out there somewhere, trying to find his way, wondering, like his father, what in the world any of this means and if hope, salvation, redemption, might be hiding in the shadows.

# 23

HALLOWEEN CAME. JAKE PLACED A large bowl of candy near his apartment door with a small sign that read *Take whatever you want* and headed out to spend most of the night along the seashore near the lighthouse. Although there weren't many kids in the neighborhood, greeting a few smiling children at the door was the last thing he wanted to do. A small campfire near the rocks and a thermos of strong coffee was a better way to spend the night. He got the idea of the sign from an old lady who lived alone in a house a few blocks away from where he grew up. The sign was so she wouldn't have to keep getting up to answer the continually ringing doorbell. But her note was a little more direct. It read *Take ONE!* As a kid, Jake was tolerant of the "take one" demand. He understood it. But the capitalization did bother him. So did the exclamation point. Jake felt disciplined.

Jake spent Thanksgiving at Sean's. He got the impression Sean and his wife, Emily, didn't like the thought of him being alone. Everyone else from the radio station had someplace to be, including Angela who ended up going back to Portland for a couple days to see the old beau.

It was pleasant enough at Sean's. Good food. They watched the football games. His wife spent most of the evening after the meal on the phone, catching up with her family in Arizona. Then, in early December, Angela invited a crowd to her apartment for a holiday dinner. "I haven't had a party at my place since I came here," she said. "I want to cook a meal and have a great little bash."

Sean and Emily, Steve, who worked the morning drive shift, Karla, who did middays, Robbie, Sean's part-time assistant, Angela, and Jake sat around a rectangular table temporarily set-up in her living room. Angela picked up the table a few days before at a thrift store.

"I made a ham," Angela said, placing a large, overflowing platter in the table's center. "It seemed festive."

"It looks festive," Emily said, eyeing the honey glaze and the small red poinsettia leaves Angela used for garnish.

"No one's vegetarian, right?" Angela asked nervously.

"Used to be," said Robbie, laughing. "Back in college. Lasted like a week, until I started craving animal blood." Robbie had studied anthropology at Cal State but was thrown out after he was caught selling dope to a professor. An offense like that didn't mean much to the radio industry. In fact, it could be an asset. None of this mattered because Robbie was a musical encyclopedia, and Sean needed the help.

"Good, because if you don't eat this, you'll have to fill up on carrots, asparagus and sweet potatoes," Angela said.

After the meal, the group lingered around the table. Most sipped Amaretto. Jake drank coffee and picked at a slice of angel food cake covered in strawberries.

"Looks like they got Clinton by the balls," Karla blurted, reaching for a refill of Amaretto. It had been a year of sex, cigars, and confessions—the biggest sex scandal in American political history—Bill Clinton, getting a blowjob from White House intern Monica Lewinsky, toying with her clitoris with a stogie and cumming on her dress, and all of it happening in the Oval Office. Congress wanted to impeach him.

"He's dead meat," said Sean. "Still like the guy."

"He's a pig," Angela said, "but yeah, I have to say, I still like him, too."

"They're laughing at us in France," Jake said.

"I'm so sick of hearing that," said Karla. "I know, it's true, but this isn't fucking France."

"Ah, the Puritan morality of America," Jake said, knowing those words would throw an accelerant on the conversational fire.

Steve pulled a pack of Winston's from his shirt pocket. "You mind?" he asked Angela. She nodded approval. "I wonder if we'd still like the guy if the economy sucked." Steve lit his cigarette with a blue Bic lighter.

"Hillary going to divorce him?" asked Karla.

"I'd kick the fucker out," Angela said.

"Not while he's still in the White House," said Sean. "That's not going to happen."

"If this had nothing to do with the presidency, the country, all that, what would you do?" Jake asked.

"Gone!" said Angela.

"Cut his dick off," said Emily, gesturing with a table knife.

"And if it were the other way around," said Sean, "I don't know what I'd do."

"Really?" asked Emily. "You wouldn't toss my ass to the road?"

"I don't think so," he answered seriously.

"You mean to say, if I slept with Ed Harris, you'd be okay with that?" Emily asked.

"Jesus, you and Ed Harris," said Sean, grinning.

"He's hot," said Karla.

"You too?" Sean asked surprisingly. "What's with that guy?"

Emily leaned on Karla's shoulder and whispered, "I'd fuck him."

Everyone laughed.

"If there were no repercussions, no guilt, any of that, who would you sleep with?" Jake asked.

"God, not this question," said Robbie.

"Come on," Jake encouraged.

"It changes by the week," joked Steve.

"By the day," added Robbie.

"Guys and their dicks," laughed Angela.

"You're the one who said you'd fuck Ed Harris!" Jake said.

Angela smiled. "Well, I would," she said softly.

"Does it have to be a celebrity?" asked Sean.

"Now you're getting into dangerous territory," Emily said, her eyes emitting laser beams toward Sean.

"No one from work," demanded Karla.

"Jesus, no," said Robbie. "Not a good plan, especially since we're all drinking."

Jake lifted his coffee to remind Robbie. "Most of us," Jake said.

"I've got a few things in the kitchen cabinet," Angela said, responding to Robbie's suggestion. "I'm sure I can pull up some heavier stuff." Angela moved toward the kitchen with enthusiasm.

"Carmen Electra," said Steve emphatically.

"Shit, *I'd* do Carmen Electra," said Karla, smiling.

"You know who's hot," Jake said, "Shania Twain."

"She could be your daughter," said Robbie.

"But she's not," Jake laughed. "Angela, what about you?"

Angela placed a half-empty bottle of Myers rum on the table, along with a nearly full bottle of Jack Daniels. As she returned to the kitchen for some Coke and ginger ale, Jake asked, "Angela, you got some sugar, maybe a little whipped cream?"

"Jake?" she asked suspiciously, reaching for the refrigerator door.

"A little won't hurt," he said. She knew Jake was teasing.

"Come on, man. Don't," Sean said quietly, thinking Jake might be serious.

Angela put the mixers in front of them and handed Jake a packet of sugar and a tub of Cool Whip. "Best I can do," she said to the room then leaned into Jake and whispered, "I'm not your keeper."

Jake had indulged here and there about a year after finding sobriety. But it never sent him back to that bad place. He sipped a beer, had a taste of someone else's wine. All the therapists and twelve step programs demanded one stay away from all of it, never touch it again. Jake knew that was the best way to go. But in those early stages, finding he could just have a little had been a comfort, a sign of strength, he believed. Time had added more strength. And now, even the minor urge to drink was nonexistent, and watching others indulge, like Sean with the beer at Goonie's or friends with wine at Thanksgiving, added no more anxiety.

Angela sighed then smiled at her guests. "It's a cliché, but I wouldn't toss Brad Pitt out of bed," she moaned seductively.

"Ah, that's a given, girl," said Karla.

"And Clooney," said Emily, " Matt Damon and Kevin Costner and . . ."

"Jeff Goldblum!" exclaimed Angela.

"What?" Sean said. Steve and Jake laughed.

"The geeky, goofy guy from *The Bill Chill*?" said Robbie. "Seriously?"

"Angela, are you drunk?" asked Karla.

"I can see doing him," added Emily.

"He's real. He's sincere," Angela insisted. "I've seen him on talk shows."

"Goldblum, really?" Jake asked.

"He's not the characters he plays," Angela replied. "You know that, right?"

"So there's hope for the rest of us," Steve said, sticking his index finger in his glass to mix the rum and Coke.

"New question," Jake interrupted, pushing the whiskey bottle to the center of the table. Angela winked.

"Bring it," Angela said, touching his shoulder.

"Why are we here in Oregon?" Jake asked.

"You know my story. Grew up in the Northwest, lived in Portland. Always liked the coast," Angela answered.

"Doing what I want to do. Good place for it," said Sean.

"Honestly, it's the lifestyle," said Steve. "Progressive, marijuana, artsy, liberal. It fits me."

"Not why I came here, but those may be the reasons I stay," added Karla.

"We all came or stayed because we were looking for something, didn't we?" asked Angela.

"Or looking to be found," Jake added.

"It's the suicide law," said Robbie.

"What?" Emily asked.

"Physician-assisted suicide, it's legal."

"So you came here so it's easier to kill yourself," Angela said sarcastically.

"I'm a native. But that law is about humanity. It's about people first," Robbie said. "I think it says a lot about how people think around here."

"Well, when I'm ready to cash it in," Jake said, "I'll think of you, Robbie, and thank you." Jake lifted his coffee mug in a toast. Everyone joined in.

"To suicide," said Karla.

"'It's painless,' as they say," said Steve.

Voices fell silent for the first time in nearly a half-hour. The only sound was ice delicately clinking against drinking glasses.

When Jake was 15, like most teenagers, he thought about taking his life. Every kid does it. For most, it's a fleeting thing. He doesn't remember what prompted those thoughts but it likely had something to do with a girl, sex, or fitting in. Jake was not alone in that experience. And for some, the thought can return in adulthood. Most manage the internal threat. But the reality is, a heart still aches, no matter the age.

"Tipper Gore was right, you know?" Sean said, pretending to be pompous. "Rock-n-Roll kills people."

"What was the song she said girls were listening to and wanted to end it all?" asked Emily.

"'Darling Nikki.' Prince," Jake answered. "But it wasn't about suicide, it was about sex."

"Same thing," said Steve, lifting his glass to his lips, hiding his smile.

Angela smacked his arm. "Please. Don't go there."

"Something about a girl with a lot of sex toys," said Sean. "Nikki is grinding, masturbating. It's pretty explicit."

"Never heard the song, but I got to now," Robbie said, sticking his tongue out in a mock French kiss.

"What have you always wanted to do that you haven't yet?" Jake asked.

"Carmen Electra," said Steve, smiling.

Angela smacked his arm again.

"Seriously," Jake added.

"Go to Africa," said Robbie.

"I want to write a book, a novel, the great American story," said Karla.

"I think we all secretly want to do that," said Angela.

"Everyone's got a story," said Emily, twirling the ice in her glass.

"Space travel," said Sean.

"Run with the bulls," Jake said.

"Seriously?" asked Karla.

"I'd do that," said Steve, "with Carmen on my shoulders."

"Give it up, man," said Angela.

"Why do people do that?" asked Robbie.

"It's the adrenaline," Jake said. "I had a friend from New York who did it, wanted me to go with him. I didn't. I regret it."

"Still got time," said Sean.

"Ah, how I long to be gored," added Steve, now on his third rum and Coke.

"Seems like a young man's thing," said Karla.

"Or woman," added Angela.

"When you're young, you think you can do everything, *everything*," Jake said. "But then when you get older, you know that's far from the truth. Still, you think age brings wisdom. It doesn't. We don't know shit."

"So does this have something to do with the bulls?" asked Karla.

"You're young, you think you're immortal. You can't get hurt. You get older, and you're not so reckless. You think you're smarter. Still, the odds are no different. And we're really not any smarter with age. We are just more aware of the time running out."

"And with the remaining time, you want to *live*," added Angela, looking directly at Jake.

"You're supposed to be reckless, irresponsible in your youth, right? Then you get older and everyone expects you to regret it. But you shouldn't. Instead, you should celebrate it," Jake said.

"Forgive yourself," said Emily.

"Living life is reckless. Believe me, I know. And yes, we end up paying for it in so many ways. But Jesus, life shouldn't be about playing it safe, no matter how much time we have," Jake added, confident in his belief.

"So, run with the fucking bulls," added Steve.

Jake raised his coffee mug in another toast. "Yep, run with the fucking bulls!"

"Since I'm the youngest in his room, should I go out and run around in highway traffic, lay my body across the train tracks, swim in the stormy ocean?" Robbie asked mockingly.

"Go for it," said Steve.

"All of us should do it," Jake said emphatically. Light was quickly entering the darkened rooms of Jake's head, throwing out vivid beams of discovery, like finding a four leaf clover and then another and another. "Will we have to face the consequences? Sure. Face them we should, and then do it again and again and again. That's fucking life, man!"

"Who's up for a swim?" asked Karla.

"You serious?" Sean questioned.

Angela stood from the table and looked out the small window in her kitchen. "No rain. Maybe a bit windy."

"The water is fucking freezing," said Karla.

"Fuck it!" said Steve. "Let's do it!"

Jake smiled, tossed back the last of his coffee, stood up, and pounded a fist on the table. "Who's in?"

Everyone quickly looked at one another. Then one-by-one, they each rose from the table. Angela lived four blocks from the entrance to the beach, a part of the coast with fewer rocks. It would take only minutes to walk there. Nights on the Oregon coast can be especially dark, even with an unusually clear sky, so they knew it would be difficult to navigate the waters. And then, of course, the water temperature would be frigid, as it always was in the Pacific Northwest but especially in December. Angela grabbed some blankets and several extra coats from her closet. An unusually clear night allowed a big moon to cast shadows on the sandy beach. One after the other, they ran, jumped, and dove into the Pacific, laughing, shrieking into the clear, bitter air. The adventure lasted only minutes. It was all their bodies could stand. They ran back to Angela's, hugging each other's soaked bodies, howling at the night, believing the tighter they embraced and the louder they screamed, the warmer they'd be.

# 24

JAKE AWOKE NAKED UNDERNEATH A bed sheet and an old fleece blanket. On the floor, a pile of still wet clothes, a pair of sweatpants, and two other blankets—the remnants of what he'd worn home from the oceanfront. After bounding out of the ocean, he wrapped blankets around his body—one covering his head—then rushed back to Angela's and drove home, the smell of salty ocean water mixing with the dry air from the car's heater.

Jake remembered a dream. It came to him as he stared at the ceiling from his bed. Lisa had emerged out of the ocean waters to the beach. She was a mermaid, half fish and half beautiful, unclothed woman. Her eyes were large, oval spheres of sapphire, locking in on his as he sat near the rocks of the lighthouse. She beckoned Jake to the water, waving her hand to encourage him. Ancient mythology, Jake remembered from a class in college, claimed the first mermaid was a goddess who fell in love with a mere mortal, a shepherd, and unintentionally killed him. She jumped into the ocean, but the water could not conceal her beauty, and only half of her was transformed. Was it her punishment? A curse? Or was it the gods' way of never permitting her to consummate her love for the mortal? In the dream, as Lisa summoned Jake, he found himself frozen, unable to move. She reached out a hand. Jake did the same, but they could not overcome the distance. And as Lisa slowly returned to the sea, another hand reached from behind to touch his shoulder. It was Sarah's, the way Jake remembered her from the summer before his senior year, the summer she came to see him in Pittsburgh, joined him at the radio station where he interned. In the dream, Jake turned and touched her hand and stood to hold her in his arms. Then from behind him, an incredible wave formed in the ocean, enveloping the coastline and toppling them into the swirling water. They held each other in the turbulent tide, lost each other for a moment but found one another again, the powerful sea somehow forcing them together. In the morning light, Jake could smell the sea, the salt in his apartment, emanating from the wet clothes. But he wanted to believe it could have been the lingering perfume of the women in his dream.

Jake wrapped the sheet over his shoulder and shuffled into the kitchen. On the counter was a half-empty liter of Pepsi. He took a sip and wet his finger to wipe away a day-old coffee stain on the edge of the stainless steel sink. The refracted sunlight streaming through the window suggested early morning, but in his clockless apartment he couldn't be certain of the time. Jake returned to the bed and sat on its edge, staring at the wet clothes on the floor. *Shit. My wallet.* He dug through the pile and found his jeans. In the rear pocket was the now soggy leather of his billfold and inside, Lisa's soaked letter. He delicately peeled it open, pulling the folds away from one another. The ink had blurred, some of it running in tiny streaks down the pages. Jake unwrapped all of it and placed each page in separate spots on the kitchen counter. Standing in silence, his arms pressed against the counter's edge to keep his balance, he breathed deeply and read aloud the letter's words, making certain the sea had not erased them.

Sean wanted Jake to follow up on Lisa's letter, to reach out. Angela had suggested the same. It had been many weeks since receiving it and from what Jake could calculate, several months since it was written. There was no return address, nothing that would directly lead to Lisa and certainly not to Jake's son. Angela didn't understand why Jake wasn't even trying. "Let me help you," she insisted several times. Producing a radio show meant research, tracking down information and often times finding people who weren't always the easiest to find. Jake ignored her offer. Sean, on the other hand, was more consistently persistent. He was leaving notes in Jake's mailbox at the station or dropping emails regularly, reading, *How's it going? Looking for anyone lately? Maybe I can help.* Sean remembered Lisa from their college days. And even though it was believed Lisa never graduated, Sean thought the college alumni association could help track her down. The association's quarterly magazine had published an "Alumni Spotlight" on Sean several years ago, and he had some connections. But Jake remained reluctant. There was a young man out there, a man Jake certainly ached to know somehow, to talk to, to look in his eyes, to ask about his dreams. But that was all about Jake. The boy has a father, undoubtedly a good man who taught him how to swing a baseball bat, wrestled with him on the living room floor, held him on his shoulders to see Fourth of July fireworks. Jake didn't think there would be much good to gain in stepping out of the shadowy past. He remembered what Kierkegaard had said. It was something about how life can only be understood backwards but only lived forwards. And while there was no doubt Jake was trying to wrestle all that came before—the death of his brother, the loss of Sarah, Lisa's disappearance, and now the birth of a son—he was better off when his eyes were looking straight into the morning sun, not over a shoulder at the setting moon.

Jake drew the bed sheet around him, pulling it tighter on his shoulders. He could see his reflection in the glass of the microwave—the white sheet, disheveled hair, and the two-day beard presenting either the image of a Jesus-era prophet or an unstable prison escapee.

Jake had just enough ground beans to make a half pot of coffee. He wanted a cigarette again, but even if he had a pack, it would now be saturated in salt water and buried in the soppy clothes. He was in no hurry to start the day, to be anywhere. And it was hard not to think of the rest of the holiday season. Jake didn't want to consider what he might do for Christmas. Maybe drive down the coast in the morning, maybe all the way to San Francisco. He could call his sister from there, wish her a good holiday, and then spend time roaming around North Beach and the Haight. Or go north to Seattle. He had never been there. And what about New Years? Always hated that holiday. It was a cultural command to have a good time, to attend a fake party, blow an annoying horn, and drink shitty champagne. Maybe he'd do nothing. Hole up in his apartment, listen to music, read, and hermit his way into 1999.

The coffee was weak, but Jake downed two cups anyway. He straightened up the apartment and tossed the wet clothes in the washing machine. Jake showered, scrubbing crusty Pacific salt out of hair and skin, and dressed for Tina's. There'd be better coffee there, and newspapers. He grabbed a few dollar bills from inside his waterlogged wallet, tucked his key in his front pocket, and reexamined Lisa's letter on the counter. The seawater was slowly evaporating, pages gradually drying, but the damage was now more evident. The words were still there, legible but streaky. Most of the ink had faded from deep blue to a faint, shadowy gray.

Tina had added a small holiday bell to the front door for Christmas. It jingled as Jake walked in.

"You look like you could use a double," Tina said, smiling from behind the coffee bar. She was a slender woman, built for speed as some guys used to say about skinny girls back in school. Her boyishly cropped red hair accentuated her porcelain skin and her small, cute nose. Jake's mother used to call them "button noses." Tina was probably thirty-five. She looked twenty-five. She was not model pretty in the classic way, but she still made men notice. It was the way she stood, her hip titled just so, defined shoulders, and the graceful nature of her upper back, which she always seemed to show off to some degree in scooped-out blouses.

"Didn't expect to see you today," Jake said. "But nice to."

Tina had given one of the crew a day off. Her employee wanted to go to Eugene to visit family.

"Big espresso?" Tina asked.

Jake nodded.

Tina's place had become a large part of Jake's life. He met Sean there to discuss the radio job, the real estate agent who helped him find his apartment, and of course he and Brenda had their sessions at Tina's. Angela and Jake worked on pre-show prep there, too.

"Tough night?" Tina asked, raising her voice over the whir of the espresso machine.

"Lots of coffee. No drinking for me. But I did end up in the ocean last night with some friends."

Tina peeked from behind the tall coffee maker. "What?" she asked, like the mother of a little boy who just admitted he'd been sticking his finger in an electrical outlet.

"I know, I know."

"You want to die?" Tina asked, scolding him.

"We all just needed to give fate the finger."

"Don't make a habit of that," she said, shaking her head. "That ocean is dangerous."

"Well, I'm here, standing before you. Guess I made it."

"Your New Year's resolution should be to stay out of the ocean in winter," Tina added, handing Jake a white cup with two shots of espresso, the brown oily foam sitting at the edge of the cup's rim. "Drink up, Aquaman."

"Do you make resolutions?" Jake asked.

"I have."

"Keep them?"

"Some."

Jake sipped from the cup. "Never made a resolution," he said.

"Oh come on, everyone has."

"Nope. If I'm going to commit to something, why do it on just that one day?"

"Just tradition, I guess."

Jake sat on a stool near the counter and downed the remaining coffee.

"Another?" Tina asked.

He nodded.

"One year I resolved to stop expecting men to make me happy," Tina added.

"How'd that go?"

"Still trying to keep that one," Tina laughed, stepping back behind the espresso machine.

Jake recalled Sarah making resolutions on New Year's Day. She vowed to quit smoking once. It worked for a couple of weeks. She resolved to read more, challenging herself to finish a new book every semester, one that wasn't part of the school curriculum. Jake doesn't remember how she did with that one. And then there was the resolution in their senior year. Sarah vowed to be more understanding, to listen more, to stop being so quick to judge. Jake recalled reminding her how she was already one of the most tolerant, considerate people he knew. He remembers secretly thinking how maybe he should have resolved something for himself that year; maybe promised to be less selfish, more attentive. It was all about Jake, back then. It was for years. Maybe it still was.

"Any resolutions for this year?" he questioned.

"Still sorting it out," she answered. "Maybe I'll give up coffee."

"Funny," Jake said.

"And you?" Tina asked, handing him a fresh cup of espresso. "Good way to start something new."

Jake purposely delayed his response and focused his attention on the coffee, lifting the cup slowly to his lips, pausing and then sipping. *Resolutions are clichés*, he thought. *They are the false beliefs on how we all can renew ourselves, be better people. One never really transforms*, he thought. *Instead, adjustments are made, maneuvers and repositions. And sometimes you just get good at hiding who you really are, ducking behind false hopes and playing roles demanded to be played by bosses, families, lovers.* Still, there was something emerging now just below the surface that allowed Jake the faith to believe that resolutions could be about moving forward. *Maybe, if done right,* he thought, *the perfect resolution is one that truly resolves something, that permits you to look back on the continuum and finish what's been started, free yourself somehow, shed an old skin.* Jake's mind was churning; in milliseconds clarity came into focus like a series of rapid-fire snapshots. *All those popular resolutions,* Jake thought, *the ones all of us make at midnight with a glass of cheap champagne, are about changing into what you believe will somehow make you a better person. But what if a resolution was instead about accepting an old self so that the new self can emerge, a way to look the past in the eye, to wrap your arms around it?* It all came to him so fast, so purely. *Maybe the way to honestly go forward,* Jake now believed, *was to look back—if only for a moment, if only for one night.*

Jake sat taller in his stool. He carefully placed the coffee cup on the counter. "I think it may be time," Jake said aloud.

Tina smiled. "Be careful what you commit to," she said, turned, and began grinding beans for another customer's drink.

There's a song on the radio. You know the tune but can't remember the artist. The brain fires off and on, sputtering, trying to trigger a memory. You work through the alphabet...A, B, C, D...hoping to spark something that reveals the singer's or the band's name. Then it's there. You are startled awake. It's immediate, satisfying, a small burst of endorphins. This is what it was like when the idea came to Jake, a hot white spotlight on the espresso-dark recesses of his brain.

Tina turned off the coffee grinder.

"I'm going to do something special this New Year," Jake said, hopping from the stool and drumming his fingers on the counter, a release of energy suddenly igniting. "Not a resolution, exactly. But a reunion of the unresolved."

"Got to help me on this one," said Tina.

Jake chugged the last of his coffee and threw a five-dollar bill on the counter. "Thanks, Tina. You've done more than you know," he said. Then he leaned over the counter, grabbed Tina's face, and kissed her on the lips. "I absolutely love you!"

Tina eyes widened, her face flushed. "What the hell's with you?" she asked, giggling as she watched Jake hurry out the front door, rush past the big window, down the sidewalk, and out of sight.

# 25

NEARLY EVERY SUNDAY NIGHT DURING Jake's high school years he'd practice with his band in the basement of his parents' home, a cramped dusty space littered with the electrical wires from amplifiers. The guys even crammed a full drum set into one corner. They played covers of the Eagles, America, and The Rolling Stones. Jake and the drummer were the only ones with any formal musical background. The lead guitarist was self-taught, and the bass player was a singer in the high school choir but never played an instrument of any kind before. All the guys encouraged him to buy an electric bass and amplifier, despite his ignorance of the instrument. Jake devised a simple system to teach him a few notes and how and when to play them. Next to the song lyrics on a sheet of paper, Jake would mark a series of pluses and minuses beside the words, corresponding to a simple bass line. It worked.

The first gig was in the summer between Jake's freshman and sophomore years at a summer festival in a small suburb outside Pittsburgh. The band was paid $25. The call confirming it came to Jake's house, and for hours he tried to contact the other band members and give them the good news. He telephoned their homes, drove his car to their houses but couldn't find any of them. Jake had tremendous news, and there was no one to tell.

This is exactly how Jake felt sitting in a misty drizzle on the small stoop outside Angela's apartment door. He had an idea, a very good one, he believed, and the one person who could help him pull it off was nowhere to be found. Jake had repeatedly knocked on her door, thinking she was sleeping or in the shower. He checked with neighbors, hoping they might know where she was or when she'd return. But no one knew. So, Jake sat and waited for Angela while the idea percolated inside him.

Using the tradition of New Year's resolutions, Jake would face the people of his life, confront the past where he was most comfortable—on the radio. Angela and Jake would seek out his old boss Ted, his New York boss, Winston Jenkins, and his sister would be part of it, too. And of course, no matter how hard it would be, Sarah and Lisa would be there, each one joining Jake live on the radio. They'd all say what they've wanted to say for years, resolving everything. This would be Jake's resolution, even though it was impossible to imagine how anyone might agree to such a plan on a New Year's Eve night, or any night.

"Jake, is that you? Are you all right?" Angela asked, startling him. She had cut through a strand of trees in a small lot next to her place and unintentionally snuck up on him.

"There you are," Jake said eagerly. "We need to talk."

"What's happened?"

"I have an idea for a New Year's show, and I need your help."

"And you've come to my place? Now?"

"We need to talk about this," he said, relieving Angela of one of three grocery bags she was juggling.

"You sure you're okay?" she said, repositioning the remaining bags in her arms, reorganizing her load and her thoughts.

"I'm ready to do something that could really, really be good. Good for the listeners and good for me," Jake answered as Angela balanced one bag between her hip and the wall near her door and reached into the back pocket of her jeans for the key.

"Okay," she said with uncertainty, pushing open the door. "Just put the bag on the table. I'll put things away. Keep talking."

"I want to get Sarah on the radio with me. Lisa too."

"What are you talking about?" Angela asked, bewildered.

Jake laid out the plan, why he thought facing all the debris and unresolved matters of the past would be a perfect New Year's Eve theme for the show and why the radio was the right place to do it and why it was the right time.

"I have been hiding, avoiding all of this for years. I got lost in my work, lost in fame, disappearing from a relationship that may have been one of the best things in my life. I drank, did drugs, all to avoid facing Sarah, Michael, Lisa. And a son, for God's sake."

Angela placed a carton of milk in the refrigerator, a box of cereal on a cabinet shelf, coffee beans in an airtight container.

"I don't like resolutions. But this is different. This is an acknowledgment of the past so I can get on with the future. I resolve to come to terms with my demons."

Angela listened to every word without interruption. She folded the last of the three paper bags and placed them under the sink. Angela leaned her back against the kitchen counter, crossed her arms, and then asked disapprovingly, "Are you nuts?"

Jake said nothing.

"Jake, this is so self-absorbed," she said, scolding him. "It's an exercise in public psychoanalysis and a bad idea."

Jake paused, then after quickly organizing his thoughts, he said, "I guess I can see that, but it's also a universal thing. Don't we all want to face our past somehow? The audience would get that. They'd relate."

"And you want me to help you track everyone down?"

Jake nodded.

Angela shook her head and reached for a half-empty bottle of Pinot Noir on top of the refrigerator. She pulled the cork and poured a small juice glass half-full and took a sip. "You okay with this?" she asked.

"No worries," Jake responded.

"It's just that you seem, well, a bit more anxious," Angela said.

"Forget about it."

Angela re-corked the bottle.

"Look, Jake. You need to rethink this," she insisted. "You really think people are going to agree to this?"

"I need *you* to convince them," Jake asserted.

Angela placed the bottle back on top of the refrigerator and shook her head. "You're exploiting them," she said.

"Some might say that. I wouldn't."

Angela sipped the last of the small amount of wine and let it sit inside her mouth for a moment, not to savor the drink but instead, to allow time to think.

"It's research. It's what you do. And, of course, you do it very well," Jake said, attempting to playfully convince her.

"Fuck you," Angela said, grinning. "Sometimes you are just a turd."

"That's why I love you," Jake smiled. "I promise this will be good."

While waiting outside Angela's apartment, he'd written down names and places where the search could begin. They studied the list together, jotting down more ideas and connective threads. They discussed how to best approach each person, how they might convince them to agree to be on the radio.

"And, Jake, what about your son?" Angela asked hesitatingly.

Jake swallowed and sighed. "I want him, Angela. I want him on the radio."

"You realize what you are asking?"

"I know," he said, taking a deep breath. "I know."

When Jake and his friends, members of that unpolished little band played its simple three-chord anthems to a crowd of about 100 people at that festival so many years ago, they didn't think once about who was standing before them. They played every song for themselves, every one seeping with sharp, sustained notes of teenage rebellion, the beautiful sounds of what each of them wanted to hear. It was an hour of self-indulgence, musical masturbation for four teenage boys who never considered the festivalgoers' musical tastes, what they wanted to hear, or what might inspire the audience to sing along. But despite the disregard, those spectators, huddling in front of the small outdoor portable stage on that warm June day, clapped and cheered until the final power chord.

Before Jake left Angela's place Sunday afternoon, she encouraged him to talk to Brenda about the New Year's show. Angela's doubts remained, and she secretly believed Brenda might encourage Jake to drop the plan. Jake was scheduled to meet with Brenda the next morning at Tina's.

———

"You seem unusually, maybe I should say, uncharacteristically, animated this morning," Brenda said, sitting down in one of the overstuffed chairs next to the window.

Jake had been at Tina's for nearly an hour, writing down more thoughts about the show, looking over what he and Angela had considered, how he would confront his guests, the characters in his life. When Brenda entered the coffee shop, Jake called out to her the way a father does to a child at an amusement park, enthusiastically encouraging them to join him on the newest, wildest ride.

"I have some things I want to run by you," he said, opening his black Moleskine on the table, dog-eared pages nearly outnumbering the others.

"I have this idea for a radio show on New Year's Eve that will bring everything we have been discussing into play."

"Really?" she asked, attempting to be nonjudgmental, noncommittal.

"It's fabulous," Jake said. "It's tricky though, and I've been told it's terribly selfish, even exploitive. But I think it's just what I need. And I honestly believe the audience will relate to it."

For well over an hour, Brenda and Jake talked about the ups, downs, and the dangers. And Brenda considered his heart, emotions, psyche, and his head.

"It all sounds like a bit of a romantic fantasy, Jake," Brenda said. "You do realize this is not likely to work out exactly like you see it or hear it in your brain? Are you ready for that?"

"Yes," he said.

"It seems to feed into your dysfunction. You are not learning to be real in the world, only on the radio," she added.

"Are to telling me not to do this?"

"I support you, Jake. But I don't support this idea," Brenda said.

Brenda knew Jake found his strength, comfort, and confidence on the radio. But she was hoping to get him to learn to transfer all of that to his life, not just his work. Jake believed he was his truest self when he was behind a microphone; it was where he was willing to be honest and exposed. But that was not necessarily healthy. *Why do you feel the radio is the only place where you can be yourself, the only place to express your true feelings and thoughts?* Brenda would ask. Jake didn't have an answer. *We need to work on getting the real you out of the studio and into the world.*

"I can't stop you," Brenda said, "but I want to make it clear: you should find a way to do this without the power of an FM transmitter and an audience of thousands."

The two were in agreement on one thing: when Jake was on the radio, he allowed his heart, soul, and spirit to be revealed more honestly than anywhere else. And he and Brenda recognized that his night radio gig on an artful station along the coast of Oregon had confirmed this reality. Jake saw radio as his platform. Brenda believed radio was his crutch.

After Brenda left Tina's, Jake sat in his chair and stared at the ceiling. All he could think about was how he and Angela were going to find the people on his list and how they were going to persuade them that coming on the radio on New Year's Eve to talk about the past was a good idea.

# 26

ANGELA NEARLY THREW JAKE OUT of the studio. It had been over a week since he launched what she still believed was a foolhardy idea, even though she had been working to find and contact the names on his list. Jake had been a royal pain in the ass, asking far too many questions for Angela's liking.

"Let me do my job, damn it," she demanded, stuffing her notebooks and a few newspapers in her messenger bag as she wrapped up for the night at the station.

"I agreed to let you do your fucking work, but I would like to know where the hell we are," Jake barked, like a cop interrogating a suspect.

"You know I don't like this. I'm not for it," Angela said, throwing her bag over her shoulder, the strap across her chest. "But here I am, and all I freakin' ask is that you just let me do it. I'll let you know when I have it worked out, if I can at all."

It's true, Angela was never sold on the idea, and that's why, despite his impatience, Jake was grateful for her work. He needed her.

"Okay, okay," Jake said, arms up in the air as if surrendering. He backed away from Angela and pushed his weight against the studio console. "I'll let you do your thing."

    

Angela shook her head. "Take a couple of days. Get away." She readjusted her bag, grabbed her car keys from the small desk where she worked, and walked out.

Before heading home, Jake sat at the computer in Angela's studio and sent Sean an email.

*Do you have some camping gear I can borrow?*

Jake was ready for a few nights on the Oregon coast. It would be chilly, but Sean had good gear and he could build a fire.

Jake was about eight years old when his father took him on his first and only overnight fishing trip. He didn't know where they were, but he remembers setting up a tent near a small lake and two rushing streams that fed into it. The two of them fished all day. His father expertly twisted long, bloody nightcrawlers on the hooks of his Zebco pole and Jake's kid-sized Superman rod. His mother had made egg salad sandwiches on white bread for lunch. His dad drank cans of Iron City beer while Jake slurped Cokes. After nearly a day of fishing, they had had only two bites. No fish. Jake was bored, at times tossing flat stones in the water and rocks at unsuspecting birds while his rod lay abandoned on the shoreline. But his father was undeterred. When Jake was tired of waiting for a nibble on the line, his dad took over, placing a red and white bobber on the line's end, leaning the pole on a thick stick from a nearby fallen tree branch and digging the pole's handle into the shore's dirt. He encouraged Jake to be patient, but he was realistic about a boy's tolerance of a long day of fishing. Jake wanted to catch a fish but didn't want to work for it. His father understood and was quite aware that forbearance would only materialize after several fishing trips, not just one, but could be aided with the catch of a single fish.

By late afternoon on the last day, they had nothing, and Jake's dad began to pack up the gear. He strapped the rolled-up tent and sleeping bags over his back, his rod and an overly large landing net in his hand. Jake rested his pole on his shoulder like Opie on the *Andy Griffith Show* and carried the now empty lunch cooler. As they walked over a small wooden bridge toward the trailhead, Jake hoisted himself to the first rung of the railing and looked into a swirling pool of clear water.

"Dad!

Just below the water's surface were dozens of fish, big ones, so close together they were crashing into each other, caged between fallen branches and smooth rocks.

Jake's dad lifted the gear off his back and rested it and his rod against the railing. He pulled on the landing net's white nylon mesh, testing its strength, and bent over the railing, reaching the net to the water. Jake's eyes widened and his heart raced. They were going to get a fish, a good one. His father dipped the net into the pool, waving it in the stream and dropping it below the surface. The more he worked the water, the more muddy it got, camouflaging the fish. His dad pulled the net out several times, letting the water settle, re-exposing the fish, then he'd go at it again, each time muttering unintelligible words. Jake's eyes darted between the swiftly maneuvering fish and his father, silently encouraging his dad to keep at it, despite his ever-apparent frustration. The water muddied yet again, but this time Jake's father snapped the net skyward; the water rushed out of the woven grids of the netting and splashed back into the stream. And there, wrestling and flopping at the bottom of the net, was a single fish, the sun glistening off the beads of water it was violently flinging from its slippery brown body.

Jake's father filled the empty cooler with stream water and gently slid the fish, a catfish, inside. He placed the cooler in the trunk of the Pontiac, and all the way home with the front windows down, his dad sang along with the country songs on the radio, and Jake worried what this fish was going to taste like.

It was the unmistakable musky odor of rotting fish that had plucked that story out of the deep corner of his memory. It was faint in the air at the beginning of Jake's hike south from the campsite at Beverly Beach, becoming more pungent as he traveled. Jake walked over a small sand mound near towering dunes, and there, sitting on a rock cropping, was a woman, about 50 years old with salt and pepper hair and weathered skin. She was smoking a cigarette, staring out to the cold ocean waters, and gently crying. Jake stood at a distance at first, and then she noticed him.

"Are you all right?" Jake asked softly.

"A whale," she said, pausing to blow smoke from her mouth. She nodded to her left toward the Pacific. "It's just sad."

Jake was puzzled.

"Over this dune, on the beach," she said, sniffling.

Jake climbed past a few large rocks and over a small dune, and there, lying motionless on the sand, was the massive animal, the tide lightly lapping against its shiny, gray and black skin. It was just over fifty feet. The tail itself was at least eight feet wide. The skin was scraped and scarred; barnacles clung to its underbelly. And all around the whale someone had ceremoniously placed rocks and large pieces of driftwood in a perfect circle, a crude memorial. Jake could see a small bouquet of blue flowers planted in the sand, still thriving despite the salty air.

Jake whispered to no one, "My God," and walked part of the way back to the woman. "How long has it been there?" he asked.

"A few days. It was nearly dead when they found it," she said. "It laid there, fighting for its life, and there wasn't a damn thing anyone could do about it."

"What about the Coast Guard?"

"They think it's about fifteen tons," she said. "No one's going to move that fast enough to save it." The woman wiped away moisture from the corner of her right eye and flicked her cigarette into a tiny pool of tidewater behind her.

The woman said people had come down on the beach in their SUVs to take pictures, to touch it, and some even prayed for the whale.

"A preacher from Florence was here. He blessed it."

She tapped out another cigarette from her pack and lit it with a cheap drugstore lighter.

"Some scientist says it's a humpback," she said, inhaling deeply. Then gazing toward the ocean, she added, "It was a noble death."

"How long have you been here?" Jake asked.

"A few hours. Been here each day to sit and just look at it and have a little cry."

"Too bad it can't talk."

"It's not unusual, you know. We get whales from time to time on the beach. There was one a couple years ago a little north of here," she said. "Doesn't make it less sad, though. Another day or two and the smell will get really bad."

Jake asked the woman if there was anything he could do for her. She shook her head and smiled sadly. "Just thanks for coming to say goodbye," she said, like a relative thanking visitors who had come to the wake.

Jake maneuvered the rocks, walked to the beach, and stood before the whale; the only sounds were the melancholy screech of a distant seagull and the rhythm of waves against the sandy shore. He behaved as if he were at a gravesite, walking slowly and respectfully around the whale's memorial. There are those who believe whales have a personality, their social nature allowing for what some consider human-like qualities. The song they sing underwater is a haunting language. Jake could hear the forlorn echoes in his head, a sense of grief enveloping him as if someone had draped his heart with a heavy blanket of dark blue.

Jake spent most of the remainder of the day sitting on a rock near the whale. Most of the crowds had arrived just after the whale was first spotted, so over several hours he saw only a few tourists, campers, and locals coming to gawk and take photos. A man who said he was from the local fire department and another from the Coast Guard arrived to take some measurements of the whale. They said there had been talk of using a large Coast

Guard cutter to drag the whale's body out to sea, something that had been done in northern England when a whale beached there years ago. But there were others who thought it might be best to bring in construction equipment and large backhoes to bury the humpback on the beach. Jake didn't know how he thought about any of this. He was only certain the days were numbered to view the body of this great mammal and mourn its death.

As Jake sat alone near this enormous animal and watched the sun float behind the horizon beyond the Pacific Ocean in the patchy, gray skies of a December evening, he was certain his heart was breaking.

# 27

"ARE YOU ABSOLUTELY READY TO do this?" Angela asked.
"I am," he said unconvincingly.

"No matter how it goes?"

"No matter how it goes."

Earlier that afternoon at a small table near the window at Tina's Café, Angela and Jake went over how everything would play out on the air. She had proceeded in much the same way she had for dozens of other shows, doing all the necessary digging, researching, making the phone calls, but this time, most importantly, negotiating with the people of Jake's past. Angela told Jake there had been heated dialogue, arguments about privacy, and intense discussions that required heavy persuasion. But from some there had also been nearly immediate agreement, the ones she categorized as "less controversial." Angela did not succeed with everything she had set out to do, all Jake had asked and wanted. But as she pushed the spiral notebook across the table with the names of those who had agreed to be on the air that New Year's Eve night, Angela knew she had accomplished a great deal, despite her reluctance. She knew she had assembled a human tapestry of Jake's past, a list of those he believed he needed to face. And she now knew far more about what Jake was up against that night, the entire spectrum of it, than he ever could. So when she asked, "Are you ready?" she could instead have easily pleaded with Jake to abandon the plan while there was still time.

Jake moved his eyes down the list, his index finger softly tapping each name in the notebook. He took a deep breath and another as the names triggered individual memories. His eyes moistened. He was hot and cold at the same time, as if a fever was attacking. Faces flashed in his mind's eye—short silent films and faded snapshots. If one were ever to be charged with the crime of melancholia, it would be the testimony of Jake's producer that would convict him.

The name at the top of the list was Ted Lawson. Jake feared he had died. But Angela found him retired and living in Nags Head, North Carolina. Jake had never properly thanked Ted for giving him a chance, taking a risk. There was Jimmy Felton, the owner of the butcher shop in Memphis where Jake had worked, the one with the turkeys, and the New York boss, the man who had fired him after the breakdown. Angela said the old program director agreed to be there only if Jake apologized on the air. *All those years, and he still wants me to say I was sorry?* Jake thought. Jake's sister was also on the list. He had talked to Mary a few times over the years but never about Michael.

At the bottom of the list were the final three names—names Jake had hoped but also feared would be there. The names were neatly printed in the deep black ink of a felt pen, each underlined for emphasis, for importance. This was real now, no longer an emotional exercise. Jake had to somehow find the courage—at least to this point—to be honest with all that had been fermenting in his heart and soul for years and do it with a mix of empathy, caring, and grace. He could have cancelled everything at that moment, but it no longer seemed a choice. Every one of the people behind those names had agreed to take an enormous, unmatched leap of faith. Jake knew why he wanted them there that night on the air—at least he thought he did—but why each had agreed to be there, the reason they were compelled, remained a mystery. Whatever it was that brought them to this night—trust, redemption, revenge, anger, curiosity—had to be respected. If they'd agreed to this unprecedented reunion, then it was no longer just about Jake, no longer a selfish endeavor. Jake was quite aware of this. This night was as much about them and each one of their stories as it was about Jake. Angela had done all the work, the negotiating, the hard discussion. So for the guests to agree to this night without ever talking to Jake was remarkable. All the years of hiding, and Jake was still at it, hiding—this time behind Angela. It must have seemed so insincere, cowardly. None of this had ever been clearer to Jake than it was at Tina's that afternoon.

"You found them, Angela," Jake whispered, afraid if he spoke any louder he'd scare the names off the page.

Angela smiled. "Do you want to know the particulars?" she asked cautiously.

Jake's silence was his answer.

"Sarah is in Philadelphia, working for the *Inquirer* in the advertising division."

"Married?"

"You want to know all the details right now?" she asked. Angela and Jake had agreed to stay away from filling in every blank before going on the air. "It might be best to tell you some of this, Jake," she said.

"And Lisa?" Jake asked.

"That's a complicated story," Angela said hesitantly. "Let's talk about Samuel first."

This was the first time anyone had said his name out loud. It was right there in Lisa's letter, but Jake had never said his name, vocalized it, neither had the others who had read the letter. Not Brenda. Not Sean.

Jake put his face in his hand, his palm covering his mouth.

"It's exactly what the letter said," Angela said, reaching out to touch Jake's hand. "It's all true."

Jake's eyelids became heavy blinds, falling over his eyes to blacken the room.

"But there's something more here," Angela added.

His eyes opened to meet hers, reluctantly encouraging more words.

"Samuel knows," she said.

"Knows?" he asked.

"Lisa found him. It was not long after she wrote the letter to you. They've talked."

Jake inhaled but couldn't get enough air.

"He knows about you," Angela added.

"How much?"

"Enough. Lisa found him working in San Francisco about a year ago. She hired an investigator. Samuel was angry of course, but he came around in time after she . . ." Angela's voice cracked. She placed her hands on her lips, her fingers pointing up as if she were about to pray. "I feel like I really must tell you more, Jake."

In his heart, Jake wanted to know it all. But for this night to be authentic, the stories had to be spontaneous. If all were to be revealed before going on the air, the conversations would be predictable for both sides, rendering them uninteresting. To keep them fresh, some things just could not be disclosed beforehand. Jake was more than conflicted about this, but as a broadcaster he understood it and knew he had to be committed to it. But of course, this night's show was about far more than broadcasting, presenting a program Jake hoped listeners would find entertaining, thought-provoking, stimulating.

"How important can it be, Angela?" Jake questioned. "Lisa has agreed, Samuel has agreed, and Sarah has agreed. I don't think there could be anything that would blind-side me so badly. I'm taking a big risk here already."

Angela entwined her slender fingers through Jake's and shook them lightly. "I'm just trying to protect you," she said.

He looked again at the three final names. "They're all okay with this, right?" Jake asked, his eyes still on the list.

The corners of Angela's mouth moved slowly upward.

"Samuel." Jake ran a finger over the printed name, saying it slowly as if to be sure he knew exactly how to pronounce it. "It's a good name."

"It's a good name, Jake."

For the next half-hour, Angela and Jake went over the format of the show, discussing music, songs that fit a theme, how many commercials were on the program log, the anticipated length of segments. It had been agreed to begin the show as usual, with Jake outlining for the audience the plan for the night. Then, at 10:30 p.m. they'd begin to bring on the air the names on the list, one-by-one. Jake wanted to keep the time slots loose, allowing room for whatever the conversations would bring, wherever they would take him. Each would need space to breathe. And even with all the preparation, not once did Jake consider what to do if something went badly. In fact, he wasn't exactly sure what "badly" could mean. The parameters were far different than they had ever been, less about the details of a radio broadcast and more about all the emotions swirling around in his chest and head. That, of course, made things highly unpredictable, placing Jake on a tightrope far above a very flimsy net.

Angela stood to refill her hot tea at the café's counter, leaving Jake alone as the last rays of sun flooded through the picture window and across the café tables and on the names written on white notebook pages.

# 28

TINA'S PLACE CLOSED EARLY FOR the holiday night, so with nowhere else to go, Angela and Jake arrived at the radio station almost three hours before the show's start, far earlier than usual. She said she was going to re-check the phone numbers for each guest. Despite talking to each one just a day ago, Angela wanted to confirm they could be reached when it was time. If this was going to proceed, it was going to proceed without a hitch. And Jake? He could have gone over the notes made for this show, walked through the spiral notebook of questions and comments he'd been keeping for weeks, or re-read the letter from Lisa, carefully reexamining every word. Instead, he sat in one of the seldom-used older studios, put on his headphones, and listened to music—Neil Young, Bob Dylan, Joni Mitchell, Leonard Cohen, Credence, Richie Havens. He bounced around through a stack of CDs, randomly choosing songs. One might think Jake would have chosen the songs with absolute purpose, each for its poignancy and relevance, a soundtrack for the performance to come. But he didn't want music to be a reflection of what was in his heart; he wanted the music to shape his heart. Rather than the notes and lyrics confirming the emotions that were bleeding out from vessels inside, soiling his skin and clothes for anyone who wanted to see, he hoped the music would instead rocket him away to some other place, a distant star.

Late one night in the summer before Jake's senior year when Sarah had visited in Pittsburgh, the two hopped the evening's last trolley up the incline to the top of Mt. Washington, more than 350-feet above the Monongahela River from downtown. There were several concrete platforms with iron fences that jutted out over the mountainside, allowing for unobstructed views of the skyline, a triangle of shimmering buildings shining like jewelry, the light bleeding into the rivers that surrounded the city. They stood alone just after midnight on one of the viewing areas, arms around each other. For a long time they said nothing, gazing out at the artificial light engulfing the night. Then Sarah paused and looked up into the sky, washed out by the power of a city's electricity. "Do you think there are stars out there tonight?" she asked softly. The splendor of bright lights wasn't enough. No matter how spectacular the view, Sarah wanted more than man-made glitter. She longed for the natural brilliance of celestial bodies. That night came back to Jake as the music played through his headphones and the year's final stars flickered on the other side of the studio's window glass, albeit most behind clouds. It was a different season now, and Oregon was a different place, a new astronomical sky. Still, many of the stars out there were the same ones that shimmered beyond the illuminated city far above Jake and Sarah so many years ago.

———

"This is Jake Mulholland. I want to introduce you to a man who was always the consummate professional, even when hot girls tried to strip him naked while he read the news." Jake announced this at 10:40 p.m. New Year's Eve, after beginning the show with a montage of songs he liked from the past year: "One Headlight" by The Wallflowers, "Everlong" by Foo Fighters, "Wrong Way" by Sublime. And now it was time to introduce the guests.

"Ted Lawson and I worked together at a little radio station outside Pittsburgh, Pennsylvania. I was an intern and he was the program director. And with all these years behind us, I hope he understands that I wish I had done then what I'm doing tonight."

Ted sounded nearly the same, his voice only slightly weaker, sadder somehow. He told stories of the station's drunken morning man, the station owner's over-the-top obsession with Crystal Gayle and her long silky hair, and of course most of the details of the day Ted lost his clothes and a bit of his cool during a noon newscast.

"Tell me the truth now Ted. You were aroused, right?" Jake asked, laughing through the question.

"Well Jake, I think it best I keep that to myself," Ted snickered, still trying to be the ultimate pro.

"Ted, I hate to say this, but you really didn't keep that to yourself, if you know what I mean?"

They laughed.

Jake then told inside jokes about old colleagues, trying his best to let the audience in on the stories. And through it all, Jake tried to be as sincere as his heart allowed, to truly thank Ted for his guidance and support. Maybe it was a little corny, but Jake needed to do this and was certain Ted appreciated it.

"I would likely be working as a used car salesman if you had not been there the summer I interned."

"You're too kind, Jake. You had talent. Still do, my friend."

"And thank you again, Ted. But don't go yet. I have a special guest."

Jake's pause was purposeful.

"Toni, are you there?" Jake asked, after pressing the button to put another phone call on the air.

"Jake, honey! It is so good to hear you!"

"Geez Louise!" gasped Ted. "Toni, is that you?"

"Still got your clothes on, Ted?" Toni giggled, her voice still sultry and velvet.

"You two know each other?" Jake joked.

"Now, Jake, while I was on hold, I heard you ask old Ted there if he was aroused."

"I did, Toni. Do you have something to say about that?"

She cleared her throat. "I certainly do." She sighed and added, "He certainly was."

"And Ted, I'm not sure you know about my little episode on a Saturday morning not long after your little moment?"

"Jake. You're going to tell that story?" shrieked Toni.

"Oh, come on. What's he going to do, fire us?" Jake smirked. While Toni giggled in the background, he told Ted and the audience his own stripping story.

"I should have fired your butts," Ted joked. "Both of you."

Jake thanked Ted again, blew Toni a kiss over the microphone, and wished them both well, a good New Year, and offered an invitation to come visit Oregon sometime, knowing neither ever would.

Next was Jake's boss from Memphis. The owner of the meat market, closed long ago, but Jimmy Felton was going strong.

"You hated those turkeys, Jake," Jimmy laughed, the crackles from a long-time smoker's throat resonating deep.

"But you got me to love them, Jimmy. I won't eat one on Thanksgiving anymore, just can't do it. But I have come to respect those goofy birds," Jake said sarcastically.

"So, why am I here?" Jimmy asked. "Why me, of all people?"

"I never told you this, but when you gave me that disgusting job, you were just about the only one who would have paid me to do anything."

"Hey, you showed up for work, worked hard. I didn't need to know anything else."

"But I never told you I had a big time radio job in New York, and I got as low as I could go. Losing it, losing myself. And you were there."

"Wow. Well, Jake, I don't know what to say, really," Jimmy said, his voice trailing at the end of the sentence. "I didn't even know you were on the radio."

"I just wanted to thank you, wish you the best, and tell you that because of people like you, I'm in a better place. I've found a new life, and I'm going to be okay."

"Twenty years later?" he asked, laughing.

"I never said I was punctual with my feelings, Jimmy."

Jake hoped he was resonating with the audience. He wondered aloud on the radio about how all of us look back on our lives and realize there are times when one person comes into the world at just the right time, someone who at that instant may have seemed inconsequential but turns out to be a catalyst for something new. In a lifetime there are dozens of saviors, angels like Jimmy, who are never fully seen. Kindness at the perfect moment, a smile from a stranger, an unexpected touch, all of this was the work of God, a collective goodness. Jimmy was the embodiment of that. He wasn't just a man who gave another a much-needed job at a time of desperation, he was a rescuer, reaching out a hand in the dark and holding it for as long as needed. This came natural to Jimmy, and he never hesitated showing it.

"We all could learn something from you, Jimmy," Jake said on the air.

Jimmy's two sons didn't have an interest in turkeys or the meat market, so when they graduated from college, Jimmy closed the place, taking an early retirement. He had made some pretty good money over the years, still lived with his wife in Tennessee near a big lake, and fished every morning.

"Life is good, Jake. Remember that," Jimmy said.

"You're a good man, Jimmy. Godspeed."

Jimmy wished Jake luck, thanked him for thinking of him, and offered to buy Jake a beer if he ever again came back to Memphis.

The next guest was hesitant from the very first time Angela contacted him. But after several phone calls and lots of discussion, she finally convinced Jake's New York boss—the one who fired him from the radio station, the one who wanted to press charges—to come on the air.

"Jake Mulholland. How are you?" Winston Jenkins asked, his tone tentative, business-like.

"Didn't you want to just slug me?" Jake asked. "Clock me?"

"Sure. I wanted to kick your ass," he replied, clearly harboring a bit of anger despite all the years. "But I knew you were screwed up."

"You might have been one of the best things to ever happen to me," Jake said. Winston's silence suggested surprise. "I needed to be fired and maybe, just maybe, needed to be punched."

"I felt sorry for you, Jake. And, you certainly didn't know it then, but I did honestly want to help."

"I was a sorry character."

"What happened to you after all that? After the rehab?" he asked. "I know you're back on the radio now, of course, but there are some lost years."

Jake explained to Winston and the audience about the redemption in a meat market in Memphis, about the meditations at Graceland, and the trip west, and the new radio station.

"Sounds like you found peace," Winston said reflectively. Jake hadn't thought of it quite that way until Winston said those words.

"Maybe I did," Jake said.

"We're all looking for it," Winston added. "Even me."

"I guess that's true."

"Years after you left," Winston said, "I found myself in rehab, you know. My wife left me. Really got low."

It was not what Jake expected to hear. He was stunned at Winston's honesty. "So sorry, Winston.

"Vodka."

"I never knew."

"I had it under control, I thought."

"How long?"

"Ten years sober."

The two talked for a half-hour about addiction, falling off the wagon, about friends and family who helped and hurt the cause. And then the calls started coming in. Jake put listeners on the air, some who claimed to be struggling with drink and drugs and others who were proud of their work toward sobriety. It was an unexpected topic on an unlikely night with an improbable ally.

"I guess we have more in common than we ever thought," Winston said.

Jake smiled into the microphone. "I am incredibly grateful for you being here, Winston. You may not believe this, but I have thought of you often."

It was time for a break. Jake played Neil Young's "Old Man," Cream's version of "Crossroads," and Strawberry Alarm Clock's "Incense and Peppermints," and primed himself for what could be the most difficult conversations of his life.

# 29

"HAPPY NEW YEAR, EVERYONE," JAKE announced just as the clock struck midnight. "This again is Jake Mulholland. We have some people on the phone who want to offer wishes to all of us, to the ones they love." All ten listener-lines were full. Jake started putting them on the air.

"Happy New Year to my best friend. Maria, I love you. This will be a better year, my love."

"Let the year be one of peace for the world and for each other."

"No resolutions, just hope to live life to the fullest. And it starts now."

"Happy New Year, Mark, wherever you are."

"Rachel, you are my soulmate. This year, I will get you back."

"I miss you baby, but this is the year I finally get over you."

"It's been one year since we became a couple, and this year, Laura, will even be better."

"I resolve to be kind."

"My resolution is to finally lose that twenty pounds, again."

"I will tell the people I love how I feel, starting now. I love you all!"

The voices of young and old, women and men crowded the airwaves, some sad, some hopeful. Several drunk. It was a cel-ebration, an exercise in group-expression. Some of the messages were clichés others tinged with personal longing and love, desperation and hope, a communal wish for new starts, new beginnings, new commitments. These were the first voices of a brand new year, one after the other reaching out for renewal.

As listeners continued to present their hopes, Jake looked into his coffee cup. He hadn't taken a sip in some time, and the liquid had cooled to the temperature of the room, the cream forming khaki clouds across the top. There were shades of brown, the milky hues a mix of dark and light, just like the sky above the Pacific in winter, a marine sky—one that could open up and spray rain on the beaches at any moment. The heavens on the Oregon coast sometimes seem to be filled with imminent tears when in fact they are empty, dry from the crying of an earlier day.

Jake could see Angela through the studio window, smiling and giving the thumbs-up sign. He wasn't sure if that was praise for the show or encouragement for what he would face. Jake returned a smile and pushed the phone button, bringing up the last listener with a wish for the New Year.

"And you, my friend, have the final word for all the others who have shared their hopes tonight," Jake said.

"Jake?"

The voice was vaguely familiar, but one word wasn't enough for certain recognition.

"You're on the air. Go right ahead."

"Jake, it's your sister, Mary."

Jake glared at Angela through the studio glass.

"Jake?" Mary questioned again.

"Well, this is a bit of a surprise."

"I thought you knew I'd be on the show?"

"Yes. Yes, I did. Just not right now." Jake scowled at Angela. She shrugged, and he playfully gave Angela the finger.

Jake thought he'd have a breather, a chance to gather his emotions before his sister came on the air, but deep down Jake knew it wouldn't matter. Maybe just jumping right to it was a better idea. Apparently Angela thought so.

"Happy New Year, brother."

"It's been too long."

"I think this was such a cool idea to have people on the show with you tonight like this."

"I'm really glad you're here."

"So, what do we talk about?" Mary asked. Jake immediately thought Angela had not prepped her.

"What's your wish for the New Year?" Jake asked, perspiration forming across his forehead.

"I have some resolutions," she said. Jake could hear her smile. "I'm giving up Mountain Dew. That's one."

"Holy crap." Jake's sister had been a Dew addict since she was twelve. "That's a huge deal, everyone. She's been drinking buckets of the stuff."

"And," she added, laughing, "I'm going back to church."

"Church? *Catholic* church?" Jake's sister had despised religious services. When the family stopped going to mass on Sundays, Jake was certain his sister silently celebrated for years. In fact, he figured she'd become an atheist.

"No. Unitarian," she answered.

"How did this happen?"

"Getting older. Seeking some peace," Mary said.

Jake's sister had not married. No children. She had worked as a personal secretary to the president of a trucking company for the last twenty years. She played softball with a league on the weekends and took an occasional few days to stay at a rented lakeside cottage in Deep Creek, Maryland. She used to ski in Pennsylvania's mountains during the winter, but a car accident had left her with an ankle with a metal pin in it. It had been a decade since she'd been on a slope. She visited the gravesite of her parents every Sunday afternoon, sitting on the ground near the markers and talking out loud to them about her latest boyfriend, the weather, how she missed her mother's blueberry pie at Thanksgiving, and once asking her father for advice on how to lay a laminate floor. In some ways, she had become closer to her parents after their deaths. The anguish of her parents losing a son had always hung in the air; Mary had grown up with it all around her, watching her parents, especially her mother, silently suffer. As a kid, a teenager, and a young woman she would consciously avoid being too close to the pain, too close to the family. But now, she longed for the intimacy she once had shunned.

"This may seem like a question out of nowhere," Jake said, convinced procrastination could only make things harder. "Do you ever think about Michael?"

There was silence on Mary's end. Too much silence; dead air was a broadcast sin. But tonight, silence was to be forgiven.

Jake heard his sister swallow.

"I don't have clear recollections, but he is there, Jake, always there," she said. "It was so hard living with the sorrow." There was more silence, then a sigh. "And what about you? How are you?"

The hair on the back of Jake's neck felt moist from sweat. His face flushed, and the corner of his mouth twitched as if involuntarily trying to control what words he might say. The conversation, a very public one, suddenly felt private, as if no one else in the world were listening.

Jake wiped a hand over his eyes. "Do you forgive me?" Jake asked.

The question frightened him. The answer petrified him. And maybe, Jake thought, this wasn't a question at all. Maybe it was instead a kind of prayer, a plea.

There was silence again.

"Mary?" he asked.

Jake could hear a slight exhale. Then she said, "Of course. You were just a kid."

"Kid in charge of his brother. In charge of his safety."

"You did nothing wrong, Jake," she said haltingly. "And I was so young. How could I judge you?"

"I've been so afraid of what you might say."

"It was hard," Mary said, her voice softening. "I watched Mom struggle."

"I dream about our bedroom," Jake said, remembering the room he and Michael shared. "I see everything there, the way Mom left it."

For years after Michael's death, the bedroom never changed. The books his mother had read to him remained on the shelves, a big stuffed Dalmatian from Kennywood Park sat in the corner of the room, his clothes hung in the closet. A watercolor painting was still taped to the wall near the bedroom door, a painting of yellow and purple and red, a child's abstract picture of his brother. His mother had written in blue pen across the bottom, *Michael's Big Brother Jake.*

"Do you remember the Matchbox cars?" Mary asked.

Jake had collected metal Matchbox cars and had given some of them to Michael—a 1961 Chevy Impala, a blue 1966 Mustang, a white Corvair.

"I can see them on the small dresser. They never moved; dust gathered around them," Jake recollected.

"You never played with them again?" Mary asked.

"Not after Michael." There was a good deal that didn't happen after Michael. "I wonder, Mary. In the spirit of the new day, the renewal for the New Year, is it finally time to get past it?"

"I am, I think. But I'm not sure what that really means." Mary hesitated, her sigh magnified through the telephone line. "It must be different for you."

At that moment Jake realized he had not truly thought about how it was for anyone else but himself—not his sister, not his mother or father. The tragedy seemed all his. Intellectually, in reality of course, it wasn't. But when he put a small light on that delicate section of his heart, Jake had only seen Jake.

For the next several minutes, Jake recalled the story of he and Michael in the woods, something he had revealed to only a few people and certainly never told on the radio. His words were simple, direct, bullet points from a tragedy. Jake could see Angela through the studio glass, her expression empty as if her feelings had been paralyzed. Mary said nothing, but Jake could hear her every breath, as if to take in and let out all the heartbreak. He continued to talk, knowing if he paused even for an instant to settle himself he would struggle to begin again. For those minutes, Jake had forgotten that he was on the radio, disregarded the significance of the night. He was more alone than he had ever been.

"Jake?" Mary asked quietly after Jake completed the story and allowed stillness to linger.

"I'm here," he said softly.

"I've never, ever heard you tell the details of what happened," his sister said woefully.

"It's time," Jake said.

"It's okay, Jake," Mary said, her voice wavering.

"Michael said to me once, how much he loved dogs. He wanted to pet every single one he saw."

"Even as a little boy?" his sister added.

"You remember the Collie we had?"

"I've seen pictures," she said. It was a loyal dog, following Jake and Michael, nudging them when they weren't paying close enough attention to her.

"Sally was getting old, and Michael loved to lay his head on her belly while she slept on the floor. The dog never moved. She'd be as still as could be. She wouldn't let anyone else do that. No one. No one but Michael."

"So sweet," his sister said.

"I'm happy Michael did not see Sally die," Jake said, thinking of the hot summer evening when Sally began to breathe erratically. Barely able to move with her arthritic hips and no longer able to control her bladder, his father placed her on a large old blanket in a cool space in the basement. Three days later her heart gave out.

"I saw a dead whale on the beach once," Jake said to Mary and the audience. "It was a magnificent sight, a magnificent animal, but such sadness surrounded it."

"In Oregon?" she asked.

"Not far from here. The town was so taken with the whale's death and showed it with tributes on the beach. It was beautiful," Jake said.

"A whale's funeral," she said. "A grand goodbye."

It was right then that Jake began to accept the infinite nature of things, acknowledging with certainty that there is incompleteness, that it's an unfinished world. Nothing wholly goes away, dissolves or disappears. Pieces of everything remain in the ashes. Even in death, the soul endures. And goodbyes are never really forever. That whale will be remembered, his story told over and over, like so many other stories in our lives. Maybe Jake had always known this, but only now, on this night, was he able to confront it.

"I hope the next time we talk, Mary, won't be so long from now," he said.

"Come visit, Jake. Come stay for a few days," she insisted.

Jake believed Mary meant what she said.

Jake took a break to play commercials, one for a local muffler shop and two national spots for Chevy and Sears. And before playing Led Zeppelin's "What is and What Should Never Be," and then Joni Mitchell's "A Case of You," Jake prepared the listeners for what was to come.

"I have three more guests tonight. And these three may be the most important people in my life, for different reasons, but still the most influential." Jake had prepared some words to say but tossed them aside. Jake was now talking exclusively from somewhere deep in his gut, through the vessels of his heart, spontaneously, honestly.

"The first is a woman—a beautiful, delightful girl—who may have been the love of my life. But she was also the one I abandoned, the one I let slip away, the one I may have never deserved."

For a long time, Jake had harbored that belief, holding it in the fog of years.

"The second is also a woman—one who intrigued me, delighted me—and in one impassioned night, we became forever linked."

Jake looked to Angela and smiled, then closed his eyes as if to regenerate courage.

"And my final guest will be . . ." Jake swallowed and exhaled, felt his mouth go suddenly dry. "My final guest...will be...my son. A man I have never met. You will meet him as I do."

Jake pressed the button on the CD player and heard the intense and sensitively penetrating voice of Robert Plant sing the opening lines of one of Zeppelin's most psychedelic songs.

# 30

O F ALL THE MEMORIES JAKE had of Sarah—her playfulness at the party where they first got to know each other, the breakfasts she brought to the radio station, how she and his mother would talk for hours on the porch of his parents' home—there was one that resonated most. It was that single strand of her hair that would fall from her loosely tied ponytail and spill over the corner of her eye. She would gently smooth it back behind her ear. It was such a delicate motion. Sometimes she'd do it when they'd be talking but mostly when she was alone quietly studying or reading, unaware Jake was watching.

"Line three," Angela said through the intercom into Jake's studio, keeping her eyes on his. "You can do this, Jake," she said.

The final chords of "A Case of You" played in his headphones.

"Happy New Year to you. It's turning into quite a night for a lot of us, I'm sure. That goes for me too. I've been facing my past and reconstructing my future right before you, right here on the radio as we go head first into a new year. A new kind of resolution, you might say."

Jake could see the blinking light on the phone bank, number-three flashing off and on, a silent, ominous tempo.

"A little self-indulgent, but I hope that you can see some of your own past in this night and can somehow gain a little inspiration on how you may want to face it, embrace it, and move through your own new day."

Jake wondered if he was going too far, getting too preachy.

"Or maybe you just don't give a damn what my life has been like and don't believe there is any connection to yours. And that's okay. I get it. Who the hell am I to suggest you and I have anything in common?" he said, attempting to temper the mood and gather more courage to open line three. "But that said, I must move forward with tonight."

Jake swallowed and wiped a hand across his face as if to cleanse it and erase the thoughts inside his head.

"The woman I am about to bring on the show may have been my soulmate. But many years ago, I was reckless, and I rejected her. I lost sight of what she meant, what could have been. I was heartless, a coward. In fact, I'm amazed she has agreed to be on the show with me tonight. I see this as a miracle and a blessing."

Jake pressed the button for the phone line.

"Her name is Sarah, and I am honored to have her here. Sarah, are you there?" He would not have blamed her if she had disappeared from the line, hung up, and abandoned him as he did her.

"Yes. It's me, Jake. It's me," Sarah said timidly.

"Sarah." Jake clenched his jaw to steady himself. "I can't tell you what this means."

"I'm not sure why I'm here, Jake. Not sure why I said I would do this," she said, sounding both distant and attentive at the same time. "I must admit, your producer—is it Angela—she kept after me, despite my reluctance."

"You said 'no' several times, didn't you?" Jake asked, assuming the answer.

"I did. Then I told her I'd think about it. Not sure why."

"Just as a way to get her to back off, I'll bet."

"Why would I want to do this?" Sarah asked. "I'm still not sure of that answer."

"For whatever reason you are here, Sarah. Even if it's to tell me off, what a bastard I was, I am."

"You broke my heart, Jake. Just walked away." Her voice was tender but tense. "I know it's been a long time, and time heals. That's probably why I'm here. But—and I guess I don't really expect you to respond to this—but I just don't understand—why do people just leave?"

It was a question that had hung in the air for so many years, one that was too big, too existential, too much for either of them or anyone to answer.

"We all do things we don't completely understand, Sarah," Jake said. "But that's not really an answer, is it?"

"So what is it you want to say to me? Why am I here?" Sarah asked. "I agreed to this, but I'm not here to be Miss Congeniality. I'm sure you know that?"

Sarah had not heard any of the earlier segments of the radio show. She wasn't on the phone line during the conversations, and she was thousands of miles away, too far to tune in to the frequency. Yes, Lisa had told Sarah about the night at the radio station, the pregnancy, and giving the boy up for adoption, but Sarah may not have known the details about Lisa's contact with Jake, the letter. And in Angela's conversations with Sarah, nothing of this was revealed.

"It may seem cliché, and it's far too late, and you can tell me to go to hell, but I wanted you to know I'm so terribly sorry and that I believe with all my heart I may have lost the only person who could've saved me."

Sarah sighed. "I'm over you, Jake. I've been over you a long time," she said. "And those words, Jake, they're really all about you, aren't they? It's about making you feel good somehow. Somehow getting this off your chest."

"You are right. Maybe this is pure selfishness," he said.

"That's exactly what it is."

"I'm sorry."

"I'm married. Live out east. He's an architect. We have a good home," Sarah said.

An image of a strong-jawed man, athletic, well-dressed, appeared in his mind's eye. He was a good man, Jake believed.

"You don't have to do this, Sarah."

"I'm here. Aren't I?"

Jake was struggling to go on, skeptical of how long Sarah would be able to balance her emotions and keep from verbally walloping him. And at the same time quickly scanning his brain for an avenue to take that would reveal authenticity and prove he was not exploiting the story.

"Sarah, please understand I will stop this conversation whenever you want."

"It's okay," she said. "We're adults, right? And, again, I'm here, aren't I? It was a long time ago."

"Okay," Jake said. "Let's talk not about where we've been but where we are."

"All right."

"Kids?" Jake asked reluctantly.

"Two. Girls," Sarah answered. Speaking about her children softened the edge in her voice. "They are the loves of my life." Then she paused, preparing herself for what she was about to ask. "And what about you, Jake?"

There are questions all of us are undoubtedly asked when we first meet or reconnect with someone: *What do you do?* They want to know what you do for a living. *Married?* Most people assume by a certain age that you are or have been. *Do you have children?* Jake had never been presented with that question before. And now he was being asked by the woman he'd once loved, maybe still did—the one he abandoned, the one who already knew the answer to the question.

"Yes. A son."

And in that very instant, in a flash of time, Jake had the sensation that he was more complete than he'd ever been.

"Is he like you, Jake?" Sarah asked, as if she were unaware of all of it.

Whatever it was years ago that propelled Jake to run from Sarah had long ago evaporated. All that mattered now was this conversation. It made no difference that Sarah wasn't being forthcoming, unable or unwilling to tell Jake what she already knew about his son. She seemingly wanted Jake to reveal the truth on his own.

"That would be for others to say, I think," he answered. "But I like to believe he has the good things of me, minus the bad."

"And his mom, is he like her?" she asked.

If Jake hesitated it might suggest he did not want to mention Lisa, but calling Sarah out, revealing she already knew the answers, also felt wrong. So he continued to unearth the story as if it might be the first time Sarah had heard any of it.

"His mother and I met a long time ago," Jake said carefully.

"Before or after us, Jake?" Sarah asked, testing him, her voice more deliberate.

If this had been a private conversation at a secluded table in a dark quiet restaurant, Jake would have reached across to touch Sarah's hands and opened his heart. At least that's what Jake hoped he would have done. Truth was, he may have attempted to lie his way out of it. This was a public conversation being broadcast to anyone who could tune in to the high fidelity sounds of an FM radio station in the first hours of the New Year. Thousands of ears could hear everything he had to say, taking in each word to interpret and judge. The listeners knew nothing of the dance Sarah and Jake were doing, but they deserved the full story. Still, Jake wondered if he was simply using, exploiting the people he cared about, creating a spectacle, a pathetic soap opera.

"Sarah, it's time to be honest."

"It might be," she said.

"I want to tell the whole story on the air, one that is terribly difficult for me." There was silence then the soft yet scruffy sounds of the phone being adjusted against Sarah's face. "Sarah?" Jake asked.

"Jake," Sarah answered finally, "I knew about Lisa from the beginning."

Jake spun his head around toward the studio glass, his eyes locking on Angela, as if she could somehow rescue him from the mess he was getting into. Angela smiled awkwardly and mouthed, *You can do this*. Nothing at that moment gave Jake the belief that he could. He was fueled only by the fear of falling apart.

"About the night at the station?" Jake asked, terrified of what Sarah might say.

"There were rumors, talk at school," she said, her voice thinner, less assertive. "I pretended not to hear it all. I guess I didn't want to hear."

"Sarah, my God, I'm sorry."

"I didn't want to believe."

"Why didn't you say something to me?"

"I was in denial, I guess," she said.

"Jesus."

"Long time ago," Sarah said, trying to dismiss it.

For just an instant, Jake forgot he was on the radio, forgot about the listeners and allowed a hush to overtake the space, a long stillness that seemed the only appropriate response to the emotions that hung heavy on the airwaves.

"Then you know about the baby," he said, testing how much of the truth Sarah was willing to tell.

"Lisa wrote me. You must know that," Sarah said, clearing her throat. "Said she wanted to get it all out, tell everything," she added. "It was her diagnosis that gave her the courage."

Jake shuttered and glanced back to Angela. Time had somehow been suspended.

"Oh, Jake," Sarah gasped. At that second, she knew she had revealed a secret. "Lisa is sick, Jake. She wrote me about the night, the boy, and also about her health."

Through the studio glass, he could see Angela's eyes. They appeared to have sunken deep into their sockets, hiding from the role of a witness.

"I don't know what to say, Sarah." Jake could take only a shallow breath, as if drowning.

"I'm sorry," Sarah said.

"She wrote me, but it was only about the boy," Jake said.

"About your son, yes. She told me she didn't want to tell you about the diagnosis in a letter."

"I don't understand."

"It's just how she wanted it."

The phone line went quiet. Jake thought Sarah might have hung up.

Then after the pause, Sarah added, "She thought it better not to tell you everything at once."

"Forgive me, Sarah," he said. "But what can you tell me?"

There was a beat of silence, like the quiet after a communal prayer in church.

"Lisa's dying," Sarah whispered.

Lisa had cancer. And after tracking Samuel down, reconnecting with him, Lisa's death would now leave her son without his real mother. That was a devastating thought for Lisa. Samuel had his adoptive parents, certainly, but Lisa believed her son needed her, needed his real parents in his life. It may have been an overstated belief, an imagined reality, but it was Lisa's truth. That's why she set out to find Jake. And if she couldn't find him, she would reach out to anyone who might know where he was. Sarah, she thought, may have been that person. So she told Sarah everything. And although Sarah acknowledged and ultimately accepted what happened between Lisa and Jake so many years ago, Sarah knew nothing about Samuel until she'd received Lisa's confessional letter.

"It was a mistake, Sarah," Jake said.

"I know," she said, exposing hesitant forgiveness. "I hated you for it."

"Love only matters when you nurture it," he said.

"There were times I believed it was all about me."

"I hurt you."

"It was a long time ago."

"Are you happy?" Jake asked.

"I'm not going to somehow make you feel better by telling you that I am. And I'm not going to make you feel better by asking if you're happy."

"I deserve that."

Several seconds passed then Sarah said, "Not sure anyone is really happy."

"Content, maybe?"

"Depends on when you ask."

"It's an effort."

"That I'm sure of," she said, her voice trailing.

Jake imagined those mornings when Sarah brought breakfast to him at the college radio station, nights they listened to music at his trailer when Jake would play guitar and she'd lean her body on his, tucking her head between his neck and shoulder when he sang. Jake wanted to hold Sarah in his arms.

And then there was Lisa. What was Jake to do with what he had now been told?

"Have you kept in touch with Lisa since she told you?" he asked, cautiously.

"You should reach out to her, Jake," she said.

Sarah was unaware that Lisa was next up on the radio. And Jake was not about to tell her.

"I hope I can," he said. There was a difficult silence. "I promise I'll let you know where I am, what I'm doing. I hope you would want me to."

"I would," she said. "I can do that, too."

"I would like that, Sarah."

"I wish for you everything you have ever wanted, Jake."

"If that could ever be possible," he said.

"Goodbye, Jake."

There was the unmistakable click of a phone call's end and Sarah was gone.

There's a theory of time that says lives are not lived in the present, lives are not a live feed like a TV broadcast but rather a delayed transmission, a thousandth of a second pause between what happens and the moment when they are experienced.

"Say something, Jake," Angela commanded through the intercom and into his headphones.

There's another theory of time that claims it moves uniquely for each of us, that our individual continuum is exclusive. For someone in motion, time moves differently from another standing still. Or for some, the days turn to nights more quickly, and evening envelops us sooner.

Jake exhaled. "Heartbreak on the radio," he announced.

Jake spent the next couple minutes thanking listeners for being with him, indulging his narcissism, as he called it, and allowing him to tell his stories. Then Jake asked them to stay with him to meet the mother of his child and the son he never knew he had.

From the other side of the studio glass, Angela gave Jake a sad yet encouraging smile and then played a Burger King commercial.

# 31

JAKE WAS EIGHT YEARS OLD when a baseball hit him in the face, splitting his lip and spraying blood on his chin and Little League baseball uniform. He was trying to play shortstop. He wasn't sure why the coach put him in a position that required quickness and a good arm, neither of which he had. The ball was a two-hopper, ripped right at Jake. He squatted and quickly opened his Bill Mazeroski Rawlings glove, hoping for a miracle. Instead of the ball skipping a foot off the playing field where his glove was waiting, it bounded higher, losing no velocity and crashing into his mouth. Jake fell to his knees, dropped his glove to the dirt and in dazed silence, instinctively reached for the pain. It was when Jake pulled his hands away from his quickly swelling lip that he saw the crimson red on his fingers, and he began to cry.

Like the violent grounder, the conversation with Sarah had stunned Jake, and for several minutes during the commercials, he was quiet, unreactive. Jake was waiting for the blood.

After the baseball injury, and ice on his lip for several innings, his father asked if Jake was ready to get back in the game, fearing he would be too frightened to return. Jake put his hat on his head, grabbed his glove, and ran to the shortstop position.

"Jake, you want to play a few songs or something before we move on?" Angela asked through the intercom. "Might be a good idea. Get your bearings."

"No, I'm ready," he said into the intercom box, dismissing her suggestion. Jake lifted his coffee mug and downed what he'd been nursing for more than an hour. It was cold, the dark roast now bitter. "Lisa is line two?"

"Jake," Angela said. His eyes were locked on the sparse notes he'd made for the show, and he was not about to look up. "Jake," Angela said again, "it's still okay to call this off."

Jake lifted his head slowly and fastened his eyes on Angela. "This is my stuff, my past, my heartbreak, and my show."

He rubbed his eyes with his index fingers and inhaled, filling his lungs with air as if to keep afloat.

"Heard from Sean?" Jake asked Angela. Sean was only partially aware of what had been planned for the night.

"He called," answered Angela. "He just asked if you were okay."

"Nothing about the show?"

Angela shook her head.

Jake interpreted this as Sean's provisional approval, reminding himself again that this program was about him but that it had to resonate with listeners. Sean must have believed Jake was somehow getting that done.

"Happy New Year, Bandon," Jake announced at the end of the cluster of commercials. "This is your friend Jake. And tonight, I thank you for coming along for a ride with me, a road trip to my past as we all head to the future. These are the people of my life. But they could be yours. They are, in so many ways, all of our stories."

Jake leaned back in the chair, hit the cough button, and then continued.

"It's time to consider resolutions, positive changes for a New Year. And tonight, I am doing just that. But like all of us, getting to a new day can first mean coming to grips with the days that came before."

Jake's heartbeat had begun to find its normal rhythm. It no longer thumped or raced.

"There've been raw emotions tonight, surprises that have shaken my soul, and my producer, Angela, has even asked if I wanted to stop, walk away from what I had planned for the final segments. She asked because she's worried about me, and I appreciate that." Jake winked through the glass. Angela smiled. "But I've come this far, and all of you've been right along with me, some even calling in to share with Angela your own heartbreaks, the mistakes you made, your life twists. You too have been, in your own way, where I am tonight."

Angela gave another thumbs-up through the glass. Not the kind a coach gives one of his star players executing at high levels but the kind a mother gives her son who is sitting alone on a stage, reaching deep into his resources to make his way through his very first piano recital.

"Thank you for that, Angela," Jake continued. "It means more than you'll know."

He stared at the blinking light on phone line two, trying to find air in his lungs. Lisa had not heard the radio conversation with Sarah, but now on hold, she could hear all Jake was saying and about to say.

"On the phone . . ." Jake said, pausing to adjust in his chair " . . .is Lisa. You've heard a bit about her already. Lisa is the mother of my child. A child I hope to meet for the first time in a couple of minutes. I will be forever grateful for this opportunity and although I am nervous . . ." He swallowed. "I am buoyed by this incredible moment."

Jake shared with the audience more details of that night at the radio station and the letter that had arrived so unexpectedly, and how the bigger story here, although a long time in coming, was in many ways unfolding before everyone, on the radio, in a surreal yet strangely appropriate account of love, mistakes, and some measure of forgiveness.

"Lisa?" Jake asked timidly after pushing the phone line button, sweat forming on his temples. "Are you there?"

For a fleeting second, Jake saw images of Lisa, little films in the head. He saw her standing outside the Student Union, her athletic body. She was in the field where they played touch football. He saw her through the studio glass at the college radio station reading the news, and he saw her body on the floor of the station's office space underneath his.

"I'm here, Jake. Happy New Year." Her voice was weak, soft.

"Lisa," he said, drawing out the syllables in her name as if to savor them. "I feel so privileged that you are here. I am *amazed* you are here."

"I think it's important that I be here," she said, tiptoeing around the obvious. "This may have been your idea, Jake, but I agreed because the truth about everything is important. It's all I can do for Samuel."

Lisa hadn't heard any of the earlier conversations on the radio. She was out of frequency range. And although Lisa told Angela about her illness when they first started to discuss coming on the show and suggested she reveal it to Jake, Angela never did. It was too hard for Angela, and Jake was insistent on spontaneity. And so now Jake was struggling to come to grips with the news and wondering if he should tell Lisa what Sarah had revealed or allow Lisa to unfold the story when she was ready.

"I needed you here on this New Year's Day for a very selfish reason, you know?" Jake asked. "It was time." Jake took a breath and it resonated in his headset. "It was the letter," he said, "and ...our son...that prompted this."

"It took a long time for me to find you."

"I'm indebted to your tenacity."

Jake told the audience more about what was in the letter, how and when he received it, and how he wrestled with the news it held.

"I didn't hear it, but I know you've spoken with Sarah on the air," Lisa said.

"Yes," Jake said, his voice unsteady. "She told me, Lisa. She told me everything."

"Now you know," she said. "Whether it came from Angela, Sarah, or me."

"Lisa, I'm so sorry." Nothing Jake had ever said to anyone had weighed as heavy on him as this. Yet, there was peace in the sadness.

"I'm past the anger," Lisa said. "First you refuse to believe. But you eventually accept enough to live the life you have left."

Jake rested his elbows on the console and his head in his hands. Angela whispered through his headset, "You're okay. You're okay."

"I called you, I reached out. I tried to find you," Jake said. "I didn't know what happened. We had that night. Then you disappeared."

"I thought about an abortion," Lisa said. "But it wasn't going to happen."

Jake could think only of her openness, honesty. He wiped his hand across his eyes. "Your family?" he asked.

"I was old enough. I could have gone ahead with it."

"And the boyfriend?"

"For so many years, he believed the baby I gave away was his."

"You told him everything," Jake said, confirming what he knew.

"I had to go all the way."

"Oh, Lisa."

"We were married shortly before the birth. We finally separated and divorced."

"Lisa, I don't . . ."

"It's okay, Jake," Lisa said, interrupting. "A lot of time has passed. That night for us was just that—one night—and a long time ago. But Samuel is right now."

"Samuel. It's a good name," Jake said.

"It means *God has heard*. He has heard my prayers," Lisa said, her voice quivering.

"I want to know about him, Lisa. Tell me about him."

Lisa knew nothing of Samuel's life for so many years, but after finding him, Samuel's life became her passion.

"He's going to school at Berkeley. Anthropology."

"Smart."

"Always was," she said proudly. "Plays piano. Played some baseball for a time but got tired of it in high school and quit the team."

"What position?"

"Catcher."

"Always athletic?"

"Sort of. Never a star. That's what he would say," she answered. "Got into a little trouble in the eleventh grade."

"What kind of trouble?"

"He had a few beers," Lisa said haltingly.

"Nothing unusual there."

"He was drunk, Jake," she continued. "Two other kids in the car. He hit a tree."

The back of Jake's neck became hot.

"It happened a couple of years ago," Lisa added. "And now his mother is dying."

"The accident, Lisa? Is he okay?"

"He broke his collarbone. It healed. But his friend lost an arm. The other friend died at the scene." The words came like reportage, no detectable emotion. Lisa had learned to anesthetize the grief. "Samuel lost his license, but the judge was sympathetic. He got probation."

"My God, Lisa."

"I'm grateful he's alive. He's here," she said. "I'm grateful for the people who raised him, loved him."

"I am, too," he sighed. "I am, too." Jake thought of his own father and all that he had been. He prayed Samuel had been as blessed.

It was clear to Jake that Lisa had come to terms with her health and what her dying would mean to her son. She knew she couldn't go back and change things and had somehow found a way to accept that. Jake, however, never considered all the baggage Lisa and all the others on the air that night would be carrying. He was selfishly trying to get rid of his own battered luggage and now, thrust into his arms, were several more satchels, fully packed. But unlike what he may have done years before, Jake was now ready to carry as much as he could strap across his back.

"I'm here, Lisa. He's my son. He's *our* son," he said.

"I am brokenhearted that it took tragedy—my sickness—to get us to this place. I struggle with it every day."

"I'm so thankful."

"Prayers answered, again," Lisa said.

"And you? Tell me about you, Lisa."

"Simply, I'm dying. It's lung cancer. Inoperable. Rare."

"How?"

"Didn't smoke."

"Nothing they can do?"

"Tried," she said, pausing. "I'm told I have a few months, maybe." Lisa was silent again and then, in a halting breath, she said, "It could be a tough ending."

"Come to Oregon."

"Jake?"

"Come to Oregon. Stay with me."

"Jake, I . . ."

"Death with Dignity," he said. "The right to die law here."

"Are you asking me if I want to commit suicide?"

Jake suddenly realized what he was doing on live radio, asking a terminally ill woman to come to his home and let him help her kill herself.

"It's an option," he said less urgently.

"Jake, I can't. I couldn't," she said with some uncertainty.

Oregon's physician-assisted suicide law had been passed a few years before. It was the first in the U.S., and it was groundbreaking. There were restrictions, yes, but Lisa was dying, and the law would permit her to choose the time of her own death before the pain, the suffering, the indignity of a lung cancer death. It was all Jake could offer, a kind of gift. She could move in with him, he could care for her, and she could make her own decisions about what is the only thing in the world that is truly, fundamentally our own—our life.

"I don't mean to blindside you. This is such an incredibly important choice. I feel terrible. Please forgive me for bringing it up so bluntly. I'm sorry."

"It's okay."

"But honestly, it is something to think about," Jake said cautiously. "Lisa, the offer stands. I really do mean it."

Jake didn't know if he could truly help her, if Oregon could help. He didn't know the details of the law. The offer was instinctual, coming from deep inside somewhere, an eruption, unrealistic and presumptuous. Who was he to suggest how Lisa should die, advise her how to spend her final days? Did he believe somehow that now, with the truth laid out in front of them, that he had some say in all this? Jake only knew what he'd read, seen, and heard on the news. But he was sure it could be done without ceremony, painless. Despite detailed paperwork and a doctor's diagnosis, the final process was apparently a simple matter of swallowing the prescription, a bitter dose of the barbiturate secobarbital. After the law was passed, there had been dozens of news stories about doctors telling the terminally ill how to mix it with a liquid—like water or fruit juice—or swirl the pill into applesauce. One physician described the death as quiet, effortless. One newspaper story even chronicled the last weeks of someone they identified as Mrs. S., a woman who had been struggling with malignant lymphoma for years. She went through all the traditional treatment, but the cancer spread to her bones and spinal cord. Physicians put her on anti-depressants to stave off, ironically, thoughts of suicide. There was a lot of pain and doctors said it would only get worse, more difficult. After a couple of weeks of talking, arguing, crying with her husband and two daughters, Mrs. S. asked her physician about taking her life. A doctor wrote a prescription, and in two days she was dead. Mrs. S.'s ashes were spread over her backyard garden, and a small ceremony was held for family and friends somewhere along a pine forest trail near her home where she had once walked her dogs.

Jake wouldn't have blamed Lisa if she had told him right then and there to back off and shut the hell up. Still, he silently prayed Lisa would understand that he, through the thousands of miles and all the years, was wrapping his arms around her.

"I've never been in this situation before. Death is brand new, you know," she said, trying to smile through her words, a gallows humor. "I don't know how I'm supposed to feel, what I'm supposed to do. But I understand for certain, reaching out to you, telling the truth, and maybe even coming on this radio show were the right things to do."

"It's very brave, Lisa."

"Dying is such an interesting experience," she said with a sudden lightness in her voice. For a few seconds, neither of them spoke and then tenderly filling the empty space, Lisa asked, "Jake, do you want to meet him?"

# 32

"YOU'LL ONLY REALLY GET IT when you have a son," his father bellowed. Jake was sixteen. He and his friends snatched a fifth of some cheap whiskey from Joey Schumacker's house. Joey swiped it out of his dad's liquor cabinet, one of those tall, stand-alone pieces of furniture with a bar top and a space in the back for a few scotch tumblers, a couple of shot glasses, and a few bottles. The three of them—Joey, Billy Thompson and Jake—mixed the whiskey with Coca-Cola and finished all of it, laughing their way to sleep on a couple of old fabric couches in Joey's basement. Joey's dad and mom were divorced, and his mother had been out most of the evening, probably on a date. She didn't even know the boys were downstairs. No one did. Joey's mom returned somewhere around midnight but only after she, Billy's dad, and Jake's father frantically searched the neighborhood, walking the streets, knocking on doors, and calling friends, driving cars, and shouting names out the windows. When they returned home, frustrated and anxious, Joey's mom heard the basement toilet flush. Billy had gotten up to take a piss. Joey's mom was embarrassed. She never thought to look under her own roof. Joey's mom was relieved, hugging her son. Billy's father thought it was a hoot and laughed his way through the explanation. But Jake's dad was pissed—a simmering, seething caldron of pissed. Jake never forgot his father's face, red from ear to ear. And he could still hear his voice, stern and resolute through clenched teeth. "What the hell is wrong with you? Jesus Christ, do you realize what you've done to your mother for hours? She's about to lose her mind. Jesus, Mary, and Joseph!"

The following morning Jake's dad grounded his son for a month, and when he finished delivering the sentence, he said those words: *You'll only get it when you have a son.*

Jake hadn't thought of that story in years, but there it was, appearing in his head as he anticipated the next voice on the phone. "This is Samuel."

It was a deep voice, deeper than expected. Samuel offered only those few words, but it was enough to detect a sweetness, a certain sincerity, mixed with distance and longing.

"Samuel, I am so pleased to meet you." It was an odd response, Jake thought. But that was all he had. He could never have prepared the right words. There were none.

"Good to meet you," Samuel said, a reflex reply, the way you answer *Good* when someone asks *How's it going?* "Are we on the air?" he asked.

Jake had not considered the layers of this kind of conversation. There were the words, of course, but he never could have imagined the rumblings of emotion in the gut, smothering and strangling the natural process of communication.

"Yes, we are, Samuel. You're okay with that?" Jake nervously looked at his notes.

"I guess," he answered.

"Samuel, I know this has to be hard, awkward; maybe you really don't want to be here tonight. And me, well, who am I to you, really, right?"

"Uh huh," he said.

Samuel was spending the holiday with Lisa. His adoptive parents understood.

"There are some things I would hope to say to you tonight." It had been weeks since writing down what Jake wanted to say to Samuel. He worked and re-worked the list and read it out loud again and again. Now, with a live microphone inches from his mouth, Jake abandoned all the preparation. "I would understand if you hung up the phone right now. Not in anger but out of ambivalence. What do you care? What can I do for you? What do I bring to the table at this point in your life?"

"Yeah, okay," Samuel said.

"All that I can do now is hope that I can get to know you. Not to get in your way, change your life, or even try to be an integral part of your world in some way." Jake believed he sounded like every other absent father, missing dad, parent trying to find redemption. It was pathetic, he thought. Still, he prayed Samuel sensed some sincerity. Jake took air in his lungs, held it, and went on. "I just want to know who you are," he added. "And maybe from there, well, we can see where it goes."

"I think I'm more curious than anything. The news is pretty fresh," Samuel said. "You're a stranger."

"Are you angry?" Jake asked.

"I wish it wasn't like this," Samuel said coolly, as if to brush away something unpleasant. "I had great parents, you know?"

"I'm sure of it," Jake said. "Tell me who you are, what you're like, what makes you happy."

"Good people. I like being with good people. And music. Music can say anything and everything."

Jake could sense strength, confidence, but yet tender vulnerability.

"What're you listening to?" Jake asked enthusiastically, hoping he had found common ground, a place to start.

"Foo Fighters. The Smashing Pumpkins."

"Do you know the Primitive Radio Gods?"

"Sure. 'Standing Outside a Broken Phone Booth.'"

"You have the *Rocket* CD?

"'Chain Reaction?'"

"Love that song," Jake said.

For the next ten minutes they talked about Nirvana, Neil Young, Pearl Jam. Samuel had been listening to old blues records, finding some vinyl in a shop outside Berkeley, obscure players like Papa Charlie McCoy and Professor Longhair. The talk turned to Jazz. Miles Davis' *Kind of Blue* was Samuel's favorite. It was one of Jake's, too. Jake asked about the Wallflowers, the band formed by Dylan's son, Jakob. Samuel thought they were a little too commercial but liked that Jakob didn't flaunt the Dylan lineage. Beatles or Stones? Samuel was a Stones guy. Jake made the point that there were few who could ever match the combination of Lennon and McCartney. Samuel made his point about Jagger and Richards. Samuel knew his music. And Jake was strangely proud, a father gloating over his son. He listened to Samuel talk about how you miss the best parts if you're not listening to the bass lines in Beatles' songs. "McCartney," Samuel said, "was an incredible bassist. Just listen to 'Taxman.'" Jake offered "Paperback Writer." And the best guitarist? "Jimmy Page," Samuel trumpeted. "Not Hendrix?" Jake asked. "Not Clapton?" Samuel was more inclined to include Metallica's Kirk Hammett or Stevie Ray Vaughn.

In the early 90s, there was this story about David Crosby in the cafeteria at UCLA Medical Center after a follow-up appointment to the lifesaving liver transplant he had after nearly killing himself with drugs. He sat over bad soup and cold coffee and talked to his long-lost son, Raymond. Crosby was a teenager when he got his girlfriend pregnant. The baby was given up for adoption. Raymond searched out his real father when he was thirty years old and discovered the name David Crosby on adoption records, never believing it was the rocker. Of course, it was. When he heard Crosby was near death, waiting for a transplant, Raymond reached out. And there they were, talking in the hospital cafeteria days after the operation had saved his father's life. And what did they talk about? What was the bond? Music. Raymond had soaked up the Beatles and Elton John, remembered The Byrds—the band Crosby founded in the 1960s—but never bought an album. It was the same for Crosby, Stills, and Nash. He appreciated them, but their music never found a way to his CD player. But Raymond, himself, *did* play. He was an accomplished keyboardist and had played in some bands in California. Not long after that meeting, when Crosby's health improved and the guilt of giving away a son began to slowly slip away, the two formed a band; they played at a few theaters in San Juan Capistrano and Santa Ana. Music was the link, the medicine to heal, and the thread that kept them together. They may never have been father and son in any traditional way, but what they were now may have been more important. They were friends.

"Do you play?" Jake asked.

"I took stand-up bass lessons in middle school, never kept it up," Samuel said.

"It's hard."

"But a few years ago, I started playing drums. Bought a snare, banged around. Kind of taught myself."

"And you still bang around?"

"Full set. Took a few lessons but mostly figured it out on my own."

"I'll bet you're good," Jake said, sounding eerily like his own father.

"I'm all right," Samuel said modestly.

The two were finding a way in and out of each other, a good bit of the nervousness, guilt, and anxiety fading. They were two men talking about music, like a couple of guys at the bar on a Sunday afternoon watching Pittsburgh beat Cleveland—beers in hand, nothing to prove, nothing to solve, just a clear singular focus on only what was right in front of them.

But, like Sunday afternoons, nothing lasts.

"Did you love my mother?" Samuel asked, as if he had been holding that question close to his chest for a very long time.

Jake wanted to say yes. He wanted to give him that gift.

"She's a special lady, Samuel."

"*Did* you love her?" he insisted.

"I'm sure I did, the way a young man loves any woman who is fun, smart, sweet, and pretty." Jake looked through the glass, searching for support from Angela. She pointed to her heart and mouthed *tell the truth.*

"I'm not stupid," Samuel said ardently.

"Okay," Jake said slowly, as a way to prepare. "I was attracted to your mother, Samuel. She was full of energy, and yes, she was a great looking lady. But," he paused, "I can't say I loved her. No."

"Uh huh," Samuel said, hesitating.

"Truth is, and your mother knows this, I was in love with someone else."

"Okay," he said.

"I'm just trying to be honest, Samuel. All these years, all that went on, I think you deserve it even if it's hard."

"Yeah, I guess," he said.

"Your mother is a magnificent person."

"I know that," Samuel said softly. Then with resolve he added, "And that has nothing to do with you."

"Nothing," Jake said. "You're right."

"None of this is easy," Samuel said. There was now an edge in his voice.

"No, it's not," Jake replied.

"I'm angry, you know. But not sure who to be angry with," he said. "I probably should go." It was an abrupt end to the conversation but not unexpected.

"I am so immensely privileged that you were here tonight, came on the air with me. You didn't have to do any of this."

"Yeah," Samuel said. "I'm still figuring it out."

"I hope we can continue to talk?" Jake asked.

"I guess we will."

"It was amazing to meet you, Samuel. You'll never know."

"Thanks," he said.

Jake could hear Samuel hand the phone to his mother. He leaned back in the studio chair and ignored the quiet on the airwaves. Jake was wordless, paralyzed.

"Jake?" Angela asked through the intercom. "You're still on the air, you know?"

Jake placed his elbows on the sound console and leaned into the microphone. "This was the most incredible and most difficult night of my life," he confessed to his audience.

"Hello?" Lisa said, returning to the phone and the radio.

"Lisa. There is no way, no possible way, to thank you," said Jake.

"Not sure why I did it, but I did," she said warmly.

"Are you all right?" Jake asked.

"Yeah, I'm okay."

"Please Lisa, think about Oregon. Think about what I said."

"It's so gracious, but you don't know what you're getting into," she said. "And it's been so long. We really don't know each other anymore." Jake and his audience then heard a soft, tempered moan and Lisa added, "I hope you're happy, Jake." Her voice trembled. "Happy New Year."

"Happy New Year, Lisa."

Jake had thought a long time about what song to play at the end of the night's show. Angela had it cued and ready to go. He nodded to her through the studio glass to let it begin, "A Simple Twist of Fate"—Bob Dylan's classic song of longing and regret—rang out in Jake's headphones. He was now more certain than ever that he had made the right choice on how to begin the New Year, despite his broken heart.

# 33

THE DRIVE FROM BANDON TO UC Berkeley was nine hours—
524 miles—and all of it along U.S. 101. The coastal highway
runs the entire way down the continent, but most of a traveler's
attention is paid to the stretch from San Francisco south to Los
Angeles, the stunning beauty of California Highway One. There
is grandeur in the cliff side roadway, the drive through Carmel,
the trek across the Bixby Bridge, the 714 foot span that appears
to gracefully drape over the rough, rocky edge of the raw land
battered by the foamy Pacific. But the run from Bandon toward
northernmost California has its own splendor, is less traveled,
and in many ways is a dreamier ride.

Jake and Samuel crossed the border from Oregon to
California when Samuel spoke for the first time in more than
an hour and some seventy miles.

"I kept some of her ashes," he said, facing the passenger
seat's side window.

Samuel's phone call to Jake came in the early morning of a
mid-July day. Lisa had died the night before, sleeping away in a
daze of drugs in a steel bed on the third floor of Philadelphia's
Jefferson Hospital. She never considered coming to Oregon for
her final days. Instead, she stayed in the home she loved in the
care of hospice nurses as long as she could. The pain eventually
became too difficult to manage at home, and it was suggested

Lisa be taken back to the hospital. Three days later she was cremated and family and friends came to her home for a small ceremony. A Unitarian minister quoted Henry David Thoreau, "'Heaven is under our feet, as well as over our heads,'" he said. Lisa had given up Catholicism many years ago. Samuel took the ashes from a small tin decorated with cardinals and Lilly's of the Valley and released them into the triangular patch of ground full of marigolds and impatiens and pots of giant geraniums just beyond the front door of Lisa's home.

"I put a tiny bit inside one of her pill boxes and kept it," Samuel added.

When Lisa knew the end was near, she asked for Samuel. He came to her side. And in the last week, Samuel telephoned Jake each day to tell him how his mother looked, if she was lucid, what she was able to say, and what the doctors were predicting.

"It's for you," Samuel said, pulling from his backpack a small teak box about the size of a quarter. On the lid, painted in black was the Chinese symbol for forever. He held it in his outstretched hand.

Jake took his eyes from the highway for a moment, turning them toward Samuel and the box resting in his palm. He then returned his eyes to the road, stretching out before the two of them and stared through the driver's side window at the landscape zipping by. "Was this what your mother wanted you to do?" Jake asked.

"No," Samuel said, "it's something *I* wanted."

Not long after Lisa's death, Samuel returned to see his adoptive parents and came to Bandon to stay with Jake and Angela for a little while. Angela had moved into Jake's apartment earlier in the year. After the New Year's show and the honesty of that night, he discovered how much he wanted, needed, Angela near. For a long time, his feelings for her had been muted by the shared work, their pasts, and their own vulnerability. He didn't know that he loved her but believed he could. Jake believed she felt the same. And while Samuel visited, Angela allowed a father and his son a great deal of space and quiet support. Angela would make coffee and eggs in the morning and give the two the time they needed to be together. Jake and Samuel walked the beach in the afternoons, and most evenings before going to the radio station, Samuel would drum the coffee table with his fingers and palms while Jake played the guitar. They talked about books, school, baseball, football, and always music. Samuel learned he could tell a good joke and knew a great deal about the Toltec civilization, an ancient Mesoamerican culture of wise men and artists, something he had been introduced to in his classes at Berkeley. But there would also be times he would be insular, quietly anxious, telling Jake there were still times he felt like a stranger. And then there was his mother, a woman he had grown to know, learned to love, and now missed desperately. But despite that emotional journey, Samuel still wrestled with her decision to give him away. Samuel had remained close to his adoptive parents but had found himself compelled to get to know his real mother and now his real father. It was a way to know himself.

"You keep it, Samuel," Jake said. "The ashes should be yours."

Samuel slowly wrapped his fingers around the box. He folded his arms across his lap and closed his eyes, holding the box against his chest. There were many hours ahead and hundreds of miles to go before they'd have to say goodbye on the sidewalk outside a ground floor apartment on Sacramento Street a dozen blocks east of the University of California at Berkeley.

———

A fog had formed along the ocean near the Coquille River Lighthouse just as the lantern began to gently pulsate, a substitute for the fallen sun. It was a familiar summer night on the Oregon coast, and it was good to be home. Jake had taken several days to return from Berkeley, stopping to sit alone on the beaches and watch the tides. Now, as night overtook day and the music of the seagulls faded, Jake desired only to be with Angela near the rocks and salty water, allowing the moist, heavy air to blanket them.

In Angela's backpack was a bottle of red wine and another of grapefruit juice, along with two clear plastic cups.

"It's a Pinot Noir. Willamette Valley," Angela said, pouring a small amount into a cup. "You're okay with this, right?" she asked. Jake smiled, momentarily looking at the glass and then her. She poured the juice in the other cup.

"Welcome home," Angela said, lifting her glass in the air to lightly tap it against Jake's.

They sipped and looked out toward the sea.

"This is home," Jake said, gently breaking the settled-in stillness.

"It is, Jake," Angela said. Jake could feel her watching him. Then, placing an arm around his neck, she said, "It's a pretty good place to be."

Jake again tapped his cup to hers.

Jake and Angela had only one place to be that night, right where they were. She leaned into him, her shoulder against his, her head softly resting on the base of his neck, her tussled hair folding over his upper back. Despite the salty ocean breeze blowing across them, Jake could smell the sweetness of her skin, lingering in the dampness. He could sense her heartbeat, her warmth. Jake wanted to forever embrace the moment. Angela's Nirvana CDs were now on the shelf next to Dylan, her dresses in his closet, her hand lotion next to the books on the night-stand, her night gown tucked under her pillow on the bed, the oversized plain white cup from which she drank her morning tea right beside his black City Lights bookstore mug inside the kitchen cabinet, her make-up on the bathroom counter next to his shaving gel. Love was no longer something Jake kept in a locked drawer only to open and pull out when it was convenient. He had learned it was now worthy of risk, of drowning in its deep waters. Standing on its shore offered only regret, revealing an insipid selfish love that dulled the real thing. Scars were inevitable, but Jake knew now that scars held the best stories, the ones that mattered, and there was redemption in the healing. People point at bloody skin and slow-healing scabs and ask, *what happened?* And when we are ready, we are more than pleased to share the details and the pain.

The fog thickened, draping over Jake and Angela like a fleece jacket gently placed across their shoulders. And as it rolled in off the ancient sea, the chill from the saturated air disappeared, the ocean breeze calmed, the fog strangely comforting them as the lighthouse signal silently beamed through the haze to the black ocean waters, reaching out forever.

ACKNOWLEDGMENTS


Thanks always to my sons for their inspiration, my wife for her support and love, and to all those in the glory days of Rock-n-Roll radio who made it such a joy to experience. Thanks to the Ernest Hemingway Foundation of Oak Park, Illinois for allowing me the time and space to complete this book as the writer-in-residence at the Hemingway birthplace home.

And thank you, forever, Gloria and Norman, my mother and father, for they were the best storytellers I have ever known.

David W. Berner is an award-winning journalist, writer, broadcaster, and teacher.

He has been the receipt of a honor from the Society of Midland Authors, presented with a Book-of-the-Year Award from the Chicago Writers Association, a Grand Prize Award from Royal Dragonfly, and has been named a finalist for the Eric Hoffer Grand Prize Award.

David has been the writer-in-residence at the Jack Kerouac Project in Orlando, Florida and at the Ernest Hemingway Birthplace Home in Oak Park, Illinois. His broadcast reporting and audio documentaries have aired on the CBS Radio Network and a number of public radio stations across America.

He teaches at Columbia College Chicago and lives outside Chicago with his wife and dog Sam.